"Where is your lady?" Angel said more softly. "She didn't leave this boat."

"She ain't fizzed into vapor, Angel. Keep looking: she's here, unless you missed something."

"*Eas-y!*" Angel's disapproval can sear a steak. We hunted through every damn inch of that boat: below decks, the several lounge areas, library, tackle room, and the navigation room.

I sagged with discouragement and twenty-four sleepless hours. Angel, who hadn't slept either, looked fresh as a petunia. He suggested one last look around the deck.

As I traipsed again around the stern, too moody to worry about somebody reporting our trespass, something off the deck side caught the corner of my eye. Something that flicked white in the dark water.

She was tucked away off the far side of the yacht, pink night flimsy a dead giveaway, billowing on the water's surface. Under it her pale arms and legs dangled like tentacles. Muff's dark red hair was tangled in the crusty links of the anchor chain. I was grateful I couldn't see her face.

Bantam Books offers the finest in classic and modern American mysteries.
Ask your bookseller for the books you have missed.

Stuart Palmer

THE PENGUIN POOL
   MURDER
THE PUZZLE OF THE HAPPY
   HOOLIGAN
THE PUZZLE OF THE RED
   STALLION
THE PUZZLE OF THE SILVER
   PERSIAN

Craig Rice

THE FOURTH POSTMAN
HAVING WONDERFUL CRIME
MY KINGDOM FOR A HEARSE
THE LUCKY STIFF

Rex Stout

BAD FOR BUSINESS
BROKEN VASE
DEATH OF A DUDE
DEATH TIMES THREE
DOUBLE FOR DEATH
FER-DE-LANCE
THE FINAL DEDUCTION
GAMBIT
THE RUBBER BAND
SOME BURIED CAESAR
TOO MANY CLIENTS

Max Allan Collins

THE DARK CITY

Victoria Silver

DEATH OF A HARVARD
   FRESHMAN
DEATH OF A RADCLIFFE
   ROOMMATE

William Kienzle

THE ROSARY MURDERS

Joseph Louis

MADELAINE

M. J. Adamson

NOT UNTIL A HOT FEBRUARY
A FEBRUARY FACE
COMING SOON: REMEMBER
   MARCH

Richard Fliegel

THE NEXT TO DIE

Conrad Haynes

BISHOP'S GAMBIT, DECLINED
COMING SOON: TURNABOUT

Barbara Paul

FIRST GRAVEDIGGER
THE FOURTH WALL
KILL FEE
THE RENEWABLE VIRGIN
COMING SOON: BUT HE WAS
   ALREADY DEAD WHEN I
   GOT THERE

PIECES OF CREAM

○

Richard Hilary

BANTAM BOOKS
TORONTO • NEW YORK • LONDON • SYDNEY • AUCKLAND

PIECES OF CREAM

A Bantam Book / October 1987

ISBN 0-553-26666-7

Published simultaneously in the United States and Canada

Bantam Books are published by Bantam Books, Inc. Its trademark,
consisting of the words "Bantam Books" and the portrayal of a
rooster, is Registered in U.S. Patent and Trademark Office and in
other countries. Marca Registrada. Bantam Books, Inc., 666 Fifth
Avenue, New York, New York 10103.

For Betty Rodino, and Hilary and Kay Connor

CHAPTER ONE

O

The alarm clock drilled me awake, early morning grumpy. To flip it off I had to fumble across the unaccustomed woman-body filling the other half of my mattress. My client.

The woman stirred and scissored her legs under the sheet, but didn't really come to. I propped on an elbow and looked her over.

She'd been my client of record since all of the evening before.

I'd been ready to call it a rainy day when she knocked on my office door, pointed to it by Marlene, the brass-voiced receptionist I share with four assorted small businesses. In she sailed on those showgirl legs, three years and five pounds past a dancer's prime, still with the expensively dressed mahogany hair and the perfect, sharp fingernails.

Muff Anglaise was the name I wrote in my notes. It's no crime to hand a private investigator an assumed name. Tell the truth, lying to your detective is one of the privileges you get billed for.

My sport shirt was sticky under my armpits from the June humidity. Ms. Anglaise wore a green sleeveless sundress that showed off her seashore tan. She started telling me about her ex-boyfriend in a voice that had low, rough edges from singing too loud, or cheering on horses, or maybe drinking too hard. Anyway, she'd spent a long time at it.

Three things about this boyfriend of hers. One, he'd been dead nine years. Two, he'd been murdered. Three, it happened while he was committing a felony—running numbers slips, according to the Newark PD. La Anglaise had a problem with the third item, seeing how she was named beneficiary on her boyfriend's death insurance note. The felony rap was a righteous excuse for the Good Hands people to refuse to pay.

No surprise when she mentioned the boyfriend's name.

"Jimmy the Cricket Finnochio," I said. "Why pick me out?"

"Well, why not? Your name was on the reports as finding the body. And I heard you was working privately now."

"First patrol car on the scene. Nine years ago. Tell me, you ever hear of bygones? Why you so hot on it after all these years?"

"Money'd come in handy, doesn't it always?" she said, mouth smiling more than her eyes. "Simple answer, huh? A dancer don't find much work past thirty. Last month I turned twenty-eight."

Womanly heft of her calves and thighs put her a year or two over thirty, easy.

"You don't look twenty-eight," I said.

"Should I thank you for the compliment?"

I laughed. Muff Anglaise laughed too.

"I'm just thinking. Nine years is a long time to sit on an insurance claim. New Jersey's got this law of laches? Which means, as of ten years later, the money isn't yours to claim no more."

Muff showed me her teeth, as if she didn't understand.

"How you gonna pay me, if you don't recover a penny?"

"Oh. We'll figure out something." She gave me some more tooth treatment. Then she dipped her head and swung her rope of hair from left side to right. "Don't you worry, honey."

I couldn't help chuckling. "Okay, I won't. As long as you're not carrying the torch for the Cricket after all these years?"

Her turn to chuckle at me. "Not to worry. It wasn't the world's greatest passion even then, you know?"

"Tell me something. The Cricket was a bagman in Newark, worked for New York organized crime, right? Cops figured he got himself whacked for sponging off a little extra juice?"

"Jimmy hardly let me know nothing. Listen, he was no Boy Scout, okay? We lived together, we got along and all. But Bonnie and Clyde we were not. Life insurance was my idea. So I'd have something. Jimmy only signed it because he owed me. He knew he dragged me into that kind of life."

"Kicking and screaming the whole way, right?"

"Well, it is pretty rough on a young girl. Guy she's living with floats in and out all hours of the night. Mister Tightlip. Keeps all kinds of guns around the apartment."

"Why'd you hang out, then? You got feet." My eyes automatically ran down those long legs. "Whyn't you drift?"

She raised her head with a proud gesture, like she was holding up a headdress on stage.

"Jimmy really liked me sometimes. I could tell he cared about me. A girl needs somebody to take care of her."

"Like a spider needs a fly."

Teeth flashing, she laughed with me. I've always had a weakness for women who've been around too long to bristle at the truth.

"Word around at the time was that maybe the Cricket was living up to his name. Chirping to the police. You know anything about that?"

"Well, that's it," she said, like I'd been beating around the bush. "The night he got hit, Jimmy told me he was meeting a cop. He wasn't committing no crime when it happened. You find that cop, and I recover the insurance on Jimmy. Good-bye retirement worries."

Dancers I knew almost all turned to hooking when they got older, if they didn't luck out and marry a front-row panter.

I said, "How much insurance is there?"

"You gonna get cut in plenty, if that's what you mean."

I started over. "You were dancing at the casinos when you met the Cricket?"

"That's when I started, sure."

"Big-time chorus lines must be hell to crack into."

"It's very competitive. Bunnies, they call the new girls. You would not believe how many bunnies just hop the bus from Detroit or Des Moines, come in begging for auditions. A good night's workout with the director on the rehearsal mats is what they get, most of them."

"You?"

"Not that way." She didn't sound offended.

"Your first job come through the Cricket's organized crime contacts?"

"Maybe."

"That's the other thing," I said. "Mob hits don't get solved. That's one certainty in this life. I'd be wasting my time and your dollars poking around."

Muff Anglaise sat up straight and smiled again, long neck arched, still on stage. There was rosy health under her tan.

"You ever dance in Manhattan?"

"Not much. Atlantic City for me. Right now I'm in the western revue at the Golden Nugget. I wear this cowgirl hat and this teeny vest and skirt? I wish you could see me in them. Sometimes I think I'm going to slip right out."

"Ever wear the fantail feathers and the fruit salad head-dress? What do they call them?"

"You mean the Busby Berkeley costumes? It's just what every teenaged girl with good legs dreams about."

"How about you? You like the work?"

"It's funny," Muff said, sucking on her top teeth. "People expect you to complain. They say, after all the years you've put in, the shows must be just a job to you now, what you do to pay the rent. But it's never like that. Dancing, the glamor, is still what I love, more than ever. During a show number, with all the high rollers paying so much to be out there. And after the shows, in the casinos, with the chandeliers and the class. I wouldn't ever want to live any other way."

"Where you from?"

"Not so far from where we're sitting. Hoboken. Hudson Street."

"Frank Sinatra country. What with you and him, they'll be calling it the Annex of Hollywood."

"So funny," Muff Anglaise told me. "The old neighborhood's half yuppie condos, half Rican tenements now."

"Yeah. Let me have your phone number, why don't you? Case I turn up something on Jimmy the Cricket's murder."

I jotted it down and stored the notepad in my desk. Then, since it was the cocktail hour, I invited Muff Anglaise to join me for a drink or two. We spent a pleasant hour over Canadian highballs at the Chess Club. Then I took her to eat at the Spanish Tavern, over in the Ironbound section of Newark. All through dinner and two bottles of Rioja red I kept jabbering. More chatter in one evening than is normal for me in a month. Muff Anglaise had this way of being totally absorbed in the man she was with. Hanging on every word, all smiles and laughs. Try as I might, I could pick up nothing phony about it either. This woman gave her all to being out on the town, with a man, with me. It's a precious knack, even if it comes from years of pleasing a different man every night. Worth a million to any man that lives by himself.

After the broiled lobsters and paella, we drove right over to my apartment, without even a discussion. What with the dimmed lights, the bassy jazz, and the lady's undemanding smiles, wasn't all that long before I was kissing her face and she was kissing me back. Ten minutes later I was taking the woman by the hand and leading her to my bedroom.

At one especially intense point I remember thinking that here I was, collecting the first installment on my fee.

But I didn't do much narrow-minded thinking again for an hour or so.

My pants were half pulled up and my turtleneck half tucked-in before Muff Anglaise opened her eyes. Unlike me, the lady woke up all at once.

She sat up without fussing about whether the sheet covered her top half.

"Where'd you get those muscles in your stomach, lover? You could be a percussion instrument in a Latin band. You must work out something crazy."

"Used to prize fight for a living. Long time ago. *Then* I worked out plenty. What I do now is just enough to keep myself from running down."

I finished pulling the turtleneck over my head, then bent over and buckled my shoes.

"It's really special, doing it with you," she said, watching me. "Do you feel that way too?"

"Sure."

"Then why are you getting dressed? Going someplace?"

"Got a job this morning." I did a bad job of meeting her eyes. "Sorry to run before breakfast."

"Oh."

"You feel like staying? Make yourself at home. I'll be back around three."

"Do you want me to?"

"Sure."

"Well, I think I'd better go too. It won't take me a minute to get ready."

"Listen, baby. I don't mean to be cold. I like my relationships to warm up gradual. Besides, old bachelor like me gets caught up in his work. Got this job to do before I can start in on your thing. All right?"

Into the bathroom she walked, purse, underthings, and little dress dangling from one hand. A brief glance from the door to see if I was appreciating the view.

Indeed, I was. But I wasn't unhappy about the quick-and-easy separation either. What did I know about the woman? That she danced for a living. That she was once a low-rent mobster's girlfriend. That she was still snuffling around for a score off his death. Basically, she was still a stranger. Like a hot-looking woman you follow around the market until at the checkout line you swap a few comments on the price of artichokes.

All the same, last night I couldn't get enough of her. We'd shared too many little caresses and games of affection. I could guess how she got her stage name. Crusty outside, but oh-so tender inside. But I knew nothing else about her. Made me uncomfortable with what I was feeling.

The bathroom door opened and out she stepped, made-up as thickly as the evening before, ropy hair sprayed back into place.

She had her arms folded across her breasts. "It's cold this morning. Last night it was so warm."

"You all right?"

"Must be the summer flu bug." She shuddered. "Some kind of cold. Just came over me."

"You bring a coat? I can't remember."

"Who carries a coat around, the end of June?" She tried hiding the edge in her voice with that tinselly showgirl smile.

From my tiny foyer closet I picked out an old tailored tweed jacket with a belt in back, British-style, and I fixed it around Muff's shoulders. Her skin felt clammy.

"I'll make sure you get it back," she sniffed. Her eyes looked sick, but her body was feeling me up.

"I'll make sure you don't forget, by coming to see you."

"I hope you mean that."

"Count on it, sugar."

Outside the apartment door the wind whipped a bread wrapper against my leg. "Where's your car parked?" I asked. "I'll drop you off."

"I caught a bus up. I've got a return ticket on a tour bus. They let me use it in reverse."

"You mean where they charge you eighteen bucks, then hand you back fifteen in casino chips when you arrive? Plus free lunch, a cruise, and a new hat?"

"Something like that."

"Bet everybody else on that bus has just cashed a Social Security check."

"I know. How about off the soap box, loverman?"

We had an awkward minute or two. Then she said, not looking at me, "Forgive me? I'm not myself. Being sick and all."

"Probably my charm," I said. "Makes them all swoony like, you know?"

She stirred enough to smile, then goose me, expertly.

A cab pulled over for us. I helped Muff swing in her tanned legs and shut the door on her. I handed the driver a twenty and told him where to drive.

"You're going to the airport livery station," I said, leaning in the window. "From there the limo's direct to AC. Take it, on me. It's faster and lots more comfortable." I pressed two twenties into her hand. The cabbie's face was very interested in his rearview mirror. "You're in no shape to ride the bus."

"You're a doll." She bared her teeth mechanically. "You shouldn't."

"Enjoy the shore," I said. "Me, I'm headed downtown."

"You'll come see me in Atlantic City? Please?"

Cabbie gunned his engine in neutral.

"I'll show you the Boardwalk."

"Yeah. The Boardwalk in Atlantic City. Life will be peaches and cream."

"You'll come soon, won't you?"

I stepped back and let the taxi vroom off. Muff Anglaise looked out the back window and tossed me a kiss.

The lady was my client, and I was handing *her* expense money. Always the great head for business, Barnes.

CHAPTER TWO

O

On Friday of that week, just before noontime, my friend Angel and I were jawing in my office. Yelling actually, is what we were doing. Outside my windows, down a floor, the Newark DPW was air drilling cavities and spinning cement. The racket was deafening.

Angel was silhouetted in front of the window while I meditated out loud about Jimmy Finnochio and Muff Anglaise. Angel wore a golden wig piled on the back of his head and trailing a long ponytail, reminiscent of a damsel in distress. Angel's limber body was encased in a light orange cotton jumpsuit, gold metallic belt, ankle sweatsocks, and shiny new, white kid leather high-tops. The throat of the jumpsuit was open, showing the single gold chain on Angel's brown neck. Sneakers as a fashion statement I had just started to see in Manhattan, but nowhere in Newark, which is usually months behind. How Angel stays on the edge of fashion, I'll never know. Angel hardly ever leaves Newark.

Angel was watching the road crew's pre-lunch show of industry while I griped. I had looked up the old police files on Jimmy Finnochio and then dialed up some people who would know the unofficial version, if there was one. Nobody knew nothing about nothing.

Dead-end street. The time-honored story, official and unofficial, was that Jimmy the Cricket got himself whacked nine years ago by the Philadelphia mob. He was a small-time Newark/NYC hood who'd hustled betting action with too much gusto, stepped over a territory line. The trunk of Finnochio's car was found stuffed with numbers slips.

Also with Finnochio's body. Or what was left of it.

Maybe I should save Muff Anglaise some money, I told Angel. Report that the investigation's dead. Make a date, the same time. Drive down Atlantic City way, take her out some evening. Three days I'd been thinking about her. Maybe I should take the day, hit the beach, too. From the perspective of downtown Newark, the end of June, the Boardwalk in Atlantic City sounded like the holy land.

Yes, the seashore sounded fine, Angel agreed. Angel has been my good friend ever since he hired me to shake down a street player that owed Angel some cash. Eight years ago. Two years before Angel had his sex change operation and became known forever as Angel the Sex Change. In spite of the name, Angel is accepted pretty much everywhere as a super-foxy woman.

Except by me. Angel is a good friend, and I am glad that he's happier now, but I have always been kind of uneasy with the idea of people shifting identities.

When the blond woman walked through the office door, Angel had started telling me about his vacation plans and hinting how I should fly to Mexico with him.

The blonde's entrance shut even Angel up.

This was an immaculately groomed woman. Expensive hot-weather skirt and top. Pastel leather shoes to match. Big-boned, good figure, sturdy brown legs from playing tennis. Her strawberry hair, summer short and glowing against her tan, together with the single blue-stone drops in her ears, gave her a Peter Pan look that, to my eyes, jarred with her ripe body. I found myself stumbling out of my chair. Woman who looked like that probably had pedigree papers.

Angel and I didn't say a word. I smiled at the woman, stood up and closed the window. The sudden quiet was like a cold shower after an August workout. Angel stiffened.

The woman looked inquiringly at Angel, at me, fixed for a second on our glasses and the office Black Velvet bottle, then said, "Mr. Ezell Barnes? I hope I'm not interrupting? The receptionist tried to buzz you."

Angel slid off my desk to shift a few hips at her, ready to fire off a few good lines. I said quickly, "Not at all, ma'am. We were just finishing. How can I help you, Miss . . . ?"

"Valentine. I'm Patricia Valentine."

"Ezell Barnes. Glad to meet you." I glanced at Angel, but hints are a mystery to him. So I said, "I'll be talking to you, then, Miss Lopez. Have yourself a nice afternoon."

Fuming in high gear, Angel high-topped to the door on those springy legs of his, then wheeled to wither me. "You have a nice day, too, Papi. I hope your skin problem leave you alone today." The door got slammed.

At Patricia Valentine's astonished look, I flashed a grin.

"Angel is more in the order of a friend than a client," I said. "That was his idea of a joke. Sit down, why don't you? What can I do for you?"

"'His'? You called her 'Miss Lopez.'"

"Is now, I guess. Angel went through this operation six years ago, made him into a woman, for the record."

"You guess? Does Angel's change of identity cause you difficulty, Mr. Barnes?" Her mouth bent ironically.

I shrugged. "Maybe it does. I understand Angel is a woman now. I've just known him too long to change how I feel."

"Angel is a woman now in every way, though, isn't she? Legally, anatomically, emotionally, psychologically?"

"I've backpedaled enough, don't you think? You want to sit down?"

"Thank you. I find you interesting, Mr. Barnes."

"Oh? What's on your mind?"

When Patricia Valentine sat down, backbone straight, her legs looked slimmer, less for utility. She sure could look you in the eye, though. And she wasn't used to beating around the bush.

"My sister came here recently to consult you."

I said nothing.

"She probably used the name Anglaise. It's really Valentine. Veronica."

"I talked to a woman a couple days ago," I said. "She was from Hoboken. You don't look exactly like a Hoboken type to me, Ms. Valentine."

"What story did Veronica use on you, Mr. Barnes?"

"Excuse me, Ms. Valentine. Woman that hired me talked and acted from Hoboken. Now you, on the other hand, are more Short Hills."

"Bryn Mawr, actually. Outside Philadelphia? And my sister too."

"Woman told me Hoboken." I lifted eyebrows.

"She told you all sorts of things, I'm sure. Frankly, my sister is not a stable person, Mr. Barnes. She has not been for several months. Why she concocted this Hoboken story, I can't say, but I suspect it's part of her renewed obsession with the Finnochio homicide. I'm quite sure, you see, that's why she sought you out."

I stood up and turned the cabinet-top fan so the breeze hit her more squarely.

"Isn't that so, Mr. Barnes?"

"For starters," I said, pulling up some notepaper, "what's the address and phone number at her apartment?"

She passed that little test, gave them to me number perfect from memory.

Proved she knew Muff Anglaise; didn't mean they were sisters, though.

I said carefully, "She tell you she was coming here?"

"We're not close, as sisters go, but we do share confidences, Mr. Barnes."

"Ms. Valentine, if I flapped about my clients' business to every soul that breezed in the door, I'd end up doing precious little business, wouldn't I?"

"I'm not exactly anyone who walks through your door, am I?"

My face probably showed agreement. My eyes were fixed on her shining 'do. The little pillow of curls on top of her head straightened at the sides, edges razored like pile carpeting. The left side was three inches longer than the right, making me wonder what the back of her head would look like.

All that hairdresser's work, and it wasn't even a really sexy look. They don't cut hair like that in Newark.

"Perhaps I'm not introducing this right," Patricia Valentine said, face wrinkling quizzically at my stare. "What I mean is, Veronica is my older sister, Mr. Barnes. My family's black sheep, or so my father thinks. But I feel partly responsible for what Veronica's done with her life."

I lifted an eyebrow.

"I've been a bit too supportive of my father. Too much the shining model for Veronica to compete successfully for his love."

I murmured at this image of father's love as a pole-vaulting prize.

"After Veronica took up with Jimmy Finnochio, my father turned against her. She's never set foot since inside our family's home."

"You say she's been acting erratically? When'd that start?"

"For several months Veronica has been reliving Finnochio's gangland murder. Compulsively, as though that horrid affair were still going on. Obviously, it would not be a pretty episode in anyone's life. But Veronica seemed to have adjusted adequately. It's only this summer that it has deranged her again."

Her eyes bore earnestly into me. I didn't like her confidences. They made me feel I owed her a little something in return.

I said, "Your sister seemed plenty sensible to me, Ms. Valentine. There's a reason she's been on this Finnochio killing again."

We locked eyes. She spoke first. "Well, why?"

"That's a professional confidence."

"Oh." Patricia Valentine's exasperated pink tongue played with the corner of her pink mouth.

"I'll say this much: it's no pretty explanation, but it's not a crazy one either."

"Well, good, I guess. Veronica is gold-digging again, isn't she?"

"I already told you more than I should. Enough, okay?"

"Not yet. I, at least, haven't confided everything." She paused for a reaction. I just waited with my palms on the desk.

"Veronica has disappeared," she said finally. "She has not been to her apartment for at least three days. I'm afraid she's in terrible trouble."

"Why? Your sister's a big girl, Ms. Valentine. Lots of reasons why she hasn't been home, no?"

"I don't think so. How much did Veronica tell you about her murdered boyfriend? That his former partners have been harassing her, threatening her?"

"She didn't say so to me."

"It's true, though." Her lopsided hairdo shook. "And whatever was worth killing Jimmy Finnochio over might still hurt Veronica. You know I'm right, Mr. Barnes."

"Your sister hasn't been to her apartment since she left me, that it? Has she been to work in that time, do you know?"

"The casino personnel office reports her absent, all three days."

"How about some kind of photograph I can show around down there?"

"Veronica's most recent engagement." She handed me a manila envelope containing one of those big publicity photos. Muff Anglaise headdressed and rooster-tailed, with a rhinestone or two in strategic places. She looked like a pretty statue, not the responsive woman I'd slept with. The line of print at the bottom gave me a start, though.

I'd been assuming that she still worked at the Golden Nugget Casino, like she told me. But the photo's caption read,

The Peaches and Cream Revue. City by the Sea Hotel and Casino. The Boardwalk in Atlantic City, New Jersey.

Somebody else I knew from way back also worked for City by the Sea Casino.

Face neutral, I asked Patricia Valentine for her own phone number and got it.

"You live in Atlantic City too?" I said, trying not to look too sharply at her.

"No," she said, with hardly any hesitation. "We live—that is, my father and I—now live in Freehold." When she saw me glance down at her phone number, she added, "That's just at the northern edge of the 609 area code."

"Right. That'll do it."

"You mean you'll find my sister?"

"I say I will, then I will. But she's my client too. I got to use my judgment about what's best for her as well as for you. Agreed?"

Patricia Valentine tilted her head and arched her eyebrows at me.

"Next thing is, my standard fee is one hundred fifty dollars per day. Five hundred up front. Plus expenses. And those're gonna include hotel room and meals while I'm in Atlantic City."

She smiled archly, the way some people camouflage when they feel patronizing, and tugged a checkbook from her purse. Then she put it back.

She reached into her purse again. "By chance, I think I may have that much cash with me today. You don't mind, do you? I'm just as happy not to carry so much money with me."

From a bank envelope she pulled five light green bills. She stacked them neatly on the desk between us and looked expectantly at me.

Me mind?

"Don't," she ordered, watching me rake in the bread. "Don't contact my sister when you find her. You'll undoubtedly spook her. She isn't expecting you, and she will just dash off again."

"What do you suggest?"

"Why not call me, then wait and I'll join you? We'll approach Veronica together. I'll need your professional's touch in handling her. Agreed?"

"Professional's touch" sounded nice. I nodded. She smiled again. I was working for her. Patricia Valentine stood up to leave. She smoothed the worry lines out of that pixie face with the freckled tan and the pale pink lipstick. She also smoothed the short green skirt over her hips.

"Sure," I said. "One more thing, Ms. Valentine?"

"It's Miss Valentine, by the way. I hate the sound of *Ms*., don't you? Like a sharecropper's wife."

Big grin from me. Blush from her. Looked good on her.

"Why don't you call me Patricia, Mr. Barnes?"

"Patricia? I thought the country club set all had cute names, like Tishy or Flubsy."

Blush number two. "Now we're even," Patricia said.

"Not until you call me Ezell," I answered.

"Good-bye, Ezell. I hope I'll be hearing from you soon."

"I'm leaving this very afternoon for AC. You'll hear from me tonight, or tomorrow at the latest."

Patricia nodded. I took a quick step to hold the door for her. From the back the sheared edge of her mane angled precipitously from above her right ear to mid-neck on the left. Maybe her hairdresser figured her back would always be to a wall?

"You know your way out? Back through the shoe store."

She nodded again. "It's an unconventional entryway, I must say, Ezell."

"Well, I was up here when that shoe store was a little lobby for these top floors. Shoeshine seats on one side, newsstand lining the other. Most tenants moved out when the shoe emporium moved in. But, like I say, I was already in here. Besides, the rent went down some for a while."

Patricia crinkled her eyes, treating me to a smile. I liked her the best I had all afternoon.

Back at my desk I pulled the window back up and took the street noise like a hook to the head. I watched until Patricia Valentine strode athletically into view and climbed into a new-looking BMW coupe. First she plucked the hydrant parking tag from under the wiper and carefully folded it into that purse of hers. Its neighbors were all green or plastic, I bet.

I pulled the window down too hard, so the accelerating counterweight let the sash crash into the jamb and crack the upper-right pane. I hardly noticed. A worm of worry about Muff Anglaise was crawling in my belly, along with something else I didn't take time to sort out. But I could feel juices of excitement growling up inside.

CHAPTER THREE

O

Good thing I'd finished my week's routine chores that morning. Bankdrops, mostly, where I lug receipts pouches from downtown merchants to different banks, a .38 Police Special holstered under my armpit, little .22 automatic in my jacket pocket.

Free to beat it down to Atlantic City. Big rock candy city by the sea. I told Marlene where I was headed, then hoofed out to my car. First, my own bank, to loosen Patricia Valentine's bills into smaller change and add to them from my account. After all, I don't take many working vacations. Next, my apartment, for some clothes and some equipment, including added firepower. I'd grab lunch on my way out to the Garden State Parkway. Stepping out the door, I remembered to go back in for the guidebook about Atlantic City and its history that I had bought, feeling either sentimental or anticipatory, the day after Muff said good-bye.

Before I left town I dropped by the community garden that I tend with a group of friends. And I stopped a couple times at different bars, the Pimlico and the Chess Club, looking for Angel. A little backup could not hurt, given the type of people you find in AC. Not to mention that Angel's dancing connections might be lucky in tracking down Muff Anglaise.

No soap at the bars. But when I called his apartment, Angel sounded delighted at the prospect of a few days down the shore.

"I just make good-bye to this sweet little man I got here, Easy. Then you pick me up."

Out-of-staters seem to remember New Jersey in terms of its two cross-state highways. The NJ Turnpike splits the state diagonally, running south, somebody told me once, through the priciest truck-crop farmland in the United States. Anybody that's only ridden along the northern oil-refinery stretches, through Newark, Paterson, and the like, would be surprised to hear that.

New Jerseyans scoff when other folks put the mouth on their state after seeing just the northern Turnpike horror scenery. Hardly anybody that lives in Jersey willingly drives that miserable highway anyway. Only takes you to Camden, Trenton, Fort Dix. You live in New Jersey, the drive of choice is the Garden State Parkway.

The Parkway hugs the Jersey shoreline, from Perth Amboy to Cape May. New Jersey's umbilical cord to the ocean, a fierce attachment looped of dreams and nostalgia, even for Jersey folks who are afraid of ocean water or don't set living eyes on it for years on end. On your left as you motor south, 110 miles from Newark to Atlantic City, is a ribbon of titanic salt marsh, sandy pinelands, some untouched by the super developments, tantalizing exit names: Sandy Hook, Asbury Park, Point Pleasant, Seaside Heights, Toms River, Long Beach Island, Ocean City, Avalon, Stone Harbor, Wildwood.

It's a great driving highway, unclogged with the never-ending road repair of, say, Connecticut's highways, cannily designed so headlights going the other direction stay out of your eyes. Five lanes each way in key spots. Twelve lanes total going over the Raritan Bay Bridge in Perth Amboy. Right past the Perth Amboy 1-2-3-4-5-6-7-8-9-10-11-12 Cinema.

By three-thirty I was turning my Nissan pickup loose on the Garden State's left lane. A hot, hazy afternoon, sunroof popped open. Ernie Horton sat in the back. Angel was lounging on the bucket seat next to me, smoking a cigarette and orange-sticking his nails. He had the right costume for the occasion, as always: orange sundress, rope sandals, long-billed little straw hat on the back of his curly wig. Looked like a fisherman's hat to me. I told Angel that.

"I hit you on the head with the pole, Easy, you don't be nice to Angel. Got to be nice on vacation."

"Working vacation."

"Where are we staying?" Angel asked. "I hope we staying at the Tropacabana. They got a private beach. Got these little striped tents with pointy tops."

I grunted.

"Like Camelot, you think, Papi? You could be King Lancelot and I be you Lady Godiva."

I couldn't choke the laughter down. From the king-cab jump

seat behind us, old Ernie joined in readily, though I doubt he got the joke.

"We'll be checking into separate rooms, amigo, my man," I said. "And I don't think the Tropicana. What do you hear about the City by the Sea Hotel?"

"Is pretty small, but is the most fancy-shmancy," Angel said firmly. "They got waterbeds, I think, and swimming pools, and healthy clubs. We gone stay there, Easy?"

"Could be. Where the action'll be, if I'm not reading the signals wrong. You got friends down in AC, Angel?"

Angel made his little Latin movement of the shoulders. "Sure. Plenty ladies come fron Nowork to Atlanty City. Got jobs for dancers, sometimes. And is pretty good now for hookers, to work the casinos. When they was starting off, always crack down, crack down. Now is pretty good."

"Know anybody at City by the Sea?"

"Who knows? Could be."

"But you never knew anybody called Muff Anglaise or Veronica Valentine, right?"

Angel lifted his bare shoulders delicately.

"You got family down there, Ernie," I said, giving up. "Tell me some more about this problem of theirs."

Ernie is a widower, retired now from odd jobs. He and I and a half-dozen others form a group that gardens in a vacant lot near my apartment. When I dropped by that morning to say good-bye for a few days, Ernie piped up as how he had a sister in Atlantic City that needed his help pronto. How about I give him a lift?

Ernie leaned over the back of my seat and said: "My sister Roberta got four crumb snatchers, age eight, nine, ten, eleven. She lose her husband suddenlike six years ago. She been having troubles in her neighborhood."

Ernie paused. Angel yawned. I drummed my fingers on the steering wheel. Two, three, four. "What kind of troubles, Ernie?"

"Well, the main thing she notice is, they burning down houses on her street."

"Arson? Somebody got those old buildings heavily insured?"

"And pretty near all the car windshields on that street get club-smashed," Ernie added. "Couple neighbors get clobbered, too, they come out, see if they can stop it. Folks getting scared on that block, Easy."

"Kids do it?"

"Search me," Ernie said. "Be pretty tough kids."

"Want some help with it?"

You could feel Ernie not thinking that over. "Yeah. That be okay, Easy."

We didn't say much else for a while. Up through the salt marshes the Asbury Park exit flashed. When I was seventeen we'd squeeze eight of us in a car, boys and girls, and drive at night to the rides at Asbury Park. Later it was the bars. In those days it was always Asbury Park, never Seaside Heights or the other white boardwalks. Sleep all night on the sand sometimes, after the park closed.

Out of nowhere Angel said, in a small voice, "You like this Muff lady, Easy?"

"She made me feel special, all hepped up, you know?"

Angel hissed, "But you don't truss her?"

"You kidding? She blew smoke up every pipe I got, with a smile. I didn't mind: she's only looking after herself. I do have a jump on something, though. Muff told me she worked at the Golden Nugget, but she doesn't. I think she didn't want me to wire her City by the Sea connection with a man named Charlie Faucher. Fellow from Newark, by the way. You remember him?"

Angel shook his head. "He is who?"

"Chief of the Organized Crime Bureau. They used to tell stories about him when I was shuffling a beat and riding the radio cars. After I went over to Bunco Squad, I worked on a couple task forces under Faucher. He was something, all right. Faucher knew more about Newark than the police commissioner or the mayor. Then he retired and took a cushy job with a casino. Vice president of security, he is, at City by the Sea."

"Why should Angel remember this Faucher?"

"He handled some spectacular crimes—like the Jimmy Finnochio murder, same as Muff hired me to reinvestigate. Now, it turns out, Faucher works at the same place as old Muff."

"Jersey is a very small place sometimes. How come you don't be a big wheels in Atlanty City, too, Easy? You could live in the casino all the time!"

"Casinos're all paranoid about their mafia connections," I explained. "And who in New Jersey's gonna blame them? Casino Commission's breathing down their necks all the time. Charlie Faucher had just the credentials to write his own ticket with the casinos." Angel's eyes went alive at the thought.

"Don't you remember Faucher? Hard to forget Jimmy the Cricket's murder. Especially when, two days later, they found a second body stuffed in another car trunk. Parked outside the Newark courthouse?"

"I remember that. Who was in this trunk?"

"Some accountant that did books for New York OC. Financial wizard for one of the families. Jewish man, but a gangster all the same."

"Why he get put in the trunk?"

"Who knows? But the papers loved the trunk-stuffing epidemic angle. Charlie Faucher headed that investigation too. Remember now?"

Angel sighed. "Who can keep track of all punks that are stuffed in trunks? They could have a Punk of the Month in the Trunk club in Nowork."

A few minutes later we peeled off the Parkway to speed east on the eight-lane Atlantic City Expressway, five miles of tidal marsh that makes AC technically an island and indisputably a world all its own.

On the expressway's center island the casinos provide employee parking and shuttle buses. We passed signs for Harrah's, Resorts International, Bally's, the Claridge, the Atlantis, Trump Plaza, City by the Sea, the Tropicana, Toby's Royale, the Golden Nugget, and Caesar's. Just off the right lane marched billboard after billboard, staked in the salt marshes, advertising the current entertainers. Joan Rivers and David Brenner would be at the Sands. Cosby was just finishing at Harrah's. Angel stared at the billboards solemnly.

"How much money does people win every day here, Easy?"

"You mean, net profit? I think they program it so the customers lose about ten, fifteen percent of every dollar they bet. In the long run you just pay for the fun of losing."

Angel snorted. "Some casinos pay a lot. How many casinos they got, Easy?"

"Twelve, right now. They'll be adding one a year up to 1990. Sixteen in all. Papers've been full of the elbowing by these corporations to grab the last pieces of action. Only one license hasn't been assigned yet, papers say. That one'll be it, for quite a while."

On billboards advertising the generous payoffs, the favorite symbol was a pot of gold coins spilling out of a floppy pirate's sack. FASTEST BILLION PAID. STRIKE IT RICH!

Then we were driving through Monopolyland, down dilapidated Baltic Avenue: tiny shacks, really beach bungalows serving as tenement apartments, tricked out with stoops and miniature iron railings, shoulder to shoulder down both sides of the boulevard. Not even driveways between them. Both Angel and Ernie sat up and looked intently out their windows.

"Don't look nothing like Nork," Ernie remarked.

He was right. Where Newark's miseries looked like a wino's mouthful of stumps, Atlantic City was an old, once-gaudy set of false choppers, cheapy even and too shiny, and the thin enamel all flaking off.

We turned right on New York Avenue and drove ocean-wards. Angel, beside me, gave a little gasp when the casino signs fanfared into view. Atlantic City has been chopped off at seven or eight stories, except for the curved line of casino towers skying above it all and blocking off the ocean. The way they'd rigged it, all the way across AC, you felt you were staring across a chancy desert and glimpsing the cool, mysterious mountains. Each tower sported a huge lit-up sign advertising the casino's name. Dwarfing the city, the red, green, and electric-blue signs kept grabbing my eyes, even as I twisted the wheel down bad streets, through bad traffic. Every time I'd tear my gaze from those plastic beacons, they'd blink into the corners of my eyes like street flecks.

The closer we got to the Boardwalk, the worse the city looked. Just half a block from the glitter of casino alley, Atlantic City looked more like a falling-down movie set than a live town. More of Newark may have actually collapsed, but somehow Newark didn't depress me as much. Maybe because much of Newark was built fifty years ago, when it had a solid economy, and the houses, in whatever state of repair, were stone, and brick, and solid wood. In AC things were just thrown up and patched through the decades with cheap asphalt siding, chewing gum, and rubber bands.

Like other gambling towns, Atlantic City, even with less than fifty thousand residents, had the look of a small city. The avenues were wide and the old trolley wires still dangled overhead. Yet nearly all the legitimate merchants had fled, leaving the guerrilla retailers in charge: an ornate corner furniture store was now a tee-shirt distributor; corner taverns had run down into restaurants with hand-lettered signs and boards over the windows, so you dove in blindly—if your stomach and brains were that numb.

The town's municipal buildings were newish and nondescript, and already dirty-looking, and they were set back on side streets because the traffic, utilities, and neighbors were hopeless on the main roads. The pedestrians just drifted along, nobody hustling any place, nowhere special to be, nothing urgent to do.

We crossed Atlantic and Pacific avenues and dropped squirming Ernie off behind City by the Sea casino to cool his gambling blood. Like the other casinos, City by the Sea turned a fat cow's behind towards Atlantic Avenue and the people of Atlantic City: a tall, block-wide, blank wall; whitewashed brick, cheerful logo, no doors, no windows. No openings.

I promised Ernie that we'd pick him up in a couple of hours. Angel and I watched Ernie's stick body marionette through the casino's rear entrance.

Then we drove down Atlantic, turned left on Park Place, made the circle past the neon flash of Bally's, the haughty chic of Claridge's, the windswept Vegas look of the Sands's rear lobby, and U-turned back onto Pacific. Park Place is glamorous until you notice that not one of the three casinos chips in for flowers in the communal park, and up close you can see that the fountain is ringed with Cyclone fence and barbed wire. At the end of Georgia Avenue we pulled into a Kinney System parking garage practically under the Boardwalk. Angel hopped out happily, while I told the attendant our bags should go to City by the Sea. They were not running an economy operation. The attendant didn't smile until I tipped a second five-spot on his palm.

Ah, the price of high life. Felt good thinking how old, well-heeled Patricia Valentine was picking up the expenses tab. The parking lot man offered us a lift back down to City by the Sea on his converted golf cart, but being without luggage, Angel and I decided to stroll up the Boardwalk and through the gambling palace.

The Boardwalk was wide there—at least seventy-five feet across—and swarming with summer tourists. On our left, in the eye-sparkle sun, the white beach was so broad it appeared to smear the Boardwalk/Casinos strip between it and the old city. A second later the immensity of the pounding ocean really clubbed us and made me feel sandwiched between sullen land and dangerous water. It was so hot, the sandwich felt like grilled cheese, and we were the Kraft's singles.

The constant ocean breeze took the edge off, but my underarms still broke a sweat. And the haze had me squinting hard. About half the women on the Boardwalk wore their backs bare in little sundresses, or their stomachs bare in halter tops. Plenty of female heads in curlers and babushkas, screwing in those waves for the evening's fun. Atlantic City is a nighttime town; daytime is a slow cycle of anticipation.

The men wore running shorts or bathing suits, or sometimes Bermuda shorts, with colorful tee-shirts. Once in a while a golden-age couple walked by, skirted and seersucker jacketed. There was a sprinkling of strollers too. A tram went by, loaded with sunglassed tourists. Practically everybody but the babies was wearing sunglasses.

Everybody, including babies, was clutching something, mostly shopping bags, sometimes fast food, with Boardwalk custard the big winner that sizzling afternoon.

On its Boardwalk end, City by the Sea casino/hotel was the narrowest of AC casinos. Just a fifty-foot width to anchor the ten-story facade it propped on the Boardwalk. And behind that a thirty-story hotel and executive office tower.

But to my eyes it offered the classiest-looking glitz. Each casino presented a slightly different face to the hungry crowd. The Sands went for desert resort atriums and windswept stucco. Bally's was Hollywood premiere lights and skyscraper architecture. The Claridge used the only hotel building legacied from Atlantic City's Victorian past to come on as a classy English hotel.

But you can't look too thin or too rich. Tall, skinny City by the Sea went in for continental sophistication, New Jersey style: dark blue awnings, monogrammed with intertwined C's and S's, thick beveled glass on the picture windows, real teak trim on all the windows and doors.

After the outside steam, inside was so dark and cold your eyes spun and your balance melted. Unlike most of the others, this casino didn't make its hotel guests walk through the gambling floor to register. It played hotel right up front, with the reservations desks and bellhops operating in the front lobby. While Angel waited in line to get us rooms, I walked through to peek at the casino floor. It was crammed, maybe because it was so well air-conditioned. All the tables and dice pits were full, slot machines backed up with waiting lines three deep.

First disappointment of vacation. No reservation, no rooms. A reservation made weeks in advance. We could fill ten times as many rooms, the girlish desk clerk smiled at me. She punched a code into the computer terminal facing her, found that Toby's Royale had a last-minute cancellation. Sold, I said. She offered pleasantly to send someone with our bags. I hated handing her a tip, she was so young and nice, but the service called for it. I tucked a ten-spot in her hand and asked her to take care of the bellhop.

Three blocks back up the Boardwalk, Angel and I sauntered past the parking garage to Mississippi Avenue and Toby's Royale. Toby's strove for middle-browed appeal: its outside looked papered in aluminum foil, with round cement pillars and dark green plastic everywhere. Inside, it was decorated to impersonate a Ramada Inn. Angel and I rode up a monumental escalator at the core of a concrete cylinder before arriving at the hotel check-in.

The rooms we were shown to, three doors apart, were pie-shaped, with the bathroom at the wedge's point, and floor-to-ceiling glass curving like the crust. Drapes made it twilight dark in there before the bellhop flicked on the lights. Everything was miniaturized and immobile, like a railroad stateroom. Built-in dresser and desk, swiveling color TV, one entire wall mirrored to ward off claustrophobia. Cool, dry hygienic air, though. Sanitized toilets, personal bath mat.

I stepped to the fully-draped windows, hoping there'd be a sliding door and balcony. But I guess those sheets of glass were strictly for architectural show. There was nothing you could open or vent. And when I pulleyed open the drapes, I was looking across twenty acres of asphalt roofing to the AC slums. Most guests wouldn't want or need a balcony there.

When we met at the elevator, Angel had changed into black tights and a baggy pink sweatshirt with a huge neck opening that slipped over one shoulder. Different wig—something designed for Tina Turner—long string of neck beads. The outfit was too hot for outdoor wear. Angel was planning to cruise an air-conditioned casino.

I asked him to nose around where AC dancers jiggled and learn what he could about Muff Anglaise. I had no serious doubts but that her disappearance was just a case of shacking up with some high roller for a few days. But I was still looking forward to seeing her again. I don't meet so many hot women these days.

"I'll be drifting over to Ernie's sister's place. Meet up in our rooms, maybe one or two o'clock tonight, okay?"

"Papi?"

"Yeah."

"I meet you in the Seacity casino, okay? At the dice tables."

"You mean, City by the Sea?"

Angel awarded me his biggest smile and bounced on his toes about four times. Just thinking of the high rollers you find around the craps pits put a sparkle in his eyes.

CHAPTER FOUR

○

When the speculators built Atlantic City from scratch in the 1850s, they were looking to grease parcel sales of land. So they laid the whole place out on a grid, angles sharp as a Monopoly board, avenues named after the seven seas running with the coastline, streets and avenues tagged for eastern and western states crossing them.

Utah Avenue runs down to and bounces off the casino line on the Boardwalk: two blocks of unbroken two-story duplexes thrown up a century ago, and cheaply built even then, despite an occasional Italian-looking scroll or bracket. These days, siding gaped on most of them, or was partly nailed over with strange-colored shingles. At the street's far end strips of tarpaper tended to serve in place of lavender asphalt. Ernie's sister Roberta had pink stucco smeared on her house, and lived just across the moat of Pacific Avenue, within spitting and wishful-thinking distance of City by the Sea casino/hotel.

Nobody was home when Ernie and I strolled up. We hunkered on the front stoop and jawed with the old man weighted into the lawn chair on the next-door stoop and his wife, who wouldn't come out from behind her storm door.

"She don't be long getting back, Ernie," the lady neighbor croaked. If she wasn't black, I'd swear she sounded Italian. She stood under five feet tall and was dressed in an ebony dress. And once you heard her, she looked exactly like a black Mama Celeste. "They just gone out to buy some groceries."

Ernie groaned. "That mean they left the city."

The old man said, "Yef, that's right." He tugged at the bill of a new dark blue baseball cap with USS FORRESTAL stitched across the front. "Mrs. Evans have Junior drive her and Roberta and Betty Marlowe from down the block to the supermarket. Over to Absecon, load up on food. Junior got hisself a van what they can pile a whole lot of bags in."

"Not a supermarket in this sorry town," Ernie tight-lipped to me. "Even with it's got fifty thousand year-round live-ins."

"You're kidding," I said. "Why the hell not?"

"Because," the woman said, with a tone of irony, "casinos can't have their customers buying food no place but the Boardwalk—don't make no money that way."

My eyes bugged. "That can't be the whole story. You got to have plenty of transients and such in this town, ma'am, that don't use supermarkets."

"Supermarkets afraid to come in here," hissed the old navy man from his webbed chair. "We too tough for 'em."

"Pathmark'll go any old place," Ernie retorted. "They in Newark, Jersey City, Elizabeth. They ain't afraid to come to no Atlantic City."

"Your ass they ain't."

Ernie stood up and stretched to full five feet five. My old friend has long, bowed arms that hang nearly to his knees. He was wearing a short-sleeved leisure jacket in black and white checks over his white strap tee-shirt, matching shorts, and black nylon knee socks. He adjusted the tilt on his black English driving cap. The seated old man growled.

That's when a tan van loaded with ladies and grocery bags rumbled up to the house. A big-shouldered, earnest-looking boy was at the wheel. The side door slid open and a thin, erect older woman climbed out, brown coat and veil-hat in place even in June. Behind her clambered a much younger, big-breasted woman in shorts and a sleeveless top, then an ageless hefty woman with wild eyes and a color scheme to match.

"Ernie, give a hand here," commanded the youngest woman, by way of greeting. To me, "You, too, mister. Those muscles must be good for something besides romancin' pretty women."

I'd met Ernie's sister years ago at their mother's funeral. Didn't look like she remembered me. She was thirty years younger than Ernie's sixty-two, thanks to their mother's forty years of bearing fifteen babies, five still alive. Youngest of the brood, Roberta had married a teacher in the Newark public schools when she was just sixteen, had wept at his funeral when she was twenty-two. Four young boys with healthy appetites and the row house in AC were all she was left to remember him by.

"You get the door," Ernie blustered. "Menfolk'll manhandle those bags." I grinned back at Roberta's big-eyed smile. She was a large, shapely woman, meaty, not fat.

The boy driver shook my hand solemnly when Ernie

introduced us. Junior Evans lived down the block, Ernie said, worked security in the City by the Sea casino. By the way he fussed, his van was most everything in the world to Junior. On the driver's door, in small red script letters, was spelled, *Feedbag Express*.

One step inside the front door the row house split into a narrow corridor and a flight of stairs, an arrangement that would facilitate renting the upstairs rooms when hard times struck. At the end of the corridor, left, center, and right doorways opened respectively into the living room, dining room, and kitchen. Turning right, with a grocery bag in my hands, I couldn't help but notice that Roberta's dining room was set up as a children's bedroom, with two sets of bunk beds.

In the old-fashioned kitchen, Roberta squeezed my right bicep. "When Ernie told us you'd be down this way," she said in my ear, "we all felt so glad and excited."

I smiled again and nodded. Then I excused myself and stepped outside quickly to buttonhole Ernie, who was puffing up the stairs with the last chow bag.

"The hell did you tell these people, Horton?" I demanded. "You didn't even know I was headed down here until this afternoon."

"I only said as you was good at fixing troubles." Ernie shone the eyes of a three-year-old on me and pep-stepped it up the stairs.

Back inside, Junior Evans cornered me with his bulk and grabbed for my hand, pressing it like I had marched the rats from Atlantic City. His eyes gleamed with soul.

"Hey, man . . ." I started. But Junior was nodding his head and backing away slowly, pointing his forefinger rhythmically and approvingly at me.

Roberta pressed a sweating glass into my hand.

"Drink this," she said. "Lemonade. I don't like to serve beer with Ernie around. Make yourself comfortable while the block rounds itself up."

I sat at the metal-rimmed Formica table watching Roberta stretch to reach the top cupboard shelves.

Through the doorway I could see neighbors filing into the living room. By the time I'd eaten half a plate of home-baked gingersnap cookies, the overflow was spilling into the kitchen, everybody grinning and buzzing.

Roberta led me into the living room. "Listen up now, folks." She waved the gathering to a whisper. "My brother Ernie, who most of you already know, is down from Newark, bringing his close friend, Mr. Ezell Barnes, to help us. You all know about Mr. Barnes."

There was more than a little clapping and cheering. Ernie stood up and pivoted to soak it up, while I tensed my jaw.

"You got it right, folks," Ernie interrupted, nodding like a king. "When Roberta called, tell me how you all was getting pestered by the mob, I figured there's just one man'd be best at swatting them off."

"Mob?" My choked voice was swallowed in the second ripple of approval. Too many folks blocked the way for me to grab Ernie's neck with both hands.

Ernie was in his glory. "No case too big for this man," he sang, saluting me fondly, like he'd personally hatched me. "He takes on the power boys and gets results. Why, last big case Ezell Barnes and me cracked open brang the city of Newark to its knees." Ernie pointed his forefinger at the ceiling and slowly tilted it straight at me. Every head in the room swiveled expectantly.

A casino chip was caught in my tonsils. I got out, "Lot of folks suggested that." Then I stopped coughing. "What's the problem on you all?"

"Ernie didn't tell you?" Roberta turned on Ernie with a look only relatives are allowed. "We sent him that follow-up letter explaining everything, along with a money order for one hundred dollars, like you asked for. The letter didn't spell things out clear enough for you?"

"Well," I soft-shoed, "I got a general idea, but I need more details. Incidentally, I'm not charging for this case." I aimed a fat smile at Ernie's astonished face. "All your hard-earned money's coming back to you. Now, you need some street toughs pulled off you, that it?"

It was nothing so simple. Roberta's next-door neighbor snapped quickly: "This city always been divided between the haves and the have-nots. People on this street own nothing but the clothes on our backs and the roofs over our heads."

"I understand," I said. "What about the vandals, and the—"

"Now the casinos want to branch out," Roberta interrupted, strong timbre in her voice. I remembered how pretty she used to be. "They're losing money in the gambling business, so they figure to make it up in housing, condos, and the like, close to the action."

The dignified, scrawny lady from Junior's van—Roberta's

mother-in-law—added proudly, "Our places are too expensive for them." Everybody in the room murmured.

Glancing involuntarily at the brown stain covering nearly half of Roberta's ceiling, I said cautiously, "How do you mean, 'expensive'?"

Roberta's neighbor wore his navy cap indoors. "Ain't our block been picked for them to build on? The independent appraiser said each of our lots was worth a hundred and twenty grand, being close to the ocean and the casinos and such."

"We been waiting for the pot of gold," a brillo-haired woman put in from the back, "and it's finally here." A chorus of Amens ran through the gallery. She jerked her head towards the street. "Except for them."

"I say we should cash in the chips now," the navy man's wife insisted in her Italian voice. She had changed into a bright print blouse and tugged her gray hair back in a bun. "We go a-rainbow climbing, all we gonna find on a other side is pot luck."

"Rubbish, woman." The old salt glared as best he could with seawater eyes. "We gonna land in Magnolia. These bones feel it." His wife hmmphed him back.

"Most of these folks," he said, exasperated, "they got more to lose than we do—least we got my disability income to float us."

I looked more closely at him. His legs hung like straps.

He caught my stare. "Lost my legs in the big one. Solomon Islands, greatest sea battle ever fought, bigger'n even the Spanish Armada."

"We gone be stuck here another cold winter," his wife said.

I cut in. "I don't get the whole picture."

"We got a basic disagreement here," the old man said. "As to what's a fair price for our houses. Looky, we don't mind moving, nobody minds moving, do we? So long's we get that fair price for our homes."

"How much they offering?"

"Penny ante," the brillo-haired woman chimed in. "It was pitiful, and we told them so."

"How much we talking about?"

"Ten thousand dollars per property," Junior Evans contributed quietly.

"How many properties?"

"Forty," Junior said.

"Ten thousand is no pot of gold." I turned to the navy vet.

"But it's a lot of bread for these old bungalows. Official appraisals are usually way high, you know."

His wife moaned approval and dug an elbow into her husband's side.

"Nobody wants these here shacks for nothing." The old sailor propped himself up in his chair. "Including us. It's the land. Real estate's funny. You go along, and go along, place is worthless, then the developers decide they got to have your lot, and bingo, your turn at a piece of the pie."

"They make a second offer?"

"Oh my, yes. A whole series of them." Roberta's big solid body shook. "First they torched Mr. Caldwell's house when he wasn't home. And then hoodlums jumped Alice Pierce's boy, Larvelle, and broke his arm."

"That's just the start," snorted the only white woman in the room. She looked seventy years old, but had kept her body clean and was wearing tight jeans and a vee-necked sweater the color of her white hair over tanned skin. "Vandalism is nonstop around here, what with the slashed tires and broken windows."

"Police just look the other way, I reckon?"

"Lawdy-dawdy," Roberta's mother-in-law answered. "All our police are up on the Boardwalk, making sure the out-of-town folks don't get mussed."

Junior Evans explained, "ACPD look the other way? Why, they don't need to. They plain don't never come around this neck of the woods."

"So you want I should scare off these thugs?"

"Shoot." Roberta's paralyzed neighbor waved a hand at the thought of them. "We take care of them hoods ourselves, one of these times."

"Watch yourselves," I said.

"We been talking. Plan is, we need a truck."

"A big truck." Junior grinned back at Roberta's neighbor. "Like a garbage truck."

"You got that right. Something big as a battleship. Some night we lie waiting in that truck until these cowards set to performing their evil. Then we start up our battlewagon and run them over, hard. Just like we squashed the Japs."

"That'd be manslaughter," I objected.

"Yeah!" Junior and Salty whooped it up.

My uneasiness had grown to a knot in my lungs. "Then just what did you want out of me?"

"Get the fair price for our properties, of course!" the white woman answered. "Get a second party to pay the hundred and twenty."

"I'd have to say, I'm better at the rough stuff than at free enterprise."

"Ernie said you could make a couple calls," Roberta said eagerly. "Start the ball rolling. That's all we ask for, a couple of those phone calls."

They almost hushed, waiting for me to swear an oath.

"See what I can do."

The roof threatened to rocket off the house. Only the old navy man's wife sat quietly, shaking her head.

I bumped knees out of the living room after that, fast as I could, elbow-towing Ernie, who was working up nice vehemence for the crowd about how he and I were going to kick ass.

In the kitchen the noise was so thick, Roberta had to come up and shout in my ear, "How about you stay here?"

She'd put one arm around my neck. Other people milling around us were pressing most of her lightly against me.

"Thanks plenty," I said, hastily enough to sound rude. "I'm already checked in at Toby's Royale." What I read in Roberta's eyes might have been disappointment, or reproach, or maybe a touch of envy.

"The casinos are behind this, you say?"

"Well, we've been approached by three or four developers. But lately just the one, Short Line Enterprises. Chamber of Commerce says they are a brand new outfit."

"So we don't even know who's causing all the grief?"

"Here's what we guess. Junior says they've got a scale model of a condominium building on display in City by the Sea. They don't say where they're going to build it, but isn't this the ideal spot for them, across the street?"

"First thing I got to do is pin down who we're actually dealing with."

"Check in with me tomorrow?"

"I'll keep you posted, kiddo," I said carefully. Last thing in the world I needed was to have these people checking up on me every ten minutes. Second to last was to be a shining knight in this lonely lady's life.

"Mr. Barnes." The navy vet's wife tapped my shoulder. "Could I have a word with you, in private?"

Roberta took her cue and eased on back to the living room.

"I don't want to make no scene in front of these people," she said, glancing over her shoulder. She waltzed me a couple steps towards the back door to make sure we were out of earshot. "My husband is a proud man—you got ears, you could hear that. But sometimes he let his pride get over on his good sense."

"You want to take the money and run?"

"Sure," she said confidently, then sighed. "The deed to our house is in my name. Some money come to me during the war. I bought our house for a song and dance—and that's about what it's worth today."

I nodded.

"If we lose this bluff, we gone be stuck in these shacks forever."

"You understand that if just one party out of forty sells, the others are worthless on the open market? Developers want the whole damned parcel or nothing."

She shrugged. "I know. But who can wait forever? Last time I wait, my husband went off to war and lost the use of his legs. I'm not gone wait again and lose my chance to get out of this crummy town."

"Where will you go?"

"We got a good chance to get into a veterans' retirement center in Florida. It's comfortable, and disabled veterans get first come. Ten thousand dollars's more than enough to set us up down there."

"I understand." My face felt tight. "Listen, aren't you willing to wait, just for a while, see what I can do, give all your neighbors a chance?" I bore in with my eyes.

"Well . . ." She glanced towards the living room door, then at my urgent face. "Maybe we could wait a week—no, a few days. And then, whether my husband agrees or not, I'm gonna sell."

"Fair enough," I said quickly. "Just until the end of next week."

She grabbed my forearm. "You won't tell nobody?"

"Not a soul. And thanks, ma'am."

Eyes brightening, she patted my arm and trotted off to sit again by her husband's side.

She passed Ernie Horton threading out, accepting congratulations from all sides.

I wasted no time dragging Ernie out to the truck. Junior Evans tagged after us.

"What should we do if trouble starts in the meantime?" the boy asked in his solemn way, kicking at a pebble with a big sneakered foot.

I looked at his hardened face behind the dark sunshades. A man's body steered by a boy's machismo.

"Turn the other cheek," I told him. "Unless somebody's life gets threatened. Then call me. Just let me shake things up some, all right, man? These're professional toughs."

"Where you going now?"

"Where we going, Easy?" Ernie repeated sadly, wishing he was back inside doing the hero shuffle.

"Me'n Ernie got a friend to drop in on, Junior."

"You got room for one more?"

I hesitated half a second. The boy was tall and wide, built heaps better for the night's work than old Ernie. But he was also seventeen years old. He deserved to finish his boyhood.

"I think we'll just drift, man," I said. "Catch you tomorrow?"

I fired up the little Nissan truck and wheeled down the block.

"Look," Ernie said excitedly. I glanced in the rearview. On Roberta's tiny lawn the entire neighborhood was congregated, waving us good-bye, some of the women with both hands. I groaned. Ernie leaned across me and delivered a cheerful flourish of the horn.

CHAPTER FIVE

O

Two blocks left on Pacific Avenue, driving past the tacky gold and red horizontal bars that frame Caesar's massive rear entrance, I turned on Ernie.

"Use those finger forks," I told him. "Give me the one hundred dollars."

"I ain't got it." Ernie avoided my eye. "Spent it already. Snookie spent the most of it. Damn fool drunk."

"Whyn't you come ask me? I'm good for a few bucks when you're light. You know that."

"Ain't no charity case."

"You ain't no thief either, brother." I revved the engine at the Missouri Avenue light and said sourly, "At least not up till now."

Ernie pulled his lips in and stretched the skin tight on his forehead. "Look, man," I told him. "I'll pay those folks back—I mean, it was me that took their case on for free."

Ernie stirred and began looking around him. I kept lecturing: "But you're gonna have to work the tab off, man. While we're down here, any leg work, odds and ends I need done, you earn your hundred bucks on. Sound fair?"

Ernie missed every word I said. He was craning his neck down towards the beach and bouncing up and down in his seat. The light flicked green. As we pulled off, Ernie managed to shout over his shoulder:

"This's where she was! Gol-dammy! Chicken Bone Beach! More fun than the law should allow, Easy, let me tell you on it."

"The hell is Chicken Bone Beach?"

Ernie snorted at me. "Where the colored folks have their beach. When I was in my prime."

"End of Missouri Ave, huh?"

"Sure. Blacks that work in the hotels got told to lay off the white beaches. So they go down to Missouri, instead. Forty

34

years back we used to drive down from Nork sometimes, mingle with the tingle."

"What's the name mean?"

"Well, black folks was always making picnics with fried chicken and cake, and cold drinks and such. Come a sunny day, beach'd be all full of cabanas and blankets, and every blanket have two or three tin boxes full of good things to eat. You just spend all day on the beach, eat whenever the fits strike you. The chicken always taste fine."

Ernie was so lost in memories, smiles wreathing his brow, that I pulled over to Kentucky and parked. Up half a block you could see the weathered maroon marquee of the legendary Club Harlem, with the hula-skirted Sepia girl banging on her tom-tom.

"Look," I nudged him.

"Oh," said Ernie. "Time and again entertainers from the Harlem and the *de*-funked Paradise Club'd come down the beach—the Platters, Count Basie, Chris Columbo, even Joe Louis or Nat Cole. Showgirls from the clubs called that beach Sunshine Row. Make the white folks laugh to see them getting a tan, though."

Ernie's eyes were bright. I said, "Sounds like a good time, man."

"Everybody'd be improvising gags, singing tunes, everything you could think of. Where could you go to find fun like that nowadays?"

"There a lot of black folks in Atlantic City, those days?"

"Shoot, we come down from Nork," Ernie said with relish, "there be twice the number colored down here as up there. 'Course, they originally from Philly, mostly."

"Looking for jobs in the hotels and resorts, probably."

"Well, yeah. But plenty of 'em was just looking to have theyself a *time*, just for that day. Trains from Philly'd get you here in a hour flat, those days. You never came down much yourself, did you, Easy?"

I shrugged. "A few times. And a few more times on business. By the time I was raising-hell age, the late sixties, most of Atlantic City's glamor had seeped away, you know? Crummy little amusememts and hot dog stands. Strictly third-rate entertainers at the clubs."

"You and me," Ernie said fervently, "got to catch the acts at the Club Harlem some night we're here."

"Deal," I said.

"How about tonight?"

"Not a chance." I shook my head. "Tonight you and me are gonna stake out Roberta's block, see what's cooking."

Ernie's got selective hearing. "Yeah, I sure am hungry," he said. "I know this fast-fish joint down the block, won't cost us an arm and a leg."

The seafood dive sat appropriately on Atlantic Avenue, though there was nothing nautical about the single room's decor. Salvaged coffee shop tables crammed one end, double deep-fat vat and industrial shelving were plunked at the other. You yelled your order directly at the frycook. The other customers had recently crawled from under some sink. The menu specialized in clam balls, oily fritters that sank to the pit of my stomach like flounder tackle. Just as well Angel wasn't along: there'd be no end to the clam-ball jokes.

We walked out into a dark night sky, no moon on the rise, but plenty of folks out cruising and perusing in the warm weather. Stomachs whimpering, we drove back to Utah Avenue and found a three-hour parking slot, no meter, at the Pacific Avenue corner, where the streetlamp was broken. At this hour neither Roberta nor any of her neighbors were to be seen on the street. The only familiar sign was the tan van belonging to Junior Evans, still parked in front of Roberta's duplex. I adjusted the tape deck, tipped my seat back.

Took Ernie about twenty minutes to get antsy. "How they gonna come at us?" he asked three times.

The third time, I answered, "Maybe they'll pull up in a hoodmobile, sneak around with a vacuum cleaner hose, connect their tail pipe to Roberta's mail slot. Guido and Louie'd probably think it's worth a try."

"You kidding?" Ernie said, eyes wide.

When I didn't answer, he insisted, "You think something's gonna jump funny tonight, Easy?"

I had my eye on a little pack of teenagers smoking and slapping under the streetlamp at the opposite end of the block. "Give it a chance to roll slow."

By eleven o'clock houselights winked out as the elderly neighborhood tucked in for the night. Ernie had snaked down in his seat and dozed off too. I puffed on my fourth Chesterfield and kept the watch.

The traffic never totally stopped, but by one-thirty A.M. things had settled down. Head against the rest, tape player barely humming, my ears perked at the grate of thin car brakes and the crunch of road sand. When whoever it was graveled past us, I eased up enough to see an old LeMans ragtop, headlights doused, roll halfway down the block and idle double-parked.

I elbowed Ernie. "Wha?" he muttered.

"Silverfishes've crawled out," I whispered. "Cover my tail. I get sandbagged, you raise the alarm."

Both doors of the convertible finned out, and twin dark figures faded into the shadows of the building line, but not before I saw that one was lugging a big suitcase or box, the other hefting a four-foot bar. I eased out of the truck, bent over, and moved up the block, peering for them. Too dark. I stopped my feet. They glided into the edge of thin yellow light outside Roberta's door. They appeared to be checking door numbers. Then they huddled over the dark box.

While I was snaking over to their idling convertible, one of the sneakers lifted up the box and shook it, as if in a rage, at Junior Evans's van. The other man's face was illuminated for half a second before he cupped the match. I saw his hand reach first towards his head, then, open palmed, towards Junior's van. The flicked match rode through the dark like a little chariot.

I was paralyzed, watching it happen.

An orange fireball snarled from the top of the van and undulated down its side panels.

Silhouetted in the fire, both men sprinted back towards their car, not yet clued that its engine had been cut. Or that, while the shaft of their car key was still tucked in its slot, the part you turn it with was nestled in the palm of my hand. Junior's van was burning merrily, but more quietly. Lights were still off in the houses.

I was waiting for them in the shadows. The lead man never saw me angle in until I forearm-shivered him flush under the chin. The gasoline can he was carrying clattered on the sidewalk the same time he splayed out on the road, hard. I shifted feet fast enough to square off his partner beading down, crowbar menacing me over his head.

That chump goombah stood twirling the pry bar. My eyes measured him: six inches shorter than my six-one, weight nearly up to mine, with plenty of upper body. Fancy yellow shirt opened three buttons worth, dress slacks, and pointy dress shoes.

He was still drum majoring when I faked in against him so

his elbows were braced against my back, the crowbar waving harmlessly behind me. Then I shoved him off, like grunting out a bench press, pulled my right shoulder back and tattooed him through his cover-up elbows. As solid a right hand as I ever threw in eight years of Army and professional boxing. Tactile memories flashed.

The man blew back as if I'd fire-hosed him. But I had lost track of his partner until a corner-eye movement jangled my reflexes. I ducked and slid.

But old Ernie had me covered. He had grabbed hair and was he-ain't-heavying the arsonist's back. Growling, the thug waggled from side to side. Windows yellowed in the darkened houses.

I started for them, then jerked back when the man on the ground staggered to his feet and noiselessly scooped up his crowbar. I fist-menaced him back two steps, shot a quick glance in Ernie's direction—and lickety-split banged onto my rear end as crowbarman slid right at me, kicked a leg and hooked my ankle. More mad than hurt, I crabbed around in the grit and elbowed up just as he did. I sneered the wolf's grin off that tough's ugly face, circling my fist at him like Mohammed Ali. He backed up. I stayed with him, mocking his crowbar jabs.

Fright pulled apart his face. He looked shaky enough to try pulling the bar over his shoulder for leverage. The instant he did, I hooked a left at the soft spot of his temple. When he dropped this time, he made his first sound, a little moan. He kneed and palmed feebly away from me.

I let him crawl, and jumped the other creep, who had dumped little old Ernie on the pavement and was kicking him. I clenched a hammerlock on him and screwed it up tight, whooshing the breath out of him.

This one was short as his partner but maybe thirty pounds lighter. A pint-sized thug. Small on making noise, too, hammerlock or no.

I jerked him around, partly to let the hurt stab into his shoulder, partly to check on his buddy *gavone*. But that one was up on his feet and running pretty good, thin soles whapping, towards the lights of Atlantic Avenue.

No matter. Takes but one set of vocal chords to hum. I twisted the little dude's arm up one more notch. This time he sobbed.

"Wienie's in the zipper, now, Guido," I said unhurriedly. "Who sent you here?"

Apparently all his life Guido'd studied to be a stand-up guy. He said nothing, even choked back his sobbing. That arm of his creaked when I twisted it an eighth inch more. It was ready to break in six pieces.

So I relaxed the grip all at once, spun him around and pasted him across the mouth with the back of my right fist.

He couldn't help howling, through hands pressed against his bleeding lips. "This is how I make my living, Guido. I can do this all night."

I thought he'd be cursing me at least, but all the little man did was bare his teeth and squeeze his eyes to slits. A tear slid down one pockmarked cheek.

"You think I'm gonna get tired of this, you're wrong, man." I whaled a fist in from the side against his temple, hard enough to turn on blue lights inside his head, not hard enough to drop him.

"You hired by the Short Line people?"

He was half bent. Blood trickled from his brow where the temple shot had torn the skin. His eyes were frosted. His chin was up, though, and his teeth were still ready to savage me.

"I'm gonna stop hanging half-hearted on this," I said meaningfully, and elbowed him hard above the rib cage. Choking and spitting, he sagged until his head scratched the sidewalk.

I concentrated on remembering the harmless souls this scummer was terrorizing. I hardly noticed that some of them were now standing around us, mouths open and covered by their hands.

"Who do I want to meet at Short Line?" I asked softly. "You tell me now, kid, or I beat you into the ground. There's no cops around, no Miranda rights. Just you and me."

I pulled his head up by the hair and shook it until his eyes closed. "Talk." His eyes opened, focused slowly, fixed on me as if surprised. Then he spat at me, a pitiful little dribble that didn't even reach.

That was when Junior's van exploded, shattering its windows into glass shrapnel. A rear quarter panel blew off and crashed in the street.

People kept pouring out of the row houses up and down that block, clutching their nightclothes. I dropped Guido on the sidewalk, where he puddled clutching his head, picked Ernie up and leaned him against a car, checked him over for head bruises. He was all in one piece.

Junior's van wasn't so lucky.

CHAPTER SIX

o

"No, you listen to me. You people play the Mr. Softie jingle for
a siren, driving over here? The hell took you so long?"

Stupid way to start with the AC police department, for sure,
but I was sore. Twenty minutes it had taken them to answer
the call from Roberta's neighbors. Enough time for half the
street to get torched. What if I hadn't been there?

The detective lieutenant I was making myself clear to
headed the team just finishing up on Utah Avenue at three-
fifteen A.M. Two news photographers were still lining up shots
of the picturesque wreckage, faces bored. But little Guido was
packed into a squad car. Ernie, Junior, and a few of the
neighbors were ready to go give statements at the South
Carolina Avenue police station. Utah Avenue itself held fewer
rubberneckers than a World Series game in Shea.

After my foolish opening, whatever I said next to the cops
would have poor luck. But I outdid myself by begging off a
complete statement until the morning. I wanted to meet Angel
before the casinos closed at four A.M. When he heard that, the
middle-aged cop's eyes lit up. He closed his notebook very
gently and got ready to roast me but good.

I contemplated an apology, decided I'd rather gut myself
with a fillet knife. Then, bingo, I pushed the magic button by
allowing as how I was working on something with Charlie
Faucher over at City by the Sea. After that the good lieutenant
practically dusted my jacket for me.

Leaving my truck there, I walked a block towards the ocean.
On weekdays Atlantic City casinos stay open until four A.M.,
then close six hours for cleaning and whatnot. When I hustled
into the City by the Sea casino at three-twenty A.M., the first
floor was as crowded as before. If anything, the nervous twang
that's forever in the air a casino breathes was pitched up two
notes. Probably an anxiety refrain: no crack at winning it back
for six whole hours.

Shadowy in daylight hours, the light of sixty monstrous

chandeliers was almost eye-hurting after the outside dark. The City by the Sea casino was divided among three long and narrow floors, each a football field long by fifty feet wide. Each floor was individually decorated, offered a different set of games, and attracted its own clientele. Not knowing the place well, I checked out all three floors.

On the first floor the crowd was a half notch more dressed-up than when I'd peeked that afternoon, even though the games were nearly all slot machines and Big Six wheels. Most daytrippers had fled home, leaving a higher percentage of hotel guests; it was pantsuits on the blue-haired ladies, designer jeans on the younger men. At this late hour the latter were mussed and dragging; the little old ladies looked much fresher. Probably napped through till midnight.

The dealers, coin changers, and supervisors wore their evening outfits: black tuxedoes, starched powder-blue dress shirts, bow ties. The cocktail hostesses hoisted their trays of complimentary drinks in fishnet stockings and what looked like thigh-veed swimsuits.

The decor motif here was "By the Beautiful Sea," or something to that effect. The carpet was patterned in inter-locking red and black lobsters; the oak-colored walls were festooned with ships' wheels, anchors, and nets.

A long bar occupying a third of the back wall had no free stools.

Women in brown uniforms, holding walkie-talkies, checked everybody walking in the entrance for minimum age, and probably sobriety. More of these guards prowled the up-escalator entrances. I stepped past them and rode up.

The second floor's theme was probably "Salute to These United States." Red-white-and-blue carpeting, with eagles every so often, beige Mount Rushmore wallpaper. The win-dows were draped with the kind of bunting you usually see around electioneering politicians.

They played roulette and blackjack on this floor, and there was not an inch of unoccupied floor space. All the tables spun and spat cards at breakneck pace; the sky-blue baize was constantly relittered with chips: gold, white, red, light blue, light green, all with red or black centers. On this floor the ceiling camera eyes were designed to be noticeable, situated every twenty feet in rows of smoked-glass half-moons.

Here there was a younger crowd—fewer little old ladies, anyway—and the dress ran from sport shirts and slacks to sweaters and ties, plenty of double-knit suits, flower-print dresses, and high heels.

I squeezed through the mob in fruitless search of Angel, and was glad to catch my breath on the escalator to the top floor.

A step onto the third floor's thick burgundy carpet was clearly a step up the financial ladder. Up here the windows were masked by cascaded red silk, framed by pulled-back drapes that matched the sky-blue gaming tabletops. The motif continued clear around the shoe-box dimensions of the room.

To my right, about a third of the space was devoted to baccarat: figure-eight tables railed in gleaming ebony, with five red-sueded chairs along each fat curve. The cards were dealt by the players themselves, some wearing fitted dinner coats that cheapened the casino staff's monkey suits. The baccarat women were designered to the chin, and their ears and fingers flashed glamorously whenever they moved.

First you took in the glitter, then you noticed that a pair of unblinking eyes was watching each and every player. Mere spectators were discouraged around these tables.

I slid left, into the craps pits that marched two by two for a hundred fifty feet. The decor might be the same on this side, but the atmosphere was more salty, more open and emotional. A few tuxedoes dotted this crowd, too, but the background they were dotting included a lot of string ties, denim leisure outfits, and madras jackets. Not a sweater or a pair of shorts in sight.

Up here you knew it was after three in the morning, not by the fatigue in the air, but by the unconscious body English that voodooed the dice and the faces hot with snuffling up the last curls of pleasure.

It was easy to spot Angel at one of the craps tables, serving as good luck charm and general ornament. Angel himself only plays slots and the big money wheels, alongside the blue-haired ladies. But he can be talked into holding a high roller's hand or dice for him.

Craps is about as funky as a game gets, hoarse and colorful, played in a pit. The players circling the pit look raunchier and scream their emotions like nobody else in the casino. The game's line of noise is full of sexy double meanings. Angel looked right at home here, shimmering under the spotlights in glittery toreador pants and long-sleeved ruffled top. A diamond in the raunch.

As I walked up, Angel was wrapping his octopus arms

around a sugar daddy's leisure suit, priming his pump. Together they were one big smile. Pit boss and three other casino workers hawked everything and everybody. Overhead the camera eyes, every eight feet, stared at the hands playing, cupping dice, sliding chips across felt.

A leather-faced man stood at the table tossing and catching a pair of red dice. He was thin as a grass stalk, silver pompadoured, wore a pale red leisure suit. Standing alone, he was not saying a word, but he sure was smiling and eating the attention.

I edged closer. The Come Out roll was up. Angel's little partner had three piles stacked on the Pass line. Angel was blowing in little daddy's ear for luck as the dice bounced around and came up six the hard way, double threes. At the Come Point Angel whispered something, and his friend quickly upped his bet from a tiny pile of chips still racked in front of him.

Close up, the lights were dancing over the perspiration beads on Angel's friend's red face. But the entire crowd at the pit was a team, sharing cigarettes, sips of drinks, and high emotions. Not a Don't Come, Field, or Lay bet anywhere on the board. Everybody was betting along with the dice roller, laughing, stacking piles on the Come line, snapping down single yellow and green chips on the Buy and Place lines.

It's the most fun in the world when somebody rolling the bones gets hot and a big table just floats behind him—good feelings hold everybody together like a fluffy cloud. I wanted to lay down a bet of my own, but the crowd was packed in three deep in front of me.

Silver Pompadour passed the dice down, hand to hand, for Angel to kiss, which he did with great showmanship. Back in the skinny man's hand, the dice shook, bounded crazily, banked off the table's rubber-knobbed back wall. A four fell flat, but the other cube still spun, teetered, then fell. Two. The joint exploded in ecstasy. Drenched in sweat, Angel's little man staggered three steps back from the rail and flopped down like a puppet cut from marionette strings. His comrades-in-arms scooped him up. He lit a cigarette, handed it to Angel, and smiled. He kept smiling as Angel daintily picked out a few chips from the sausages in the polished wood-rail rack, pecked him on the cheek, and slipped out of the crowd.

I stepped around the mob to meet him.

"Some game." I grinned into Angel's shining face. "Who's your pal?"

"His name is Cocktail Frank," Angel told me, busy shoving the chips into the coin pocket of his purse.

"Why's that? He wasn't tasting a drop at the craps pit."

Angel explained the name. It had nothing to do with drinking.

Then he said, "Poor man is down on his luck and is lonely. Angel help him both things."

I rolled my eyes.

"And beside, Mr. Cheapie"—Angel wagged a fistful of chips in my face—"got no grubstake from you. What is a poor girl to do?"

"Speaking of girls," I said, waltzing Angel away and towards the exit doors. "You didn't bump into any old friends that know Muff Anglaise, did you?"

"Sure," Angel said gaily. "Seen Mimi a couple hours ago."

"And?"

"And Mimi say you girlfriend got this steady thing with Mr. Jones." Angel shook his head.

"Dope," I said, meaning me. "Of course—that washed-out look of hers the next morning, sudden case of chills. Smack downside."

Angel's eyes were lowcast and serious. He'd lost more than one friend to scag.

"So where do we find her?"

Angel brightened. He looked around, then grabbed my arm and dragged me to the down escalator. On the second floor we squeezed over to the high-minimum blackjack tables. Every stool was taken, with spectators crowding them. The aisles were a frantic, jostling mess, as a few hundred seatless gamblers got the closing hour heebie-jeebies.

Angel slipped effortlessly through one table's tight pack and disappeared. Trying to follow, I made a couple of lifelong enemies and had my nose shoved against a dozen colognes and summer body aromas. When finally I reached him, near the two-hundred-fifty-dollar minimum table, Angel pointed to an overstuffed black man perched on an end stool like a crow on a telephone pole.

"Is Mr. Jones," Angel murmured.

The fat man was decked out in expensively cut royal lavender—not a color you see often in men's clothing. Embroidered cream silk shirt, couple of conspicuous rings, bright red tie and collar pin all helped the suit seem conservative. A matching lavender top hat was carefully upended on the stool beside the man. He was playing two hands.

"What is that?"

"Mimi call him the New Yorker," Angel said without irony.

"Muff scores off this character? Mimi say how often?"

"Most every night."

I put a hand on each of Angel's ruffled shoulders. "You got to help me tail this clown, soon as the casino closes up."

Angel took the opportunity to step closer to me, which made me backpedal. We did this two or three times, like we were getting a good samba step working. Crowd noise around us turned ugly.

"Stop," I said. "We got work in front of us." I turned Angel by the shoulders so we were both watching the New Yorker. We never learned if he was winning or losing, because the floor men began signaling to the dealers, and everywhere around us the games stopped. Loudspeakers thanked us over and over for another great day of excitement at City by the Sea and touted the delicious pancakes to be had at the Sea-City Deli upstairs. They were looking forward to the renewed pleasure of our company in just six short hours, at ten A.M.

The floor was one second a jammed train terminal, the next a near-empty dinosaur's bowling alley.

The New Yorker left plenty fast. Angel and I strolled discreetly a good length behind him. Suit like that, this tail job would be child's play.

Out front the New Yorker nonchalantly tipped up his top hat and adjusted it, then turned left on the Boardwalk, waddling past the taffy shop (Fralinger's Original 1883) and Dip-Stix stand like he owned the ocean. The pitch-dark night was glazed with rings of lamplight. Angel slipped on the little toreador jacket he was toting. Despite the memory of afternoon swelter, the June predawn had gone chilly and forlorn-feeling.

Outside Atlantis casino, vomiting its own puddles of late-night gamblers, a row of rolling chair pushers stood waiting, even at goddam four A.M. The New Yorker swung into one, rocking it on its ancient springs. Angel and I hopped into the next rolling chair in line. "Up the Boardwalk. And how about rolling the flaps down?"

Ahead of us the New Yorker's rolling chair barely made headway. His pusher was leaning at a steep angle, head hangdog down, straining every ounce into keeping the wheels turning.

Angel was beside himself with pleasure. We were sitting in one of the original Atlantic City rolling chairs, a Victorian luxury that my AC book said was a chief attraction and delight of the Boardwalk from the 1880s into the 1940s. The little wicker gondola had been repainted glistening white and put in running order. Otherwise the refurbishing was minimal. Little isinglass awnings could be rolled up or down, in case there's a change in the weather. For twenty-five bucks chair pushers were still ready to propel you up and down the Boardwalk for an hour.

We passed an Oriental import shop, a video arcade, a Taylor Pork Roll store, a custard shop, a tee-shirt emporium, another custard stand. For the first half mile the flood of turned-out gamblers gave the boards an artificial midday look. But the feeling was altogether different. I saw no tuxedoes. And the well-dressed, happy, but well-behaved City by the Sea clientele was swallowed in a shambling mob whose mood was distinctly tired and bitter. Several groups of local boys in denim jackets and felt hats milled around with the gamblers. A tall, white-haired woman draped in a white-fur stole cried belligerently into the lapels of a man who stared blankly over her head.

By the time we'd window-shopped behind the big man from Utah Avenue to Illinois, we had rolled past all the casinos except Resorts. Hardly another pedestrian was left in sight. The New Yorker no doubt spotted us there behind him. But I was betting that a middle-aged black man spooning with a gorgeous young looker was a plenty common sight at that hour.

Our chair pusher was anxious to get in another fare. We kept catching up to the New Yorker. I called back to him, over and over, to take it slow, but to no avail. Finally I fingered an extra twenty out of the side flap, and our chair instantly dropped to a snail's crawl.

Both chairs passed a bathhouse, crumbling concrete, doors chained and padlocked, ornamented with the spray-painted observation that AC IS A TOILET. Angel looked at it solemnly. Used to be, I told him, you could change in a public bathhouse along the Boardwalk, rent a basket for a buck to store your valuables and clothes in, then shower off after your swim. Now the beaches are pretty well locked up by the casino/hotels, and the bathhouses have been demolished or converted into rest-rooms. If you want to change and shower up, you've got to rent a hotel room, I guess.

People are taking baths of a different order these days in Atlantic City, was the gist of Angel's reply.

At Kentucky Avenue the New Yorker swung his big feet out of the chair, pumped his legs left, down the ramp, and up the tired city sidewalk. No glitter here, just the dark side of the moon. Angel and I jumped out and followed along, working hard at looking carefree and fascinated only with each other. A brown-shirted security guard passing by grinned at the picture we made. Who, us sneaking?

To most people Kentucky Avenue is just a spot on the Monopoly board. But to black folks of a certain age, it's the home of the Club Harlem, the Carnegie Hall of the old "chitlin' circuit." For half a century it was the place for black entertainers to make their mark. Billy Daniels debuted "That Old Black Magic" there in 1942. Now most top show-biz blacks are locked into exclusive contracts with the casinos.

Atop the glass block and chrome facade, the Sepia girl on the marquee still banged her drum for the old clientele that never would be back. Angel and I strolled inside after the New Yorker through the large velvet-papered bar, and stood at the door to the showroom. The New Yorker glanced down at us over his big shoulder and smiled like the full moon. Just another couple fixing to keep the old night alive. New Yorker liked that.

The room was enormous, still sassy with its old potted trees and tiny round cocktail tables. Looked to me like it would hold a thousand people. At four-thirty A.M. maybe a hundred fifty folks sat around drinking mostly soft-looking cocktails in rainbow colors.

When the hostess came back to seat us, I asked her if it always jumped like this at four A.M. Gearing up for the breakfast show at six A.M., she answered absently, all covetous eyes for Angel's metallic toreador suit. Place is half packed every summer morning for it, she told me.

At our tiny table we ordered Cape Cod cocktails and Eggs Benedict. The old gooseneck lamps aimed at the walls put stars in Angel's eyes. "You been here before, Papi?"

I shook my head. "Year I first got legal to drink, we used to talk about coming down here for a show. Then, that Easter Monday, about seven hundred people were in, feeling good, spring and all, primed for the Billy Paul show. End of the first song, bullets started flying from all directions. When the smoke cleared, a dozen were bleeding and four were dead. The whole sad massacre was over a punk heroin kingpin named Tyrone Palmer. He and the three ladies at his table had ordered eggs, got served slugs. Rival junkers."

"They catched them, no?" Angel's mouth was set in an O.

I laughed bitterly. "You kidding? And believe me, it took the edge off this old place for one long time afterwards."

"Is not too edgy now," said Angel, peering around at the tattered palm trees and patched stage curtains.

Our eggs and cranberry drinks came and went. The New Yorker drank two yellow-colored drinks, ate from a platter, drank another. The room filled, slowly at first, then more rapidly as it got near the sunrise showtime.

Angel's mouth fell open again. This time he was gaping at a jovial white man pouring champagne for four not well-dressed, but sexy, women, two white and two black. Angel was impressed by the man's indifference to expense.

Muff Anglaise appeared from nowhere and sat at the New Yorker's table.

I tried to hunch myself into a shadow, but she wouldn't have spotted me anyway. She was all smiles, goo-goo eyes, and nervous chatter for her host. Under those eye smiles of hers, frantic energy streaked, as a light bulb turns brightest just before it blows out.

Angel nudged me. "Easy," he whispered, "you catched the flu? Or is that your Muff lady?"

I nodded without turning my eyes from her.

"She need a fix pretty bad," Angel said in my ear.

I nodded again. The big man and the showgirl were passing back and forth a little saltwater taffy bag the New Yorker pulled out of his jacket. They were good at it, but looking sharp I could see Muff slip a few folded bills in with her hand and the New Yorker fingertip them out. The next round, while Muff leaned over and nuzzled his cheek with her nose, old New Yorker palmed a little bundle of what I figured were glassine packets, tipped them into the taffy bag, rolled up the top, and handed it to Muff with his part-toothed grin.

You could see the calm wash over Muff's face. Just knowing she was holding made life beautiful again for her. She sipped at an orange-colored drink, on the New Yorker's tab, then stood up to leave, holding the bag against her scarlet dress. The New

Yorker leaned forward and put his hand on her leg. My blood churned.

"Grab your purse," I told Angel out the corner of my mouth. I dropped a twenty on the table and hustled Angel out, to the you-must-be-from-Mars look of the hostess. She had a line of folks waiting for a shot at the breakfast show.

We reached the street before Muff Anglaise. I hit the curb for a cab, just in case. Kentucky Avenue was lined with them, dropping off couples. If Muff took off on foot, I'd drop a Lincoln on the cabbie and beat the pavement after her.

But she came out walking fast and hopped in a taxi. Our driver gave her a block, then jolted off without a word. Whatever you've heard, cab drivers, at least in New Jersey, are happy to do a tail job for double fare.

At first we seemed headed towards the White Horse Pike that runs directly through the pine barrens to Philadelphia. Just before Muff's cab reached it, though, it swung right onto a six-lane apron along the Atlantic City marina. SENATOR FRANK FARLEY MARINA, WATERWAY TO AMERICA'S PLAYLAND, the big sign blustered. Just across the apron stretched Trump Castle, brand new and already dated, cheap-looking brown and beige hospital tiles, shapeless lumps in place of architecture. Altogether in keeping with AC's jugular grip on the second rate. The whole enormous complex, casino and giant hotel, looked built to score off the considerable yacht traffic. In front of one of the dozen main gangways, Muff's cab screeched up, and she instantly yanked her door open. I tapped our driver's shoulder and he pulled up a hundred yards behind.

She scurried out with barely a nod, and high-heeled it on those great legs. What I could see of her face looked worn, but still softened by that infinite good-naturedness of hers. Down the narrow wooden gangway, three football fields long, yachts sardined in sternwise: aerodynamic billfishing rigs, deep-water sailboats, jumbo cabin cruisers. I could see a few names on the sterns: The *Misty Lady*, the *Sea Jumper*, the *Sea Champion*, the *Sammi Jo II*, the *Empty Pocket*. Half the home berths were in New Jersey, the other half from Maryland, Florida, New York, North Carolina, and places that sounded like the Caribbean and Europe.

Muff kept stalking down the boards, looking vulnerable, putting ever more distance between us. As she neared the end of the gangway, I saw where she was headed. The very end of each long gangway fashioned a double slip. While even a big yacht fits into a single slip, the boat Muff climbed aboard crammed that hundred-foot double slip with its raked cabins and a radar antenna the size of a municipal park sculpture.

I pulled Angel out of the cab and handed over the fare. A very elegant woman in high-heel sandals strolled down the gangway with the biggest poodle I'd ever seen.

"Ohh," cried Angel with his eye for high-life. "This is so fancy-shmancy!"

"Way too rich for Muff or old New Yorker, don't you think?"

"Very much money is in drugs, Easy."

"Angel," I said patiently. "We're looking at a yacht the size of the *Britannia*, custom built. Cost a couple million at least. Got to have a crew of four when she's at sea, anyways, and be insured and registered and all. Druggies don't have this kind of imagination for spending their profits."

"Angel would."

The two of us sat in the dingy twenty-four-hour coffee shop, one or other pair of eyes always fixed on the big boat into which Muff had disappeared. The early morning customers here were an equal mix of boatsmen and temporarily high-and-dry Trump's Castle gamblers. Was there a coffee shop anywhere else in the world where a string of natty yachtsmen could pass a woman with Angel's striking hairstyle and gold toreador suit—yet flash nary a frown or even any surprise? Even the big black lug sitting with her didn't cause a batted eye. I was learning a few Atlantic City social facts.

After most of an hour Angel began sighing and drumming his fingers next to his coffee refill, familiar signs.

"All right," I said. "This lagoon water ain't all that smells like dead crabs. I think we're going to make a move."

Angel paused his drumming and pursed his lips hopefully.

"We could slip on this boat, Easy?"

"Probably can't avoid it."

"And shanghai this Muffy?"

I hesitated. The image of Muff Anglaise pawing that smug fat junkie and then curling up with her bag of trash ate at me. Half of me wanted to charge on board that boat, like Angel suggested, and drag Muff off with me someplace.

And the other half knew what outraged reception that thick-necked approach would get. And deserve. This was a mature woman I cared about, not a teen-giggler. A woman that knew a lot of people, had done plenty, seen more. She knew something about life. A man that wanted her respect couldn't gallop all over her private business like a moony schoolboy.

When I told Angel this, he actually gasped with astonishment. It's been Angel's ambition to get rescued by a knight.

But I knew better. The minute I buttonholed her on that yacht, Muff would know I'd been tailing her, not to mention voyeurizing. I didn't want her thinking I was the standard skirt sniffer a showgirl meets plenty of.

But now that I had seen her again, I was not about to park my butt while that yacht rocked with God knows what.

"Sit tight," I told Angel. "What I'll do is touch bases with my other client. I'll be back. Keep scoping this gangway, write down everybody that comes or goes from that boat, hear?"

Angel nodded gravely. He'd done work for me before.

"If she splits, you do what you can to tail her, right?"

"Angel will cover this tramp like that ugly frown you got covers your face, Easy."

CHAPTER SEVEN

O

In the double phone booth behind the marina administration building, I unfolded the notepaper with Patricia Valentine's phone number.

Sister or not, I figured to turn her loose on Muff, check that she was okay, pump her for what was happening. I would ask Patricia to keep me out of the picture until I got next to Muff again, rekindled what we had going, showed her I wasn't out to score anything off her. Or much of anything.

I dialed the number. Patricia Valentine picked up at once and sounded almost too glad to hear from me, considering the six A.M. wakeup. On the phone you'd hardly guess her for the Little Miss Prepette she came across in my office. Her voice was lower and husky, as though her mouth were close to the receiver. Sounded more like what I remembered of Muff's voice. Well, this unlikely pair was supposed to be sisters, according to Patricia.

When I told her we had Veronica Valentine covered, Patricia's voice gloated like a big cat, sounding right in the phone booth with me. I hadn't figured she could bring out the goose bumps on me.

"Wonderful! Where is she?"

"Patricia?"

"What is it, Ezell?"

"I got a problem with this. There was something nice between me and your sister, you know? Coming between you two over your personal business'll score me no points with the lady."

"Do you have a better plan?"

"I do. I'm nervous about some things Muff probably got herself messed in. But I don't feel I have the right to confront her myself. Make a deal?"

"What?"

"I tell you where Veronica is, right this minute. You go in,

52

talk to her. Keep me out of sight, for the time being. Report back to me what's going on with her."

"Listen to me, Ezell Barnes. You have some nerve! You work for me, not vice versa."

"Well, as to that, your sister hired me too. I got to look out for both your interests."

"You sound as if your own interests are paramount." If she'd been within reach of the phone booth, my earlobes would be bleeding.

"My way or not at all," I said. "I could handle Muff myself, you know."

Over the phone her breath hissed out as if she'd been whispering in my ear.

"Veronica is not a stable person, Ezell. I think you know that. That grotesque job of hers! She consorts with horrible people. Lives in disgraceful places. You know I'm right."

"Place she's sitting at the moment is not too embarrassing, let me tell you. It's the biggest yacht I ever saw."

"Is she on drugs?"

"Possibly."

"Well, I—her family—want better things for Veronica. We want to help her."

"Me too."

"But if *you* approach her now, she'll merely frighten and fly away. She is a distressed woman, Ezell."

"I care some about her, too, Patricia. All I ask is that you fill me in on how Veronica is. Let me help look after her."

"I suppose I must agree to that condition," she said, still a little miffed.

"All right. When do we do it? Sooner the better."

"Where do I go?"

"She's on a boat, I mean a big yacht, on a slip in the Farley Marina. You know the place, near Trump·Castle?"

"Not really. Come pick me up."

"In Freehold?"

You could have counted to five. "I'm not in Freehold, actually. The number I gave you is that of a friend."

"How about you drive here?"

"I'm stranded here without a car. Please come for me. I'm just thirty minutes away."

I wasn't crazy about doing it, but twenty minutes later I had taxied to my truck and was tracking down the address she gave me. Morning was fully lit now, and I'd had no sleep at all. Took me longer than half an hour to get there. Hell of a lot longer. Down the Black Horse Pike, west through the Jersey pine barrens, mile after mile, all white sand and a sea of twisty pine trees six feet high. Cutoff onto a numbered state road, two more rights and lefts. I passed a big blueberry packing shed, a gas station/general store, two cornfields, and a huge old steam locomotive propped by the side of the road.

The next two left turns took me off the paved surface, onto one of the rutless sand strips that peel off the road on both sides. I rumbled past a rusted car cemetery, a piney's shack, through two intersections where six or more sand trails streaked off through the woods like rays from a star. By then I could feel the tall grass whipping between the pickup's tires.

I stopped in my tracks and stuck my head out the window. Before me and behind me ribboned the white sand I'd been raveling for twenty minutes. Everything else was dwarf pines and scrub oaks. Nice morning it was: clear, warming, buttermilk sky, egg-yolk sun.

I K-turned and followed my own tread marks back to the highway.

By the time I'd smoked back to the Farley Marina, it was close to nine o'clock. Even while I was parallel parking at a hydrant, Angel came tapping up to lean breathlessly in the window. First he grabbed a cigarette from the pack in my jacket pocket, frowned at finding no filter, but leaned across me to tug out the dash plug and light up. Then he said: "Easy, where you been? Is been Grand Central Station while you gone."

"What?"

"No-good hussy sneaks in there too."

"The woman you saw in my office yesterday morning?"

"Yas."

"Who else?"

"First this very handsome man pull up in a little Mercedes-Benz. He is so much good-looking, like Dr. Canova on my soap. He got wavy white hairs and is a fine figure of a man."

"Old guy?"

"Is somebody's grandfather, for sure, Easy," Angel said. "But I think he got a fire lit still."

"You'd remember him again, you saw him?"

Angel nodded.

"How long was he in there?"

"If Angel had cigarettes, could know something like that," he said, and helped his purse to a second smoke from my pack.

"You had no money? Sorry, Angel. Who else?"

"This other man that come is not so old as Dr. Canova, but he's very athletic. Keep his middle very trim, Papi, like you. Maybe he's a cop, I can't tell."

"Maybe Muff is some kind of police snitch," I said, mostly to myself. "Could be the cops are stowing her here for safe-keeping."

"This second man stays not too long, and he leaves too. And then Miss Good-for-Nothing-but-Lies come along."

"She walk right on?"

"Sure. They all of them did."

"Not like they knew the layout?"

Angel hesitated.

"My client stay long?"

"No, same as man number two."

"She yanked the wool over my peepers, Angel."

"Sure."

I climbed out of the truck and hitched my pants. "Let's go get some straight answers."

Angel tugged on my sleeve. "You don't want to hear everything?"

"There's more?" I moaned.

Angel nibbled his upper lip. "Two more men come after the club-face snoot lady leave. Come right out again."

"Our turn now."

Three minutes later we were standing alongside the big white yacht. Polished brass letters spelled POLARIS on the cabin side. Three padded planks sloped to its decks. Nothing but blindingly white fiberglass, teak, and shiny brass on that boat, magnificent and sparkling in the fresh morning light.

It was quiet enough on that deck to hear the boats in their moorings creak to the swells. Walking to the very end of the gangway, we had passed three or four tanned boys running hoses and puttering. Nobody gave us a second look.

I pulled in a chestful of the salt air and started up the nearest plank. Funny thing, jealousy. I spent one night only with Muff Anglaise, and I knew full well that she lived off men. So how come I wanted to strangle the sailor boy that laid claim to this boat and to Muff?

"Is like a fun house," Angel said, staggering up behind.

"We better announce ourselves," I muttered, not quite knowing how.

Didn't matter. All our calling stirred nothing but silence. We took the plunge down the cabin stairway. Had to sidle my broad way down the narrow steps, but then I stepped into a ritzy living room, brass light fixtures, wood-paneled walls oiled to a high sheen. Leather-padded benches ran the perimeter, bathed in light. Beyond this room was the galley, where nobody'd been cooking recently, but a pile of dirty dishes and a microwave oven told me someone was eating aboard. Crew quarters up front were cleaned out. Back through the big common room I trudged, Angel clutching two handfuls of my jacket. Four sleeping berths in the stern, two empty, two made up and ready for guests. The common bathroom was spotless.

The master cabin door stared at me defiantly. I stepped up and yanked it open. Light sliced at us as we walked in. This room was larger than my entire apartment. And a pack rat lived there. The place was tossed from top to bottom and side to side. On the floor lay the back-belted tweed jacket I had lent Muff Anglaise. I picked it up and draped it over my arm.

On the nightstand was strewn an empty set of works—bottle top, syringe, spoon, and hypodermic. There, too, were empty glassine packets stamped with the little logo you see on New York's most famous magazine.

"Easy, look here!" How long had I stood staring at the dope setup? Long enough for Angel to dig up some buried treasure on his own.

Angel's voice came from a little built-in closet near the cabin's entrance. The solid wood door had been crowbarred near its lock. The one-inch deadbolt had splintered right out of the jamb.

Inside the closet Angel was poking at a deluxe Betamax recorder. Cabled to it, a tripod-mounted camcorder was trained at the wall separating the stateroom, through which a one-foot by two-foot hole had been jigsawed. The view of the master bed was a little smoky, but clear enough for home movies.

I stepped out again. The gold-framed mirror covering the hole looked permanent as the yacht itself.

My friend finally flicked the ON button, because a television screen the size of a refrigerator suddenly bloomed in living color: a black woman's naked body was swarming all over that of an elderly white man.

I gaped like a cretin for a second. Angel bounced out of the closet, gasped indignantly, and flew back in to stab furiously at the electronic buttons.

"Don't watch nobody else make love," he called from the closet. "Where you brains, Easy?"

I followed him in, leaned over his shoulder, and pressed the STOP button.

"You know who is making love?" Angel asked.

"Just actors," I said. "Nobody I recognize."

"Is not your tramp?" Angel insisted.

"I told you, it's a commercial porno tape. Startled me, is all. Come on, let's search this tub one more time and then call it a night."

"Where is your lady?" Angel said more softly. "She didn't leave this boat."

"She ain't fizzed into vapor, Angel. Keep looking: she's here, unless you missed something."

"*Eas-y!*" Angel's disapproval can sear a steak. We hunted through every damn inch of that boat: below decks, the several lounge areas, library, tackle room of the deck level, and the navigation room above that.

I sagged with discouragement and twenty-four sleepless hours. Angel, who hadn't slept either, looked fresh as a petunia. He suggested one last look around the deck.

As I traipsed again around the stern, too moody to worry about somebody reporting our trespass, something off the deck side caught the corner of my eye. Something that flicked white in the dark water.

She was tucked away off the far side of the yacht, pink night flimsy a dead giveaway, billowing on the water's surface. Under it her pale arms and legs dangled like tentacles. Muff's dark red hair was tangled in the crusty links of the anchor chain. I was grateful I couldn't see her face.

My body shook, maybe a reflex to fish her out of the chilly black-green water. But Angel grabbed hold of my gray matter and dragged me back to reality.

"Easy, watch Angel's lips moving: *Don't Do No More Stupid Things Now*. You done plenty harm already."

I froze to the railing, gazing down at the twisted dark red hair.

Angel's voice turned tender. "We go get some sleep, Papi. Let police come here while we sleeping. Tomorrow is another day."

I nodded.

"Unless tomorrow is today, which Angel think today maybe it is."

"Let's go."

We wobbled back up the endless wood planks to the shore, climbed into my pickup, and I must have driven us back to the hotel, though I don't remember how.

CHAPTER EIGHT

O

When the knocking started at two P.M., my head throbbed like a fork caught in the garbage disposal. I slid my feet to the carpet, grabbed a towel, dropped it, picked it up and wrapped it around my middle, then opened the door to find Ernie Horton wondering what the hell was wrong with me. He himself had been stuck at the police station giving a statement until five A.M. Police were looking for me, he croaked, had I been down to headquarters yet? And had I gotten around to fixing Roberta's problem, once and for all?

I grabbed the phone and called ACPD for the second time that day. This time I gave my name and got through to the detective handling last night's arson case. Yeah, he guessed he needed a statement from me. No, today he was too busy. No big hurry. No, he had no news for me, only that the thug I'd arrested was an Italian national, and the paperwork was already being processed for his deportation.

"Greenhorn without the green card," the detective told me, voice like he was chewing on a toothpick. "A Sicilian. Mafia's been bringing in these young bucks from the old country, by way of Canada. Beefs up their organizations."

"Didn't realize we were running out of Italians," I said.

"Still plenty," he said cheerfully. "But the American dream marches on. Sons of the sons of Palermo have been to college now, can't be bothered putting some putz's fingers in the dresser drawer. So they import the talent."

"He should be in your jail."

"Costs taxpayers about five grand to prosecute a felony rap, twenty thousand dollars a year to house and feed an inmate. Short of rape or murder, an illegal alien gets shipped back to bananaland."

"You get anything out of him?"

You could hear the shrug. "Mob muscle would be crazy to tell us anything. To them nothing's worse than being a stool pigeon."

59

When I lit in, blustering about losing our only lead in a major felony, the detective lieutenant cut me off by pointing out mildly that the suspect had been brutally beaten.

"How should I report that, Barnes? Was the guinzo resisting arrest, or maybe you just lost control of yourself and savaged him? He don't understand a word of English, by the way. You want to come down to explain?"

"Rather not."

"Then mind your own business."

After I hung up I stared absentmindedly at Ernie for about ten seconds. Then I blinked.

"Give me two minutes to dress," I said. "Then you and me are gonna shake Roberta's problems out of their tree."

First stop, fancy duds for me and for Ernie, who was still sporting yesterday's leisure shorts suit. Casino lobby shops have the ritzy men's clothing these days, but I wanted to buy these clothes well off the Boardwalk.

"I know this habodasher," said Ernie. "Where I bought me my first suit, as a youngster. Better'n the Marx Brothers. Hope it still be there."

Sir Gents was still there, on a different planet from Hart Schaffner & Marx or Brooks Brothers. The old clothier lingered on Arctic Avenue long after most melodies had faded. Outside, Sir Gents's sign sang, LOOK NEAT AND SWEET, / WHEN YOU HIT THE STREET, / WITH A MUSICAL BEAT, surrounded by musical notes. Inside they specialized in outfits like the checked shorts suit Ernie already had on his back.

I set the ancient salesman and the equally ancient tailor to work finding us the most expensive and conservative suits in the joint. They had some in plastic suit bags that would do, a handsome chalk-striped gray three-piecer for Ernie, and a cream-colored two-piece for me. Both tropical weight. My suit fit well enough, but Ernie's needed work. I gave the senior citizen tailor instructions and got his promise that we could pick it up that same evening. We found white-on-white shirts and ties that didn't have tiny whales or rep stripes on them. After I handed them plastic for the bill, Patricia's five hundred advance was spent and so was a chunk of my own bread.

I walked out wearing the suit with my sunglasses, Ernie tagging by my side and swearing I looked like a movie star. By the time we stopped to pick out shoes and wear them back to my hotel room, it was four o'clock.

First thing I did was redial the number Patricia Valentine had snookered me with last night.

"Eight-two-eight, nine-three-four-nine. Has been disconnected. Eight-two-eight, nine-three-four-nine. Has been disconnected." Who else but a computer voice could get so cheerful about a disconnected number? Dead end. Paperback detectives are always calling the phone company, foxing an address out of them. Just try it some time. You'll have better luck drawing a bead on the Unkown Soldier's hometown.

Meantime I had other work on my plate.

"Don't forget to go back for your suit, no later than eight," I reminded Ernie. "Use my room all you want. I'm leaving the key on the dresser here. I can pick one up at the desk."

I'm not sure Ernie heard me. He was concentrating on Yankee TV baseball and the Canadian bottle I had sent up. As the door shut behind me you could hear Scooter Rizzuto tell Bill White. "That huckleberry is gonna get his nose clipped!"

I poked through a bright seashore afternoon up the Boardwalk to City by the Sea. I was going to see a guy about a guy.

Since he retired as a Newark detective, Charlie Faucher had risen in the world, all the way from a city under siege to the City by the Sea casino, executive top floor. The shadows were four o'clock long on the cranberry carpeting. In front of the wall-sized mural of the casino and hotel, the receptionist's glass-topped desk held a single rose in a porcelain vase.

Informed that I was an old friend of Mr. Faucher's, the career lady squinted disapproval, and instead of patching in on her intercom, walked my card through to Faucher personally. She'd rather get her head bitten off in private, if I was a wrong number.

Charlie burst out of the inner sanctum first, an inch taller than me, black head of hair combed back. "Well, goddam," he said, pretending not to grin. "What wind blew you this way?"

He grabbed my hand, leaving me no doubt he was still in enormous good shape. Navy-blue three-piece suit, red pinstripes tailored right down the tapered lines of his prosperous body. Outdoor sports had weathered his skin. His pearly caps matched the silk handkerchief that blossomed from his breast pocket.

Still crushing my hand, he turned to the secretary. "This rascal is an old streetwise pal, Loretta. We worked plainclothes together for a while in Newark. Say hello to Ezell Barnes."

Loretta said hello in a way calculated to show that twenty years in a casino office had left her no schoolgirl.

"Not exactly true," I told her modestly. "While I was humping a beat and then working Bunco, Charlie was a walking legend in the Newark PD."

Loretta smiled at me, then turned undisguised adoring eyes on Faucher, who made a face.

"Always the three-piece suits for him, even as a cop," I needled. "Most Wall Street cop I ever saw. Impressed the hell out of the street cops."

"This way, buddy." Faucher ushered me down the corridor to his office. On the thirtieth floor, high above the gambling crowd, the offices of City by the Sea Casino looked no different from those of Bell-Tel or IBM. Three-pieced junior execs beavered about in glass-walled rooms open to the view of anybody cruising by.

"So this is behind-the-scenes in an AC casino," I said. "The fish-bowl approach to personnel management."

"They better have nothing to hide," Faucher said, half grinning. "You doze off for one second in the casino business and somebody or other will lift your eyeballs."

Faucher jerked his thumb at one unoccupied desk behind the glass wall.

"This recently departed crumb bun thought it would be dandy to approve credit lines for a few dozen OC types with phony pedigrees."

"How'd that work?"

"Something new. Mob recruits a bunch of players to come in here, show us a truckload of forged credentials, Social Security numbers, the works. They set up semilegit bank accounts with maybe five thousand bucks, keep changing them, so when we call, they all check out. First they ask for a modest line of credit, usually a five-grand limit to match their bank accounts. It all checks out on paper, we give it to them, they pay it back. Next they apply for twenty-five grand, and disappear with that."

Faucher shook his head sourly. He looked around to see who was listening, and lowered his voice. "All these casino bonzos believe devoutly that as the high rollers go, so goes the house profit line. It's an old myth from the Vegas days. Welcome mat's out for anybody who wants five grand in chips."

"Must be just a drop in the bucket compared to the buckflow you boys see every day."

"That's a joke," Faucher said. "Everybody thinks a casino is a license to print your own money. I used to. Not even close. The overhead is Godzilla. Fifty con men bilking you for twenty grand apiece in one year will tear a hole in any casino's balance sheet."

He moved me towards his own office, which was plenty private.

"I pity the paisans with you on their tails. You always had it bad for Italians, didn't you?"

Faucher chuckled comfortably. "All that was overrated."

"Oh? You mean you didn't actually have a coffin delivered to Angelo Tortino's doorstep?"

Faucher laughed again.

"I think my favorite was the story about you and the Ciampelli brothers—at the Colt Lounge, down Paterson?"

"What did you hear?"

"That you broke in on the boys and their dates while they were enjoying a predinner cocktail, and you invited all four of them to kiss the shotgun you were carrying. Tommy Ciampelli was supposed to have burst into tears."

"It wasn't exactly like that," Charlie said.

"No shotgun?"

"No tears. Tommy pissed his pants, is all." Faucher watched me laugh for a second. "It's not easy to humiliate cementheads like those. You pretty much have to catch them trying to impress a first date."

"You dressed so well around headquarters, everybody thought you'd campaign for police commissioner one day."

"Except for all those wild-man stories."

"Cops'd have backed you. Every last one. You had them all convinced, man."

I sat in a ring of cube-shaped chrome chairs while Charlie fixed us drinks at the bar under the wall-sized mirror. His office, fitted behind that of his executive secretary, stretched across the entire south end of the thirtieth floor. The desk and business doings took up one tiny corner of it. Through the floor-to-ceiling glass Charlie had a gull's-eye view of the Atlantic Ocean. A stiff offshore breeze whitecapped the waves rolling nonstop to shore.

"This is a vice-president's office? I want to catch the board chairman's digs sometime."

Charlie handed me a glass, lifted his to me. After he swallowed, he said, "Bright, personable black fella like you would be worth a fortune in Atlantic City. You got your college degree finally, didn't you?"

"At night."

"I never did, you know. Wasn't essential in the old days."

"I actually got most of the way to a master's degree in criminal justice at the John Jay School. Remember when that was the thing to do, you wanted to make sergeant?"

"You didn't make sergeant, as I recall."

"Oh?" I said facetiously. "Why do you suppose that was?"

"Because those idiots would do anything to pass over a black cop, even somebody with your talents. They prefer to promote hash-eating bogtrotters." Charlie sized me up with new interest. "Seriously, Easy. I always liked working with you. This might be the place for you. Atlantic City is blacker than even Newark. Always has been, did you know that?"

I frowned skeptically.

"No, really. Right after the Civil War, soon as blacks got the leg irons off, they made for AC by the sea. Back then Newark was only a piddling two-percent black, but this beach was over twenty-five-percent colored. You know how come?"

"Black folks like to eat fried fish?"

"Work in the resort industry." Charlie sat back in his leather chair. "Pursuit of the almighty dollar."

"I'm happy where I am."

"Face it: Newark's a ghost town. Nothing but bad memories there. You look prosperous, I admit. You must have found something better than PI work, huh?"

I shrugged. "Business is decent, what with my contacts around town. Nothing glamorous, but it's comfortable."

Charlie lifted his eyebrows at that.

"Really, man. Got this regular lineup of bank drops and lockup checks that pays the rent and puts gas in my car. Every once in a while something fancier turns up, and it's gravy."

Charlie sipped his drink, looking at me.

"I'm doing something out of the ordinary now, as a matter of fact."

Charlie still kept his mouth shut. He heard too many folks' stories in a day.

"Couple days ago I got a call from a lawyer in Newark I know. He'd been contacted by this law firm in Georgia. They needed somebody to chaperone this eccentric moneybags from Atlanta looking for development opportunities in AC. My lawyer friend didn't know a soul in Atlantic City, but knew I could find my way around down here. So I hooked up with the tycoon. We hit it off pretty good. He even bought me the suit." I fingered my new cream-colored finery.

"What kind of development possibilities?" Charlie said, steadily and not so friendly.

"Dude's got cash to burn, wants to invest in Boardwalk land. Play Monopoly."

"Hotel and casino development's strictly a closed game," Faucher warned. His mouth corners turned down. "Each house already has a limited number of shareholders; nobody's selling any stock to nobody."

"Point of fact, Mr. Horton was thinking to build a joint of his own." I smiled. "Figures to levy a handsome bid on that parcel of land behind your place. Between Pacific and Atlantic on Utah Avenue?"

Charlie stood up to make more drinks, scowling and drooping like a cannon ball was in his pants. Halfway through the pouring he said smoothly, "What's he got in mind?"

"You know, truthfully, I don't think he has a clue? Real estate development is what this character does for fun. And he's so happy on his vacation, he wants to stay here in AC by the sea."

"It's not funny," Faucher told me. "If it's your idea of a joke."

"Say again, Charlie?"

"ID this clown for me." He put down the rocks glasses and grabbed a pad of paper.

"The man is loaded. Fortune's in fast food in Fulton County, Georgia. Owns a string of barbecue joints in and around Atlanta. Horton's Rib Cages. They're famous down there."

"Never heard of him."

"Don't you ever travel in the South?"

Charlie shook his head. "Fifty-two weeks a year in AC."

This late on a Friday afternoon, it'd be Monday afternoon before Faucher could check out Ernie's alias.

"Well, you turn on the radio in Atlanta, not an hour goes by you don't hear them singing about Ernie Horton, His Nibs of Ribs, the Big Boss with the Hot Sauce, the Squire with the Hickory Fire."

Faucher pushed the empty notepad away from him. "Squire? Nibs? The hell are you talking about?"

"Now tell me what bit your butt?" I said.

"The big scale model we passed, on the table in the lobby? That's our architect's rendering of the condo complex that City by the Sea is projecting for the Utah Avenue space. And here you come in with this crap."

I waved an arm. "Hey, I had no idea, Charlie, God's truth."

"Our idea is an ultra-swank time-sharing condo. Luxury beyond anything ever built in AC, or just about anywhere else in this country. Comparable to Trump Tower."

I whistled. "How big?"

"Two hundred units, around three thousand square feet each. Quarter of a million dollars buys you a month each year in it. Plus you can exchange at three or four sister complexes around the world. I mean, there are only three or four in this class." Charlie ticked them off on his fingers. "Monte Carlo Hotel, Club Carioca in Rio, the Blue Club in the south of France."

"Another port of call for the jet set to gamble and frolic," I remarked. "Jet set like that saltwater taffy, right? Dip-Stix?"

Charlie grinned. "They like baccarat and Frank Sinatra. Three million buys you a place year-round. Twenty-four-hour room service, private bridge to the casino, Jacuzzi lagoon in each apartment—you can swim laps in them."

I whistled again. "Six hundred million in receipts. How much to build?"

Faucher's grin mocked me. He stood up and refilled my glass. "Does your friend hold that kind of stake?"

"Well, I don't know. But he's willing to shell out a heap more than your casino is—for the land. According to our sources, a developer named Short Line Enterprises tried to lowball the property owners at ten grand apiece. Made the Utah Avenue folks angry. This Short Line don't sound like shrewd business partners to me, Charlie."

Charlie didn't know whether to scowl or laugh. He laughed. "You don't always get to pick your partners in OC by the sea."

"OC? Oh, man, what a switch for you!"

"I'm in security, not development. How much does your friend plan to offer for that land?"

"Whatever's fair," I said. "I heard Mr. Horton say something about forty houses at a hundred twenty grand apiece."

"For shacks," Faucher said contemptuously.

"Buildings are worthless," I agreed. "It's the lots, they sparkle when somebody lusts after them."

"I have nothing to do with City by the Sea's development plans," Charlie repeated, annoyed. "Why'd you come here to tell me about it?"

"Because the folks on Utah Avenue have been treated to a wave of terror, ever since they turned down your casino's offer. I personally grabbed one hood that torched a car on the block last night. I tried beating a little information out of him. But he kept his mouth shut."

"You were always handy with your mitts." Charlie shrugged. "I don't know a thing about it."

"Now they're shipping the goon back to Sicily, without bothering to grill him. Which way does ACPD jump, Charlie?"

He lifted his shoulders again. "Like any city PD, they jump in step with the band."

"Who knew this casino had a marching band?" I said. "What instrument did the goon I caught play? I bet something in the string section, like a piano wire."

"We could sue your ass for that, you repeat it in public," Faucher snapped. He squinted at his drink like a bug fell in it. "And we will."

"Christ."

Charlie softened a little. "Easy, I have absolutely no control over anything but internal security at this casino and its hotel. How they pry loose the deeds to that land and at what price is none of my business. Quite frankly, I don't want to know."

"Innocent people'll get hurt."

"Those people are not the innocents you think they are," Faucher scoffed. "They're playing your Mr. Ribs against the casino to up the ante. It's a scam from their angle too."

"Atlantic City's got more angles than a kaleidoscope." I shook my head.

"Oh hell," Charlie said. "This life's a bitch. I'm still mighty glad to see you again, Easy. Let's get out of here, the place sours my blood. I'll buy you a real drink in a real bar."

"Can't," I said. "Like a rain check, though."

"The only time I cool out is early morning. You still do workouts?"

"Just a little jogging. Haven't boxed in years, but I still get the roadwork in."

"How about a long swim in the ocean, tomorrow morning, early?"

My face must have flushed with alarm.

"You don't swim? That's right, you grew up in inner Newark. Want to learn? I'll show you how."

"Always wanted to stop being afraid of the water, Charlie. But I'm getting too old to change my ways."

"This is your golden chance. Swim in the goddam Atlantic Ocean."

"If I ever do take swimming lessons, they sure won't be in the ocean. Gives me the creeps, man, keeps coming on and coming on. Never stays in one place; you can't get ready for it."

"How about we just run the Boardwalk loop tomorrow morning, six o'clock?"

"Meet where?"

"Just in front of the Ocean One Mall. By the treasure map of the world."

He was looking so friendly again that halfway to the door I turned back around.

"Dancer in your casino that they found in the water last night? The one buried on page thirteen of the AC *Press*? Well, I knew her. In fact, I was working on something for her when she bought it."

Faucher's face folded into wrinkles I wouldn't have guessed he had. Then, "Busy, busy, busy," he said. "The cupcake's name was Veronica Vallee."

"Stage name she gave me was Muff Anglaise. Stop laughing for a minute, Charlie, you're not going to like this. She hired me to check into a mob hit that you and me handled years ago as cops. Remember Jimmy the Cricket Finnochio?"

"Punk that made like a spare tire." Faucher's eyes narrowed.

"The one." I nodded. "She was after me to dig around on his murder a bit, prove he was snitching to the police that night, not running OC errands. That way she'd pick up on his life insurance note before the clock ran out."

"You talk to her last night?" Charlie was concentrating so hard he turned pale under his tan.

I shook my head. "I only arrived in town and heard about it on the radio this morning. She drowned, right?"

"Not exactly true," Charlie replied. "The coroner ran a toxicology test on her blood and urine. Came up with a show of heroin."

"Got high and toppled off the boat?"

"Not very damned likely." Faucher snorted. "Get this: forty-percent pure heroin in her veins. You can bet the boys in homicide'll be sniffing around it."

"Kill a horse, that would. Kill a Sherman tank."

"Even a long-time user like her," Faucher said.

"How does a dancer that has to wear those skimpy outfits hide the track marks?"

"Medical Examiner said this one used her armpits and the underside of her tongue."

I let my breath out. "If she was so experienced a user, why would she pop a pure bag like that? She, of all people, would know it's instant death. Four percent is what they sell on the street."

"I imagine the homicide boys are asking the same question right now."

"Puzzles me," I said. "She'd gotten hold of all the old police reports of the Cricket's murder. Why didn't she talk to you about it? I mean, your name was there as the assigned detective."

"Probably didn't want the casino to know about her background with Finnochio." Faucher shrugged, making me to admire his tailor again. "If the Casino Commission has one hard and fast rule, it's that nobody—but nobody—gets hired who even faintly smells of organized crime. I had no idea this dancer was the Cricket's doll. Seems to me the name she went by in her Cricket days was Ronnie Valentine. Maybe I should have put two and two together." Charlie looked at me. "I don't like it now that I do know. What did you come up with for her?"

"Nada," I said. "I was hoping you could help."

"Could be," Charlie conceded. "Especially if you help us out on the Utah Avenue thing. We want the Rib King out of this."

"Maybe we can swap something tomorrow morning," I said. "When we run. Both do some homework between now and then."

I started to finish the long walk across his office to the door.

"Wait a second!" Charlie grinned and stepped quick to catch up to me. "Easy, until then, if the blue boys breathe down your neck, I've got police contacts in this town. No problem to run interference for you."

"Thanks, man," I said. "I was counting on you for some backup, and ditto some information."

"Two old cops." Charlie grinned. "Sadly misplaced specimens of the born public servant. Sometimes I think I played myself a fool to leave. I knew what I was doing, those days."

I made a show of surveying his office again. "Looks like you still know what's what."

Faucher's mouth twisted ironically, but his cheeks burned—

with pleasure, I thought. "Some day I'll decide these casino assholes can go squat on themselves."

I shook Charlie's mitt.

"I'll have Vallee's jacket pulled and cull it for anything helpful," he promised.

"Good. I'll have a little chat with this expert on forty-percent pure heroin."

"Local type?"

"Charlie," I said. "Give me a little room for starters, okay, man?"

"Sure." Charlie's mouth twisted again, then he winked. "Sure thing, partner." He gave me thumbs up.

CHAPTER NINE

O

George Benson headlined a special early stage show at the Club Harlem. When I walked in, after the supper crowd had settled down, Benson was breezing to a finish, the audience exploding with affection.

I shook off the offer of a table and stooled up in the lobby bar.

The bartender towered, thick body, stalky legs, like a dancing bear with a coffee mug, and a manner to match. Long hair pomaded back over his ears, diamond stick in his left lobe. Open-collared maroon shirt, gray knit trousers.

"I'm looking for some information," I said, friendly.

"I got drinks. You want news, try the tourist bureau." He blew at his coffee and slurped some.

"Or maybe I'll go swap questions and answers with the police." I grabbed his forearm before he could move off. He was hefty and tall, but I locked his arm to the bar.

"Another grunt's trouble with the law is no skin off my nose, friend," he grumbled.

"Do not pass Go," I said, still grinning. "Do not collect two hundred dollars. Go straight to Jail."

"What are you talking about?"

"Drugs. Murder."

"Sea breeze outside," he said. "How about you catch some?"

"Sea breeze in your thick woolly head," I said. "Last night me and a friend watched one of your regulars sell a dope bundle to a young lady who showed up OD dead a little later."

Hawking his eyes, I saw not a flicker of surprise. Word was around town about Muff Anglaise.

"Somebody cops drugs in here," he said soberly, "it's on them. Club's no party to it."

"Well, you know how cops are," I needled.

"What you want from us, mister?"

"The New Yorker, as if you don't know."

"I ain't his damn social secretary. He come and go as he please. He's a big boy."

71

"Put your finger on him quick." I pointed. "I'll be sitting at that table in the corner. If his fat ass don't shine in here like the harvest moon by ten o'clock, this dive's gonna crawl with cops toting sledgehammers and arrest warrants."

"Sure, my ass," he grumbled, yanking his arm loose. "You better hope that fat boy ain't in his bubble bath."

From the bar's corner table I watched him grab the phone from under the counter and dial a few quick calls. A complimentary highball floated my way. A half hour later another, along with a waitress who told me my guest was on his way.

Before the ice had melted, a little stir in the bar announced the New Yorker, who pomped his way to the padded rail. He jawed with the bartender some, then with a nod swiveled and slowly took me in. I was still wearing the cream-colored suit and my sunshades, even indoors.

Liking what he saw, the New Yorker stuck a swizzle stick in his mouth, hitched his pants, and strutted my way. His suit was lemon yellow tonight and even had little tails banging his butt on the back. Top hat and gloves were tailored of the same material.

Hulking over my table, at least six inches taller than my six-one, and three hundred pounds minimum, the New Yorker looked like Convention Hall with feet.

"Mocha Joe says you got talk for me." Swizzle stick was barely visible in the black cave of his mouth. "Talk of what?"

"Talk of the town," I said. Then, "Forget it," to his puzzled look. "Sit down." I motioned to a captain's chair. "Have a drink on me." I waved the cocktail girl over.

"I enjoy talking with a man that has style." The New Yorker carefully removed his top hat, upended it on the table. "Style is a lost art these days." He tugged at the fingers of his yellow gloves and tossed them into the mouth of the top hat. A diamond ring the size of a Cracker Jack kernel gleamed on his pinkie finger. He pointed that pinkie at me.

"Now, you take that George Benson, there. He's nothing but a North Jersey boy that made good strumming that old sugar-coated jazz guitar. But he still got the style to come back to his roots, give the Harlem boys a show after its glory days be gone. You take your other black stars, one or the other's always 'appearing nightly' down the casinos. But you think they got the style to stroll that one long block off the Boardwalk, for old times sake?"

"You are a man of finesse and polish," I said. "Anybody'd see it. Violence ain't your game." The New Yorker's stinger came. He sipped at it delicately.

"I abhor violence," he said. "Got no style."

"No way you'd dip into murder, then. I got that right?" The moon-shaped smile got tight.

" 'Course, the facts don't lie," I observed, eyes flicking to the bartender.

The smile dropped like the Times Square balloon.

"Nice figure of a woman?" I went after him. "White skin, red hair, danced in the chorus line at City by the Sea casino? Only thing is, she had this craving for liquid sky. Last night she pumped herself chockful, grabbed the moon with her bare hands."

"I read about that. Young lady don't know her limits," the New Yorker wheezed, "ain't no fault of mine."

"She overdosed on the junk you sold her last night. Cops have a bad habit of calling that manslaughter."

"Junkie got to be responsible for her own limits of consumption. It's a matter of style, you see. Girl makes a pig of herself and overdose, that's on her. Breaks my heart, don't you know, but it's all a matter of style."

"I can see you got strong ethical convictions," I mocked. "Let me appeal to your sense of legal convictions."

He tilted his big head.

"Girl shot a hot bag of H, forty-percent pure. That puts your fat black ass in the wringer."

"You got no proof it was my dope." The New Yorker was clearly tiring of me pissing on his rainbow. "I don't peddle nothing that pure. I am strictly a retailer, do no wholesaling."

"Packets had your little Mr. Monopoly insignia on them."

"Is that what you all about? Shit. That little rubber stamp been around a lot longer than me. I took my trademark from it, when I got started." The New Yorker stood up, uncomfortably like a chest freezer come to life. He drained the green liquid from his cocktail glass and swirled the foamy inside with his cow's tongue. "Been a pleasure, brother. Pardon me, got to go drain the monster."

He smoothed on his gloves, tipped the stovepipe onto his conked head, and blew off, half waddle, half swagger, not pausing by the men's room but heading for the air. I gave him thirty seconds, then dropped a ten-spot on the little round table and sauntered outside after him.

In the darkness outdoors I searchbeamed up and down the block with no luck. I dashed around the left side of the Harlem, where a vacant lot stretched between Kentucky and Illinois avenues. There he was, looming like a monstrous scarecrow, halfway across the dark cinder barrens.

I ran across the dark lot until my thudding feet alerted the giant. Top-hatted, he looked eight feet high. He stomped around to face me and shook an arm like a ship's anchor at me.

"You son of a bitch!" came growling through the brisk wind.

I never switched a stride. Four feet from him, at full sprint, I dug in my heels, gave him the Sugar Ray Leonard flurry of faked hands and head, and finally buried my right fist deep into his kidney padding. It felt too good. I waited a beat for his hoarse scream. His top hat flew off and rolled across the lot, caught by the sea wind. I ducked his big, slow haymaker, dug a second kidney shot into him, and watched his knees buckle.

He looked like the Michelin man, sinking to his knees. I backpedaled and danced a step or two, just to show him he was taking his pasting from a ex-pro. In my adrenalined state he seemed in slow motion—I could have sipped a cup of coffee and still stepped in to kick him down before he elbowed to his feet.

In all I kicked him six times, twice when he tried standing up, then four more to open up his nose and eyes with my shoes. By the end they were oxblood for genuine. Then I stood the heel of my new leather goods on the nape of his neck and let him ponder a second or so.

Suddenly my knees were tired too. "Who killed Muff Anglaise?" I said. He just lay there, a beached whale, hands in the sandy dust covering his face. Second beating I'd pummeled out in as many nights. I felt old and without finesse, a sleeve-hearted palooka beating on all the meanies 'cause his pure heart felt so bad.

I looked down at the big lemon shape and sighed. I rolled the sole of my shoe across the fatty back of his neck.

"Arrgh," he moaned.

"What you got for me, New Yorker?"

"Nothing," he kept moaning. "I don't know nothing. Bitch was my meal ticket. Take a dumb fuck to kill the gold-egg goose." He spat blood.

"What were you two into?"

"You gonna get me dead, asshole."

"I'm gonna sell you the right to walk away under your own

power," I advised him. "Price is something I can use to get at Muff Anglaise's killer."

I felt obliged to roll his neck under my heel again.

"She worked the casino," the big fat man blubbered then.

"Say again?"

"Worked the casino for me. Moved the drugs in—recreational—coke, meth, that shit. Very little scag."

"City by the Sea casino?"

"Yeah. Showgirls got to have their fun."

"She was your street dealer for the casino?"

"And the hotel. Guest with a comp suite touch the right bellhop, he ring old Muffy's number. She take the order, get back to me."

"Casino put the heat on you two?"

Flat on his belly, face in the dust, the New Yorker still managed a sour snicker. "Casino can't make it without us, sugarfoot, they want the high-rolling trade to stick. Any more'n they can afford to bird-dog the hookers coming into the hotel. Folks's here to *play*, man."

"What else?"

"Motherfucker! I been spilling my guts to you. You gonna get me killed. Son of a bitch. Let me up."

I moved two steps back and watched him hoist to his feet, moaning. I stood relaxed, hands at my side. The New Yorker slapped at his grimed-to-hell clothes, his bloody face showing no further worry about me. Hell, I had no style, lacked the killer instinct.

"Son of a bitch," he groaned again, still spanking dust from his ruined suit. Back on his feet he was so big I did a double take.

He swiveled his head to find his blown-away top hat, didn't see it, sighed, and moved his bulk in the direction of Illinois Avenue. I followed three paces behind, neither of us saying one word. He shuffled straight to a Cadillac that looked like the flagship of the Puerto Rican navy. A coupe de gauche complete with little coach lights screwed to either side of the roof.

After he got out his key and opened the driver's door, he looked over his shoulder. I stood there staring at him. I made it one cold stare.

A gang of teenagers bopped down the opposite sidewalk. They yelled a couple insults at us and moved on, snickering. I looked down at the New Yorker's legs and moved my eyes up to his face.

"That is for Muff Anglaise," I said, just after I smacked him one last time upside the head. He shuddered and grabbed his temples.

"She was a hell of a woman," I said. "You could never understand that. You got no style, you goddam pig."

CHAPTER TEN

O

A ferocious hunger welled up in me ten minutes after I put the fearsome sport on the New Yorker's ass. Believe me, I felt no regret about the beating I'd delivered the greedy hog. His sky killed Muff, upfront or backdoor. Jesus, I was hungry.

The delicatessens in the casino offered tarted-up platters of second-rate cold cuts for first-rate prices. So I deliberated between Abe's or Dock's oyster house. Abe's was five blocks closer, so I hoofed it down Atlantic Avenue. In my opinion Abe's has the best seafood in Atlantic City at any price. Along with Dock's it's the last of the old seafood restaurants, now that Arthur Treacher's original place, Hackney's, has closed its doors. Abe's has a loyal clientele that passes the word to other seafood lovers, who keep the place afloat.

The restaurant was packed to the rafters when I walked in the door at ten-thirty. One big room, thick coat of glossy white paint over a fancy pressed-tin ceiling and walnut trim well worn during its fifty years. The original ceiling fans still whirred quietly between pearly white globe lamps. The hostess sat me at a white-and-red checked table by the curved window, where I could fish-eye the foot traffic streaming by. The Atlantic City bus terminal was one block south and west of the restaurant. The faces headed up to the casino strip were a heck of a lot brighter than those trudging home.

I ordered the Neptune's Delight with fish chowder.

"You get to pick a lobster of your choice from the tank," the middle-aged waitress said. Shoulders to heels she was one straight line. Even in late June her skin was fishbelly white. She motioned me towards the lobster tank set into the outside window.

"Him," I said, peering into the swirling tank water. I tried to pick out a lobster large enough to saddle and ride.

"Good choice, Mr. Barnes," a cracking voice behind me said. "Me, I'll take the gimped-up lobster in the corner, that guy with the one claw."

I wheeled around on a dapper dan standing beneath a gray fedora, matching topcoat draped over his shoulders, matador-style.

"Nick the Twist D'Amato." He smiled, offering me his hand. I pulled my right hand back at the sight of his withered right arm. Felt funny squeezing his left hand with mine.

"Put the whole nut on my tab, doll," my new acquaintance said. He winked at me, then at the waitress, and held out to her a ten-dollar bill folded twice between his third and fourth fingers.

"We're having the same thing as friend Barnes here. Only clam chowder, the red kind, with herbs and tomatoes, like nature intended, not that white school paste."

"You bet, Mr. D'Amato." The waitress was no girl, but she switched on her eyes for the Twist.

"Something nice in a red wine, just cool, huh?"

Nick twirled his coat off with a flourish and handed it to the very wide goon lurking at his side. Under his coat Nick was regulation Frank Nitti pinstripe, complete with maroon silk shirt and silver tie, diamond stickpin, hefty gold watch with a band like bars of bullion.

"Let's grab a seat, why don't we." Nick after-you'd me back to my table. The other man, belly like a medicine ball, lumbered behind us mutely.

I jerked my head. "Who's your friend?"

"My driver," Nick said. "Mike Marano. He makes up for what I lack." Nick grinned and stuck his gnarled right hand on the table to keep me off balance.

"Why do I think you and Muscles Marinara didn't drop in to sell me a ticket to Sons of Italy night? Why the unexpected pleasure?"

"Later we can get down to business." Nick looked genuinely shocked that anyone would be so vulgar. He recovered enough to offer me a black cigar shaped like a stuffed grape leaf.

"Rather eat rat bait," I said politely, and fired up a Chesterfield.

"First we eat. Business on an empty stomach gives you agita in the banza, as my sainted mother always said."

Nick lit up the veined cigar as slick as a one-armed magician's card tricks.

We sat grinning fatuously at each other until my frozen face felt ready to crack.

"The chowder here is pretty good, for a Jew joint," Nick said finally, in a stab at entertaining conversation. Then he puffed a bunch of times on that evil cigar of his. Muscles said nothing, chewed his lip, stared into deep space.

The waitress plunked a big carafe on the table, tipped up a stemmed glass in front of each of us. Nick stubbed out the Parodi. "Hey, *salute*, Mr. Barnes." I kept leaning on my folded arms.

Abe's oyster lady dropped three bowls down in front of us. Both men tucked their napkins into their shirt collars and dropped handfuls of oyster crackers in with their clams.

I looked at my bowl of white fish chowder. "What'd you suppose clams eat, anyway? I heard sewage."

Muscles didn't raise his head or shoveling fist from the bowl. Nick's stare flooded with distaste.

"Let's get it over with," he said finally. "I hear you're in town on business. Land speculation?"

"Word travels fast in this town."

"It does if you keep your ear to the ground, Mr. Barnes. And that's my job."

"Well, you heard right," I said. "Mean something to you?"

"Let me tell you a story." Nick leaned across the table, holding his half-a-hand where I had to see it. "I started out in linen supply. Half the restaurants and hotels in town got their clean linen from me. Now somebody else handles that racket. I got too big in one of my sidelines, fresh fruits and vegetables, to worry about towels. These days every market and restaurant in Atlantic City is supplied by my trucks. You know how many trucks I got? Do you? Forty-seven trucks. You believe that? Ventnor, Margate, Longport, Brigantine too. But I am currently diversifying, would like to stick my thumb in a little land development."

I ate a huge spoonful of milky fish chowder, none too neatly. "Horatio Alger tale like that brings tears to my eyes."

Nick grinned. Muscles Mike yawned.

"You're Short Line Enterprises, aren't you?"

"I am affiliated with that concern," Nick said, delighted to be famous. "You've heard of us?"

"Nothing but dirt."

"Wouldn't it be foolish—" the Twist said, slipping in and out of falsetto. He cleared his throat. "Foolish for your people and my people to conflict over this property? Nobody wins a bidding war." He shot me a V for Victory grin. Our lobster platters arrived and the table filled up with them and with little side dishes of fried oysters, calamari rings, haddock fingers, cole slaw, french fries, onion rings, and tartar sauce. I waited until Nick started to say something, and then asked Oyster Dolly for ketchup.

"I would like," the Twist began again, "very much, to meet your key man. I believe we can make him an offer he'll find hard to turn down."

"You didn't say that right," I told him, mouth full of haddock fingers. "You're wanting to buy my man out of the game?"

"It would be cheaper in the long run for both you and me." Nick was not too busy cracking the claw on his lobster to treat me to impish dimples.

"Oh damn," I said. "Threats." I rooted in the lobster's belly with the tin fork they give you.

"You misunderstand me," Nick said earnestly. "You personally got everything to gain from me. If your principal don't want to participate in a settlement, you yourself could make something happen anyway. And then you personally could pick up the entire nut. Hey, I got high hopes for you, Mr. Barnes."

"Well, you're a nice man, Nick. It just so happens that Mr. Horton, my principal, is gonna be in town tomorrow for a few days. He's got a busy schedule, though."

"You can squeeze me in." Nick reached over and pinched my bicep. Another couple minutes, he'd be tipping me a ten-dollar bill. "Call me. When your friend gets settled in town. D'Amato Green Grocer. D-Hyphen-A-M-A-T-O. You and me can make good things happen here, sport." The liquid brown eyes were dripping with honesty.

I watched the Twist turn back to his meal. He was delicate with his food, like he respected it.

"You gonna tip that lobster a ten-spot?" I asked him.

All this while Muscles had been digging singlemindedly into his chow, emptying all his side dishes and most of his platter. At my crack, Nick elbowed the strongman into consciousness. "Let's go."

Muscles Marinara shoved his chair back, untucked his napkin, and wrapped Nick's overcoat lovingly around the boss's shoulders. He glanced mournfully at Nick's practically undented lobster.

"I'll be waiting for your call, big fella." Nick laid his good hand on my shoulder. "And by the way, don't pass on the fresh berry shortcake. Terrific with a scoop of vanilla ice cream."

Nick the Twist D'Amato strolled through the restaurant, graciously waving to a few familiar faces along the way. At the door he turned and grinned at me. He made a pistol of his one good hand, pretended to shoot me with it, slipped his fingers into a peace sign. Then he winked, and faded into the Atlantic City night.

CHAPTER ELEVEN

O

During the thin hours of morning the casino world siestas and tallies up. By law the gaming tables close down weekdays between four and ten A.M., weekends between six and ten, gamblers staggering off to lick their wounds while the maintenance elves sweep up bushels of cigarette butts and truckloads of plastic cups, and change roll wrappers.

At six sharp I padded out the elevator door in my jogging shoes and Goretex windbreaker, the buzz of vacuum cleaners filling the lobby air. Outside Toby's Royale a slice of morning sun lashed long, lean shadows across the herringbone planks of the Boardwalk. Tractors were combing beach sand, sea gulls picking at the piles of food, drink, and souvenir debris waiting to be hoppered in a garbage trailer. Spite of all, the air was fresh and spicy, like its old nickname, the Lungs of Philadelphia, promised.

Over the top bar of the Boardwalk railing in front of Toby's, I hooked one heel, then the other, and hurdle-stretched my hamstrings.

Two blocks up-beach the Ocean One Mall, tricked out as an ocean liner, stretched into the water, nine hundred feet long, three stories high. Its facade sign shouted that, inside, one hundred seventy shops offered balm to mall-withdrawal sufferers. Step inside, instantly you forgot why you came to the seashore, could convince yourself you were back in suburban Pittsburgh or west of Boston or in Woodbridge, NJ.

Shopping, opium of the masses.

No thanks, I'll stay outside rat traps like that, with the other rodents.

The Boardwalk entrance to Ocean One Mall had something I really liked, though: a treasure map of the world, wrapped in relief around the semicircular facade of the mall front. THE WORLD OF SUNKEN TREASURE. A batch of color-coded windjammers marked spots on the ocean floor where centuries ago ships went down, holds crammed with gold bars, jewels, and pieces of eight. I leaned on one of the descriptive legend cases. The treasure buried nearest to Atlantic City was a pink Spanish galleon, the *Juno*, that died in the waters off Cape May, New Jersey, in 1802.

Not a mention of Captain Kidd's treasure map, though. An old Jersey shore rumor had it that Kidd, chased by the English navy, put ashore at Toms River, NJ, and buried a fortune on a sand spit now undersea after the currents shifted.

Makes a good story for tourists. Good metaphor, too, for what makes Atlantic City tick.

"Yo-ho-ho and a bottle of Dewars," Charlie Faucher off-keyed. He was bouncing on his toes beside me.

"Handy map," I said. "Too bad everything within reach is vandalized."

Flicking a finger at me, Faucher led me trotting up the angled boards, fifty feet across.

"How long is this thing?"

"Four miles in AC," Faucher puffed, taking his time warming up. "Smaller boardwalks in Ventnor and Margate add miles more."

"When did the old Steel Pier fall?" As we passed, I looked through the chain-link fence in front at the barnacle-encrusted pilings stretching out in the surf.

"Couple years ago the pier caught fire and had to be torn down." Faucher hacked and spat.

"Place was hokey, but it sure was fun. Remember the Incomparable Diving Horse?"

"Ha, ha!" Faucher roared, then coughed. "They used to pull a pin on the trapdoor, drop that horse and the girl kicking and screaming into the kiddie pool! Jesus, and people accuse the casinos of stealing money."

"It was different, Charlie. More innocent kind of fun. People didn't lose the rent money buying a ticket to see the diving horse."

Most of the tacky old shops along the Boardwalk had been torn down, elbowed out by the casinos or just losing as a different clientele high-tided into AC. We blew past the spot where the original Planter's Peanut store used to stand. Now the shop was filled with tee-shirts and costume jewelry, but behind a front window a five-foot Mr. Peanut, gray with age, sat astride one of a row of barrel-shaped nut roasters. Old Mr. Peanut was tipping off his seat like a drunk.

"Shops are going belly-up," I complained.

"Part of the plan," Charlie huffed rhythmically. "Whole idea of a casino is self-containment. Don't let 'em sniff the outdoor air. If they got a quarter to spend on a newspaper, *you* sell it to them."

"Not to mention that Boardwalk real estate is getting too valuable to tie up in taffy shops and hot dog stands," I said.

On the beach a blue Ford tractor with four big wheels pulled a sand-grooming harrow straight down the beach. Automatically I picked up my stride to keep pace, and felt Faucher respond with a strong surge that forced me up still more.

"Yeah, in a way it's a shame," Charlie said, puffing less. "Lot of memories tied up in these little holes in the wall. But AC can't afford to live in the Belle Epoque past. The gambling industry's the only chance this town has. We'll put AC back on its feet."

"Don't make me laugh. It's been ten years since casino gambling set up shop in Atlantic City. Place looks like hell, outside the casinos. Damn hurricane ripped through here ten months ago and they still haven't replaced half the damaged boards yet. Town's flat-ass broke."

"That is on the town," Faucher said flatly. "They're taking their cut of the action, believe me. What they do with it is their responsibility. Go complain at City Hall or the State House. Don't blame me, friend."

We had outrun the living, breathing part of the Boardwalk. Everything we passed now was either new construction or condemned memories.

A concrete shell pyramided thirty stories high in front of piles of construction materials. A security guard was posted to keep the locals from unauthorized shopping.

"What's this little outhouse gonna be when it grows up?"

"Twelfth casino in town," Faucher said dourly. "The Showboat. Scheduled to open next spring."

"Looks gigantic."

"New birds flying in are profiting from our early mistakes," Charlie said. "The real money is in the hotel and condo end of things. Gambling's got overhead coming out the kazoo. Four of the eleven houses are losing money right now. Three others only broke even last year."

"Including you? How's City by the Sea making out?"

"You heard that Playboy went broke at Atlantic City, didn't you? Same problem as ours."

"I thought that whole Hefner empire just sagged away."

A gull squawked so close over our heads that Charlie and I both flinched. I laughed. Faucher looked at me seriously.

"No, we came in the same time they did. The thinking then was to build European-style casinos. Notice how our two are real long and narrow with three floors? The idea was to isolate the baccarat, blackjack, and dice tables from the riffraff pulling the one-armed bandits downstairs. It's a classier set-up; all the European casinos use it. Exclusive."

"All the other AC casinos I been in are one big hangar, look like the Convention Hall. People like that better?"

"We were betting that Americans were turning more sophisticated." He shrugged. "We were wrong. They still like to gamble all in one huge room."

"How many more casinos can this area support? That's another big one going up there just before Hackney's, ain't it?"

"The Flagship," Faucher said. "Casino corporations are mesmerized. They read every favorable statistic known to man. Mainly the one about how a quarter of the population of the United States lives within a three-hundred-mile radius of here. Fogs their minds."

"I heard Atlantic City was the number-one tourist attraction in the country. City by the Sea get plenty of day trippers?"

"Less than our share," Faucher said tightly. "Nothing works. We're trying nickel slots, two-buck blackjack minimums, everything the Casino Commission will let us get away with."

"Casino Commission keep a tight rein on things? You see one of their offices behind every craps pit, practically."

"Unlimited powers of supervision." Charlie put the quotation marks on with a rueful grin. "You read in the newspaper how the Casino Commission thinks Resorts International is stockpiling too much AC real estate? If it wants, the Commission can shut down Resorts until they divest."

"Real estate's the thing these days, huh?" I said significantly.

"It's the only game in town the big boys are playing. Monopoly for keeps."

We ran out of runnable Boardwalk at the behemoth lobster painted on the side of Hackney's old seafood house. Plywood sheets covered its windows, steel grates its doors.

"My uncle once told me he saw women dressed in lobster suits parading down the Boardwalk advertising Hackney's," I said. "Must have been the forties."

Faucher didn't hear me. "They're granting only three more

casino licenses," he said. "Boys are playing hardball to get them."

"City by the Sea in the hunt for a second license?"

"Who isn't? We've lined up a nice piece of land on the Boardwalk, ready to go," Charlie said. We had turned around at Hackney's and were following the Boardwalk dogleg back around the old Absecon Lighthouse. Set a hundred yards from the breakers, in the middle of piss-poor slums, old Ab and a little patch of sand and weeds had been designated a city park. They'd even built a little glass-enclosed information booth next to the freshly whitewashed tower. But the park was lifeless except for a skinny man in layers of clothes topped with a huge old khaki parka. He clutched an open newspaper in one hand and was shaky-legging around old Ab's base as if hunting for light to read by.

"How's it look for you?"

"Terrible. Control Commission isn't exactly wild about our application. They figure it's safer to grant licenses to newcomers than give second licenses. Harrah's and Trump's got their second licenses, for their marina houses, before this new commissioner got sworn in."

"Who's that?"

"Crusty old bird. His name is Roger Trimster, and he's the damn chairman of the damn commission now."

"Just a guess, but maybe he's not your best homey?"

"Old money," Charlie said, in a way that made me chuckle. "Lot of it. Family dates back in New Jersey to the American Revolution."

By this time construction crews were moving around the work sites. We tailgated a cluster of young women dressed in brown frocks and bonnets, as if for work in an olde tyme muffin shop. We grinned, sped past, and they laughed and waved.

"Dealers," Charlie grunted.

"What!"

"Claridge's daytime gaming staff."

From the casino front, Resorts International is standard AC tacky. But from across the enormous construction site on its side, it is one of the classier-looking hotels. Resorts had been first kid on the casino block, and was still eight city blocks from any of the other houses. They'd renovated the old Haddon Hall so the outside imitated the grand old Atlantic City style of yesterday, with shiny gambling and hostelry machinery tucked in its guts. Classy, if you overlooked the handprints and slogans of the stars—KISS MY RESORTS, DON RICKLES—pressed in the cement out front.

When I was a teenager, Haddon Hall and its Victorian twin, the Chalfonte Hotel, had been landmarks. The Chalfonte didn't survive the wrecker's ball, a more accurate forecast of things to come.

"Shame they didn't save more of the old glitz," I said to Faucher. He wasn't listening.

"Gets his pocket money from money now," Faucher said. "Years ago the family built ships. Now the old fart hangs around the Hunt Club and pretends to read the *Wall Street Journal*. I heard he breeds racehorses as a hobby."

"Jersey breeds are not all that good." I knew this from my old friend and bookie, Cosmo.

"Not a big-time champion in ages," Faucher agreed. "Maybe Trimster breeds them for platform diving." Three and a half miles, and he was running more strongly than when we started. My comments were coming out in gasps now, but Charlie could talk as easily as if he were sitting over a drink.

Looking at Faucher, I had looped to the far side of a police barricade that cordoned off a section of planking ripped into roller coaster waves by the hurricane. It was a long drop to the rock jetty below.

"You got a thing for this turkey, Charlie?"

"He takes it too seriously to suit me," Faucher said. "Thinks he's running the U.S. Olympic Committee or the Camp Fire Girls."

"How'd he get elected?"

"Elected? It's a five-year appointment. Governor looked for a good figurehead, add a little class to the commission. Rich man, from an old family, looks less corruptible. JFK rather than R. M. Nixon."

Ahead of us loomed Caesar's Palace, directly across the Boardwalk from the Ocean One Mall where we began. I started dragging my feet.

"Warmed up?"

"Wound down."

"Come on, Easy," Faucher ribbed. "You're a pro athlete. That loop was four miles, tops. It's 6:34. If we run down to Ventnor and back, we tack on another six miles. Take us another forty-five minutes. Don't you run ten miles a day?"

I thought for a second. My guts were hanging out from the torrid pace Faucher had set, and I make a point of proving nothing to nobody. Thing of it was, we still hadn't gotten to the point of our coversation.

My feet slapped the Boardwalk again.

"Let's do it."

Down from Caesar's three-story statue of baby Augustus tugging at Julius's toga, the next casino was the Atlantis, which rubbed elbows with Convention Hall. The sun was lemon creme now, and hot. I unzipped my windbreaker on the fly, stripped it off, and tied the arms around my waist.

Charlie and I pelted along, elbow to elbow, stride for stride, hitting a nice long rhythm. A couple of maintenance men stopped to watch us fly past. The Boardwalk, double width for a few hundred yards, still looked deserted, but casino and shop employee traffic was picking up.

Convention Hall had just been face-lifted, new doors and fixtures, but featuring the same granite facade I remembered. I pointed this out to Faucher, who said, "Looks the same as the day she opened in 1929. And still the world's grandest organ, all 33,000 pipes. In its day the Hall was some kind of architectural marvel. Seven acres of structural steel. Now it's full of a different kind of architectural marvel every September. God bless America."

Ernie and Snookie'd been nagging me for years to drive down to AC for the Miss America pageant. Maybe this year we would.

After another minute I said, "Were you able to pull Veronica Vallee's personnel file, learn anything?"

"No, I didn't have time yesterday. I've got a Casino Commission hearing later this morning; we make our preliminary pitch for that second license we were talking about. I spent most of last night prepping for it."

"What's that involve?"

"Everything but checking you for hemorrhoids, pal. It's the Miss America contest for casinos. First they look at your background, make sure you're an all-American type, no organized crime contacts. Which is a farce, because the mob gets strawmen to front for them anyway. Second they have to approve your architectural plans. Just imagine the cheap piles of junk some of those jokers'd throw up if somebody didn't keep tabs. Then your casino also has to be a first-class hotel. As of this year they want a minimum of four hundred rooms. There's another place where City by the Sea missed the boat when we built. And after that they monkey around with financial resources, management, and so on. That part's fairly mysterious to us ex-cops."

"Roger Trimster going to master-of-ceremony this hearing?"

"Of course." A gull's scream echoed Faucher's bitter laugh. "No way he'd miss the chance to wax self-righteous over the likes of us."

For the next mile we ran in silence, the Boardwalk planking creaking and sometimes cracking as the old boards strained to flex underfoot.

"How about you?" Faucher puffed finally. "Did you talk to your friend about Veronica Vallee's hot shot?"

"I did. Dude claimed there's bales of it floating around Atlantic City." Charlie glanced over at me, and I took the look for an invitation.

"Point of fact, he sells an ocean of dope to casino high rollers."

Faucher's brows curved down.

One, two, three. "Including the crowd at City by the Sea."

"I don't try to control what people do in their rooms," Faucher said, without lips. "So long as they keep the shit off the casino floor, it's not my job to care if they buy prostitutes or dope or little stuffed animals, if that's their thing."

"You and me're old homeys, Charlie," I rasped softly. "Let me tell you something. The situation don't reflect all that well on you, you know?"

We had started the return trip up the Boardwalk from Ventnor. In the morning mist that always rolls in from the sea, the entire Boardwalk string curved like dominoes before us, casino towers upright, other buildings only half high, plenty more knocked over. The first morning tram, empty, rumbled by on its casino hop up the boards to Resorts, where the first day trippers always landed.

"How can you just look the other way?"

Faucher gave me the Newark cop's patented you-don't-know-shit-because-you-ain't-been-there stare.

"Barnes, I'm going to explain this once because we used to work together back when. Anybody else, I'd tell him to fold it and stick it. My job is Vice President of Security Operations for the casino. Not Minister of Morality." Faucher was shouting in gasps, the first signs of tiredness he'd shown. "And not vice squad for the goddam Atlantic City police department."

"Charlie—"

"It's not my job to knock on hotel rooms, see if they're all in bed by curfew, and confiscate any dirty magazines they're reading in there."

"You get other people to do your snooping for you, Charlie?"

"What the hell are you getting at?"

"Two Italians paid me a visit last night at dinner. To warn me off the Utah Avenue properties. Strains my sense of the coincidental, you know? First, I tell you about Mr. Horton planning to develop the block behind your casino, and then two heavies show up, lean on me."

"I didn't sic them on you, man. Who were they?"

I had a serious case of ache in the legs and arms by now. Wind was raspy, but not too bad.

"The littler one called himself Nick the Twist D'Amato. His shadow was a big bone crusher."

"I know them both." Faucher's voice relaxed. "Philly gangsters, local business reps, so to speak. But I swear to God I didn't talk to them."

"How'd they find me, then?"

"Well, naturally I told a couple of our development people about Horton's plans to bid on the land. You knew I would do that."

"Yeah, but. You're not telling me *your* casino is mobbed up with Philly OC?"

"Not at all," Faucher said. "Atlantic City is a very small world, Barnes. Like on Wall Street, word travels fast. Rumors make the marketplace react. News of your friend Horton shoehorning into the action must have leaked out of our office and spread like an oil slick. You can probably expect to get more feelers from other groups, now that word's getting around town."

"Think it could turn into a bidding war?"

"Jesus, I hope not," Charlie said devoutly. "What's likely is they'll try buying you off, a lump sum to back Horton out of the game. Much cheaper for them. Frankly, I hope you take them up."

A hundred yards from the Ocean One Mall we spotted the little clump of policemen waiting for us. Couple of plain-clothesmen sheathed in raincoats against the early morning damp. Three blue uniforms. Charlie and I stopped running and walked hands on hips the last dozen steps.

I had not met any of these AC cops the night before last. The older detective said, "Morning, Charlie." Then, "Ezell Barnes?"

I nodded.

"There's been a murder. We're putting you under arrest."

"Who died?" I said, lungs burning, legs shuddering.

"Of course, you wouldn't know," the younger raincoated cop sneered. His collar was turned up even though the sun was burning off the fog.

"The deceased's name was Omar Reese," the older cop said impatiently. "Alias the New Yorker. He died around 12:45 last night. His body was found an hour ago."

"How'd he die?" I asked. "They make him wear a leisure suit in public?" Charlie let out a loud chuckle.

"You sound like a man that didn't much like Omar Reese," said the gray-haired detective. He shoved both hands into raincoat pockets and grinned facetiously.

I had no pockets, but I tried to match his grin. "I don't sound like a man that killed him, and you can tell, can't you?"

The younger cop had pulled a plastic-coated card from his breast pocket. He stepped right into my face and began to Mirandize me.

"You quarreled with Reese in a public place," the gray-haired detective piped over his partner's litany. The youngster flicked incredulous eyes at his partner. One of the bluecoats snickered.

"Around ten o'clock last night, it was," the older man told me. "A hundred fifty people can swear to it. Better yet, we've got two eyewitnesses to the beating you gave Reese a little later."

My heart sank. Plain and simple, I could not afford to spend time locked up. Too much I didn't understand was spinning around me.

"Barry," said Faucher easily. "You're barking up the wrong tree. Barnes here is an old Newark PD partner of mine. He was with me late last night, from about eleven to at least two A.M. He's clean."

"Are you clear about the time frame, Charlie?" The detective looked doubtful.

"Absolutely. We sat in my office drinking too much bourbon and yakking about old times."

"What's his business in town? Don't tell me he's a tourist."

"Come on, Barry. He's here representing an investor from Atlanta who's looking for an entrée into our development office. Naturally he contacted his old buddy."

"He beat that drug dealer something fierce, Charlie."

"Are you crying about it? I'm not. You and I both knew the New Yorker was a pimple on Atlantic City's ass."

To me Barry said mildly, "He cheat you in a drug deal?"

I shook my head. "But he fed the hot shot to that girl you found floating in the marina yesterday. I knew her. He had the beating coming."

The detective looked at Faucher, who nodded. "That's the truth, Barry. I knew the girl too."

"All right, Charlie. You guarantee this character will stay in town and out of trouble for the next few days?"

"Sure thing. And thanks, Barry."

Faucher walked with Barry back to the no-chrome cop sedan.

By now the uniformed cops had beaten a trail back to their blue-and-white cruisers. The younger plainclothesman dawdled behind Faucher and Barry like a schoolboy.

I waited for Faucher to finish with them.

When he walked back, Cheshire-catting, I said, "I owe you one, man."

He waved a hand in dismissal. "Hey, when I landed this job, first thing I did was get my friends in Newark that knew the fuzz down here to introduce us over dinner, talk about what a hero I was in north Jersey. Plus, since I've been here, I make sure I work very, very well with AC cops. These monkeys worship the boards I stand sweating on."

"You want to eat dinner tonight?"

"Sure. No, wait, I got to work later tonight. Tomorrow, maybe the next day. Give my office a call."

"Be Sunday tomorrow."

He grinned sarcastically. "You're in Atlantic City, boy. Land of the midnight sun. Casinos don't close. Nothing closes. Who keeps count of the days of the week?"

CHAPTER TWELVE

O

The ten-mile run in sea air put a growling in my gut that only a good diner breakfast could silence. Being without roadhouse diners, I hummingbirded an alternate spot.

The Taylor Pork Roll House is on the Boardwalk, just north of City by the Sea. Taylor Pork Roll is as New Jersey as Rutgers tomatoes or solid waste landfills. First time I ordered Taylor Ham out of state, they laughed at me. Looks like a slice of Canadian bacon but it's made of ground pork and spices, with a tangy bite that always sets my mouth to watering thinking about it.

With a Newark *Star-Ledger* popped from a box tucked under my arm, I stepped inside the two-story brick restaurant. My sweat was far from evaporated yet; in fact, I slid onto a stool away from the window to dodge the suddenly steamy sun. The stools ran in a long string down the front of the counter grill. Not another soul sat in the place. Too late for the casino crews, I figured, way too early for the tourists and gamblers. Hell, gamblers generally eat breakfast just before nightfall.

I studied the signboard over the counter. The waitress automatically poured coffee without a quarrel from me.

"Double Taylor Ham, three over-easies, side of home fries, blueberry pancakes, toast, and the biggest glass you got of grapefruit juice."

She smiled at my size and appetite.

"Make it diet," I said, and grinned back.

"How do you want your ham?"

"Burnt around the edges, golden brown in the middle, ma'am."

The sports section flipped right open and was feeding me yesterday's Mets-Cardinals box score when nasty storm clouds blew in. They were wearing alligator shirts in cranberry and lemon, under alligator cardigan sweaters in baby-boy blue and fire engine, over window-plaid golf slacks. They were peering

93

through the plate window at me, cupping their hands around their faces to cut the glare. Embarrassing.

One of them was a short swarthy man with a short swarthy hairline, tanned skin color in the center, gray curls at the temples. His face was darkly tanned, including a nose like a sickle, which gave him a convincingly cruel look. The Caesar statue on the Boardwalk should be so lucky as to have Al's looks. He was stocky, with an inch of hard fat around the middle. The other man was rangy big, younger, full mane waved over his ears.

Nothing to do but sip on my coffee as they swaggered through the door and up to my stool.

The short curly man stood looking at me with indescribable annoyance.

"We got a tee-off time of nine o'clock. I don't want to miss it on account of pissing around with you."

"'Scuse me for holding my bar mitzvah so early in the day," I said, and turned back to my coffee.

The rangy man parked his butt on the stool next to me. He said, "Al, what stunats said mouls got no sense of humor?"

"Here's the message," Al said briskly. "It's from Mr. Carmine Napolitano. Know who that is? The message is, you got something that belongs to him, and he wants it back."

I blew out my breath wearily. "You about the worst organized Cosa Nostra I ever heard of. I already talked to Nick the Twist late last night, Al. Liked the Twist's sales pitch better, tell you the truth."

The Jersey OC golf team exchanged puzzled looks.

"What is a twist?" said the younger greaseball on the stool.

"Your approach," I said. "You all supposed to be organized." I looked at the service door, wishing my breakfast platter would come so I could chew my food at them. But my waitress hadn't worked in Jersey all her life for nothing. She stayed put in the kitchen.

"Listen good, Barnes." Curly Locks Al leaned in close so I could smell his Old Spice. His red-brown skin was taut and shiny. "You like to joke around? Okay, joke around. I never do myself. We don't know no damned Twist. You are holding a very valuable item that belongs to my employer. A young lady named Veronica Vallee was involved in obtaining the item for Mr. Napolitano. Now it's gone, and he's holding you directly responsible, like it or not."

"I'm drawing a blank," I said, but seriously.

"Who cares?" Al glanced at his Rolex and flicked his head at the other, who stood up. "Two days to return it. When you are ready, call the Alpine Golf Club in Long Branch, and somebody'll meet with you."

"Who do I ask for?"

I had a high school math teacher once roll his eyes at me like that.

"Just say it's Ezell Barnes, is all."

"Well, what's the item? I find most things better when I know what they're supposed to be."

Al shook his head, annoyed again, then glanced at the kitchen's swinging door. He wafted Old Spice at me again. "They make you go to special school, you were a kid? The hell is the matter with you?" His voice dropped a notch. "I'm referring to a video tape cassette, idiot." He motioned to the tall man, "Rickie."

They stalked out the Pork Roll House door. The younger man stopped to practice an iron shot, then smiled to himself and parodied Al's executive bustle out of the joint.

Directly they dissolved, old waitress scooted out with my breakfast platter and an apologetic smile. The cooled food went tasteless on me.

Damn. Easy to take a very educated guess at what they wanted. That camcorder on the *Polaris* had made a special videotape of Muff Anglaise for them. Whether she knew what was going on or not. Featuring—who else?—herself and somebody worth blackmailing. Doing sex and drugs and who knows what more. Had to be. What else would these Long Branch golf bums be sniffing after?

Only thing was, Muff's killer was the one palming that item, not me.

CHAPTER THIRTEEN

O

The Casino Control Commission hearings were scheduled for eleven o'clock, and I needed to hustle. Back at my hotel I stripped, showered and shaved, and started pulling on that cream-colored suit. I got as far as the shirt before I stopped. Never in my life have I willingly put a soiled shirt on my back—something my grandmama put in me. Buttoning a sweater over the dress slacks, I grabbed my toothbrush, pasted it, and stepped into the corridor same time as the young couple staying next door. They looked headed to the beach in khaki shorts and matching raspberry polo shirts. The boy carried their beach bag of swimsuits and towels. His girl toted their paperback books and whisked his back like a wife.

"Hi, neighbor!" The woman couldn't be older than nineteen. Her little woman pleasantness was infectious.

I pulled the toothbrush out of my mouth and wiped the lather off with my hand.

They looked at each other and wrinkled their noses.

"Beautiful morning," I said feebly.

We took the elevator together, where they announced they were from northern Wisconsin. The girl kept beaming up into her boyfriend's face, and when they thought I couldn't see, the boy pinched her behind.

"Honeymoon?" I said knowingly.

"Not really," the girl exclaimed cheerfully. She and the boy exchanged more smiles. "More an anniversary vacation. We each left our spouses and got back together after two whole years of mistake."

The elevator doors opened then, to the relief of my speechless mouth. In the lobby I nosed around the men's shop until I found something soft, French-cuffed, and medium-rolled. They wouldn't put it on my hotel tab, but they sure liked my plastic.

Suited up, I dialed Angel's room, got endless brrrings,

finally a sleepy Latin voice that electrified when Angel heard it was me.

"Papi! Who could believe this! I am backstage at the Seesee casino, talk to Mimi and her friends, and the director is this pretty little boy that likes me and invite me for an audition in the revue."

"You mean a dance part? In the casino revue? Like you did with Paul Anka a couple years back? I knew you had a career in show dancing if you wanted it."

"Oh, is wonderful! I go to audition, he ask me to move this way, that way, and I get the job, Easy! Mimi been rehearsing me all the time since then. I'm gonna dance tonight. You can come see me? Please, Papi!"

"Wouldn't miss it if the seats were land-mined," I said, and meant it. "What time's it start?"

"Start at ten o'clock, and I gonna make sure you got comp tickets waiting for you and Ernie, Easy. You come see me after the show?"

"First night, you gonna be busy celebrating with the other girls and your director. I'll see the show tonight and come backstage after tomorrow's show."

I could almost hear Angel nodding over the phone.

"What's the name of this revue, amigo?"

"Is the *Pieces of Cream Revue*, Easy. Very elegant, very sexy."

"You mean, 'Peaches and Cream,' like in the song? Well, if it's elegant and sexy, you gonna fit right in, man."

"You sweet, Easy."

"Catch you later."

I hung up before Angel could blow me a kiss, then phoned Ernie Horton at Roberta's house, got Roberta.

After five minutes of pleasantries I asked her, "Can you get your neighbors together for a meeting today? Ball's starting to bounce, and you folks need to know which way."

"Oh dear." She let out her breath. "Saturday's such a bad day to get everyone together. We have a meeting set up for Sunday morning after church, though. Tomorrow morning. Will that do?"

"Have to, I guess. Ernie there?"

"Yes he is. I'll get him."

Roberta came back on the line while Ernie was getting his pants on to come to the phone. "Ernie looks so handsome in his new suit," she cooed. "That was wonderful of you, Ezell."

"It's nothing."

"But it must have cost you a lot of money. And you bearing the expense of a fancy hotel room!"

"Oh," I said breezily, "my savings are for exactly what I'm doing—going first class when I do go, and covering emergencies."

"You are such a good friend to Ernie. Are you sure you won't accept a bed at my house?"

I knew what to say to that. I asked Roberta if she had plans for that evening. Her voice was Fourth of July, trilling no, she was free, yes, she'd love to get together. Six o'clock, her house, I'd pick her up. Dress to the nines, I told her, I had tickets for the *Peaches and Cream Revue*.

Ernie barged on the line then. "Easy! What's shaking, brother?"

"Listen good, Ernie. Tomorrow morning or afternoon you and me got to play our Rib King parts for some people. Come over to my hotel around ten tomorrow morning. We got some rehearsing to do."

"You got Roberta's problem fixed, Easy?"

"Ernie, man, that's what I'm talking about for tomorrow. What'd you think I meant?"

"Nothing. Not a thing. I's just wondering if you got the mess cured, man."

"See you tomorrow morning, Ernie."

"You got it, Easy. We drink some beers together later?"

"Not today, man. I got a shitload of business."

After I hung up, there was just twenty minutes to find the Arcade Building between Caesar's and Bally's on the Boardwalk, where the Casino Commission hearings were being staged. A security guard at the marbled hall entrance directed me to the hearing room on the third floor, where I found Charlie Faucher facing front at a long table behind a microphone, flanked by platoons of other gray-suited business types.

The red-carpeted room was half filled with press and observers. I grabbed a seat in back, beyond easy recognition distance. Peering down on Faucher from an elevated bench was a gang of four hearing examiners. The middle chair among them was conspicuously vacant, though. Its bronze name wedge declared that ROGER TRIMSTER, CHAIRMAN, was missing.

Faucher was pretty slick for an old Newark cop, volleying questions and answers with the examiners until they tired first.

Other stuffed-shirt representatives of City by the Sea changed seats with Charlie and delivered mixed performances. The skeptical questioning and pious answering went on until I thought I'd faint from boredom. Finally, with a fanfare of formalities, the commissioner acting as chairman in Roger Trimster's absense gaveled the hearings to a sharp cracking close.

Briefcases snapped shut, chairs screeched back, and gray suits shuffled out, except for a small crowd at the front, where Charlie Faucher, alone among the casino crowd, chummed it up with the Casino Control Commissioners like they were old college buddies. One commissioner, a steel-haired woman in her early fifties, seemed a particular friend, laughing and touching Charlie's sleeves. The one other woman in the little crowd shone like the Statue of Liberty among the gray suits and pink noses. I knew her.

She was dressed in a summer-weight rose-and-pale-blue pinstriped dress suit, rose shoes, and carried a blue leather satchel shaped vaguely like an attorney's. No question that she knew all the commissioners well. Knew Faucher too. The entire group was smiling and laughing in a semiofficial way. I watched closely as it filtered down. Finally the lady commissioner bid a wryly gay farewell, and left Faucher to the company of Patricia Valentine.

Into the hallway I ducked, and hunched my back inside a phone booth as Faucher and Ms. Valentine arm-waisted their way past me out of the building.

I hung back a safe distance and dogged the pair down the Boardwalk to an outdoor café, where they camped under an umbrella table. At a hot dog stand diagonally across, I perched on the Boardwalk railing and watched them, aching to wolf down about three chili dogs and large fries. But I had a dinner date later. To grit down the hunger, I recollected the particulars of chopping off chickens' heads for my grandmama.

Relationships between strangers are harder to size up on surveillance than civilians might think, especially at a distance. But it was easy to see that this man and woman shared more than the Formica table between them. Faucher's body underlined his urgency like a silent film actor's. He picked up Patricia's hand and stroked it between both of his.

At that, Patricia lounged back in her chair, so Charlie had to let go. Charlie's whole body tensed. She shook her head twice, but he shook back at her, more vehemently, setting loose

strands of his carefully combed back hair. Finally she threw
her hands up and ran them over her shiny head. She oozed out
a few words as if she could not care less. Faucher flinched, but
leaned across to her like a plant to sun.

Patricia Valentine uncoiled to her pastel feet, apparently
bored, dropped a remark like a tip onto the table. Faucher
shot from his seat and clutched her elbow. Patrons at other
tables were craning their necks now. But Patricia's look dared
him, until Charlie dropped his hands. La Valentine spun on
her heels and stormed off. The other patrons buzzed and
grinned behind their menus. Faucher watched her go with
eyes that might have held despair, might have held admira-
tion. Or even amusement. I just couldn't see.

I was too busy following Patricia Valentine.

She tapped briskly up the Boardwalk toward the City by the
Sea casino, and I began to wonder if she were a casino
employee, maybe even worked for Faucher. Hustling up, I
hitched to her elbow just outside Fralinger's taffy shop.

She thought it'd be Charlie. Her infuriated face melted, and
the breath caught in her throat when she spun around.

"Imagine meeting you here," I said. "Thought you hung out
in the cranberry bogs back in the pine barrens."

Country club ladies are built sturdy, don't bolt flighty. "You
have some nerve," she insisted. "What do you want?"

"A few answers. Who on earth are you really?"

She steeled up: "I owe you nothing. You accepted my five
hundred dollars. You were well paid for the little service you
rendered. Now leave me alone."

She tried to shake me off, but I tightened my grip on her
arm. Two young business turks at the café were leaving their
rocks glasses untouched and staring hard at me manhandling
the uptown woman.

"Listen, lady, I don't hire out as an accessory to murder, at
any price. You're under arrest."

"If you don't let go of my arm," she hissed, scrunching up
her pretty eyes, "I'll kick you in the balls and then call the
police."

"Good. You'll bruise your toes and the cops'll love locking up
the woman that hired me to find Veronica Vallee. Don't forget,
she turned up dead right after I reported to you where she was
hiding."

"So *you* say." With this, Patricia did wrench free and ran
from me, X-ing the diagonaled boards. The blonder of the two

businessmen stood up from his table and buttoned his jacket. I trotted after the woman. She wheeled. "I'm walking into the nearest casino, which happens to be Bally's. It is full of bored dinner-jacketed security men who would just love to hear me yell for help and point accusingly at you, Ezell."

That logic grabbed my bicep, hard, from behind. "You have a problem with this gentleman, ma'am?"

I twisted my arm free from the tall, chunky man. His mustached friend stood a pace behind him. They both looked like ex-high school jocks now sales-representing kitchen equipment on the Boardwalk.

"Mind your own damn business!" Patricia Valentine snapped at them. She bent one sturdy nyloned leg in an unconsciously threatening gesture.

"Sor-ry, lady." The chunky one shrugged, looked at his friend, hesitated. He pointed a finger pistol at me and looked back at Patricia. "Nothing we can do for you?"

I said what I usually stick into an opening like that.

When they had walked away, snarling, Patricia put her hands on her hips and her teeth on edge. "Stay away from me!"

She stalked into Bally's without a glance for me until she was safely inside the two-story revolving door. I looked at her from the center of the Boardwalk. She risked a satirical Kukla of one hand and then disappeared.

CHAPTER FOURTEEN

○

I killed time until my six o'clock date with Roberta by shopping for a second complete set of clothes. I showered again, shaved once more, retied my tie knot. Then I turned up the air-conditioning, poured a tall, mild highball with plenty of ice and ginger ale, and sat down to read my Atlantic City book for a spell.

At quarter to six I bookmarked page 193—on a picture of Al Capone strolling the Boardwalk with a 1920s mayor of Atlantic City—washed my highball glass, took a last sideways glance in the mirror, and walked out to the landing.

When the elevator door opened, my next-door neighbors stepped out.

"Ooh, somebody has a date," the teenaged girl teased. Her boyfriend brushed his hand across her fair hair, then reached back into the car and thumbed the HOLD button.

"Do you?" Caught off guard, I nodded.

"You do? That's terrific!" The boy beamed. "We were worried about you."

I did a double take. "About me?"

He said, "You always come and go by yourself." She added, "I don't see why a nice man has to be alone, just because he's older."

"Atlantic City's a tough town to be alone in," the boy advised me, young eyes narrowed in instant world-weariness. "Too many loneliness traps."

I let my breath out, stepped into the car, and let them morale-support me out of sight. Outside Toby's I hoofed it to Roberta's house. One block west to Pacific, four blocks south to Utah. Walking up the seedy block in my shining new suit and tie, I looked as ordinary as a jolly flophouse proprietor.

The price in self-consciousness was worthwhile, though, when Roberta appeared at the door in her evening dress, a one-strap number in emerald, black, and a hint of summer colors. Sheer black stockings, black high heels. Simple—no scarves to wrap around my face in the sea breeze—and shape-hugging.

She held her face up for me to peck, and a big greenstone dangle brushed my cheek. She was a big woman, and with her hair put up, she could carry those huge earrings fine.

"You, hungry?"

"I could be."

"How about we club-hop the casinos a little, slide on down to the Golden Nugget? Then, on the way back up, I know this drugstore counter where we can dine."

Roberta took my arm and squeezed it. "This is such a wonderful idea, Ezell."

No debate from me. She held my arm and we strolled up to the Boardwalk through the City by the Sea tunnel.

From Utah Avenue south on the Boardwalk you get a fat dose of traditional carnival sleaze: custard stand, Fun Spot Arcade and Skeeball, Jackpot Souvenirs, A. Donis of London Gentlemen's and Ladies' Furnishings, now defunct, Souvenir and Tee-Shirt Factory, Candy Kitchen, featuring something spelled Macarums, Fam-a-lee Fun Playcade, then Duke Mack's night spot at California Avenue, and a Burger King.

On a June evening the Boardwalk is crammed with good-natured fun seekers, all the jitteriness of the wee hours suspended. The evening-clothes set, border-guarding the frontiers of fashion, rub elbows with the bathing-suited, tee-shirted unwashed. The predusk salt breeze is thick and honeyed, but excuse enough for the furs to pop out. Two tuxedoed men, past middle age, walked arm in arm with a magnificently coiffed woman swathed in leopard spots from ears to shins.

"Fun fur?" I whispered to Roberta.

"I don't think so."

We hit the Tropacabana, as Angel calls it, in honor of the little striped tents strewn over the beach in front of the casino. Actually, all the Boardwalk casino-hotels have little striped cabanas, distinctively shaped and colored. At midday, they add to the beach's colorfulness, however silly they look. But in the long slants of the evening sun, on the roped-off beach, there's something distant and romantic about them.

We leaned on the railing and watched the redly burning sun turn the ocean water black. Two wet-suited divers spearfished like seals beyond the breakers.

"The Atlantic Ocean," I told Roberta. "You should have seen it in the old days. It was something."

She giggled. "I never saw it until I moved down the shore. Now I love to just look at it."

"Me too." I lifted my chin at the scuba couple. "But just watching people swim in those waves gives me the heebie-jeebies."

"I've heard that a hundred years ago the city installed enormous life lines up and down the beach. They used to advertise the perfect safety of Atlantic City beaches."

"Yeah?" I turned us towards the Boardwalk. "No sign of life lines now."

"Well, now they have gambling to sell the tourists. They don't need safety."

We walked side by side, not touching, into the Tropicana, under a dark purple awning, through huge squares outlined with hundreds of electric bulbs. Just inside the casino entrance we pulled a couple slot handles with my pocket change. Roberta said she would like to try a roulette spin or two. She hadn't gambled in a casino in years, she told me.

"Got a system for you to try, if you like," I said. "Roulette tables are split up lots of ways. One of them is into thirds: 1 to 12, 13 to 24, 25 to 36. I'll stake you to this ten-dollar bill. Strictly an investment, mind you. You buy a ten-dollar chip, stick it on the line between first third and second third. Even with zero and double zero, you've got almost two chances in three of winning on any given spin. Odds are actually way in your favor that you'll win any one turn."

"I thought casino odds were stacked against the player."

"Well, they are, in the long run. The stack on this play is that your payoff is only half your bet. So you are risking ten bucks trying to win five. You willing to try?"

"I'm game for anything tonight."

"Here's what we do, then, give it more spice. Chances are good you'll win your first bet. Pick up your winnings, cash in the chips, and we'll sashay to the next casino, lay the total down, same way."

"That's the Golden Nugget."

"That's it. If you win there, we'll let the whole package ride in every casino up and down the Boardwalk."

Roberta's eyes shone, but not with greed, I didn't think. Just a plain old sense of fun.

"How much could we win?"

"Hmmm. Ten casinos on the Boardwalk. You win them all, I think you'd be holding maybe five-and-a-half bills."

"Oooh."

"Baby, you win all ten, I will personally drive you over to the marina, play the two casinos there. You win those two also, you'll have over a thousand."

"And then can we come back to the Boardwalk and go through them all a second time? Look out pot of gold!"

"That's what I like. A woman with her feet screwed to the ground."

We circled the roulette tables—mostly little old ladies, youngsters of barely legal age, and suburbanites, at this early hour—until we homed in on Lucky Dan. Roberta bought a green ten-dollar chip and split the first thirds line. *Fourteen*. My date scooped up her chips, eyes and red lips shining. Away from the table she grabbed my head and kissed me hard on the mouth. "For luck!"

Arm in arm down Boardwalk to the Golden Nugget, we passed radio station WAYV, and across from it the only sign of civic improvement I'd seen in all Atlantic City—a brand new public rest room. No doubt with the NO CLOTHES CHANGING AND NO WET BATHING SUITS signs inside it. I explained to Roberta my theory about the AC beaches being absorbed by the hotels, and she agreed. Mood she was in, I could have explained how Lucy the Elephant was an alien from space and she'd have agreed.

We passed the Ocean Park condo where, the newspapers claimed, Vic Damone, Art Linkletter, and such owned units.

"They're fixing to build one like this where your house is," I told Roberta. "Only even bigger and slicker, from what I've heard. You feel sad about that?"

Roberta made her big earrings swing and flash. "Oh no, I hope they build a beautiful resort there. I mean, our homes have been condemned anyway. I'm not moony-eyed over that dump, believe me. I have lived there almost since I got married at eighteen. We moved here from Newark after a year."

"Bet that house has some memories for you."

"Of course, but they can't repay me for living in squalor."

"Nobody told me your block was condemned. That changes plenty, no?"

"Oh yes, the whole block is finally being evacuated as

uninhabitable firetraps. We've all been ordered to move by the end of the month."

"You fixed your place up nice."

"In a row house everybody suffers when a few let their places run down so terribly."

"This turns the flame up under everybody's tail," I said. "You folks don't have time to sit back, let the bidding heat up. What will happen to your neighbors?"

"Well, the housing office is making space available in the old Connecticut Avenue project. Sounds attractive, doesn't it? The younger people, like me, will get second jobs or something to afford a better place. But the older folks will just have to move into that project, I'm afraid. They won't have a dime to their names."

"Over dinner," I said, "we'll figure out the briefing you'll give your people tomorrow."

We dawdled, hearts not in window-shopping the glittering boutiques lining the ground-floor windows of Ocean Park.

To cheer Roberta up, I told her, "You know, I have to admit. Going this way on the Boardwalk, after a short stretch of the sleaze America knew and loved, they've really cleaned it up."

"It leaves me empty, though," Roberta said softly.

"Me too."

"The old Boardwalk had a character all its own." Roberta bit her lower lip.

We strolled a half a block, and the Boardwalk came through for us. We couldn't help roaring.

"Thank heavens, we are saved!" Roberta gasped. Saved by Dip-Stix III, with the monstrous lemon revolving on top and Mr. Dip-Stix himself jumping out at us.

The Golden Nugget was our favorite casino so far: little Hyatt-style bronze hood awnings striped with light bulbs over the doors outside, cow palace motif inside. Waitresses, dealers, and security guards were all cowgirls, wranglers, and deputy marshals. Mirrors and western floy-floy on every available wall. The Disneyland of casinos.

Roberta hit her bet again, cashed her chips, and we moseyed on out.

"I like that one," she said after I collected another good luck kiss. "The dealers and security people all look so miserable and foolish wearing those costumes that you don't feel as intimidated by them."

I suggested a rolling chair to push us back up the Boardwalk.

My date was ecstatic. "I've seen these all my adult life," she oohed, "and I've never sat in one. Do you remember the old song, Easy?" She sang in high vibrato, "'There, where the saltwater air, / Brings out the ladies' charms. / There, in a rolling chair, / She'll roll right into your arms.'" We looked at each other and smiled. "It's from a silly old movie," Roberta said, full kilowatts burning in those big eyes. "It's called *Three Little Girls in Blue*. Sounds like a sad story, doesn't it? But it has a happy ending."

Seemed like we'd done nothing but smile at each other all evening.

At City by the Sea Casino and Atlantis Casino, the two multileveled European-styled houses, we rode the escalators up for one roulette spin each. City by the Sea had impressed me the night before last, but next to the other casinos, its crowds seemed smaller. And for all the upscale decor, a low-roller scent hung in the air. Bingo, bingo, for Roberta at the roulette wheels, though. Her stake had increased fivefold.

"One more roulette stop," I said outside Atlantis. "Then how about some dinner?"

At Toby's Royale, where I was staying, Roberta upped her winnings fifty percent more on a number 3 spin. Then we walked across the plaza to Ristorante Alberto. Quite a few AC restaurants have that beachy, dress-down atmosphere. I picked Alberto's because Roberta was all dressed up. Alberto's is Forty-seventh Street New York style, and I liked it the first time I went there.

We ate their specialties, Veal Piccante for Roberta, and for me, Gamberi alla Parmigiana, which the menu rhapsodized as "a delightful fantasy of shrimp in a light marinara sauce with a blend of Italian cheeses." Both would do. So would the bottle of Barolo I sprang for.

We were feeling pretty good when we walked back out on the Boardwalk.

"It's after nine," I said. "The show is at ten. Want to skip it, keep your streak alive? Or we could pick it up again afterwards?"

"I've never seen a casino floor show," Roberta said firmly, and stepped behind me to push. "I don't intend to miss my only chance."

The City by the Sea showroom was semicircular and wrapped in tiers around the stage, with little aisles everywhere for the waitresses and a sensational view from each table.

If you ever saw a Vegas or AC floor show, you've seen the *Peaches and Cream Revue* that we caught. Some folks go for that style of entertainment, I guess, but I think most tourists ante up because, like the rest of Atlantic City, floor shows are unlike any other entertainment in your life. You don't like it, exactly, but it's satisfyingly weird and fascinating while you're there.

Before the dancers came on, the clamshell-shaped hall was raucous and antsy as a bus terminal, with stocking-and-bowed waitresses scurrying to fill drink orders.

Our comp table was already inhabited by a small, dapper man I recognized as Angel's dice partner our first night in town. I told him my name and stuck out my hand, and he introduced himself, proudly I thought, as Cocktail Frank LaCroix. Roberta stifled a laugh with her hand, then burst out helplessly with it. I joined in, and so did Frank, with perfect good humor.

"Atlantic City has been my tonic," the little red-faced man said, smiling, just as our waitress returned. "But especially that Angel."

Then the house lights dimmed and an MC orated melodramatically for a time as the spotlights kept changing colors. A mostly electric band sounded bassy and blurry where we were sitting. They might have been playing "Tenth Avenue Freeze-out," for all I could tell.

Finally the beat volumed up enough to suck the dancers out onto the stage. I pointed out Angel to Roberta.

"What a cute figure," she yelled in my ear, after studying Angel for a minute. "But why is Angel glaring at us?"

"What?" Somebody had dialed up all the instruments.

"Glar-ing at us! Look, she's doing it again! Angel stuck her tongue out at us, see?"

I admitted seeing that.

Roberta put her lips on my ear and shouted, one word at a time, "Is she upset that I'm here with you? Do you two have something going?"

"Absolutely not," I hollered earnestly in her ear.

"You are rather vehement about it, no? She's gorgeous! What's a girl to think?"

I reached for Roberta's bare shoulder. "Angel doesn't think any woman is good enough for me. Wants to take care of me."

"I don't blame her," Roberta shouted, grinning. Her eyes twinkled.

"What's that they're playing?" I yelled hastily.

"What?"

"The song?"

"You don't recognize it? I sang a verse for you on the Boardwalk."

"*That's* 'Life Will Be Peaches and Cream'? Sounded like 'I Can't Get No-oh Satisfac-tion.'"

Roberta made a rueful face, shook her head. Too screaming loud now to hear if we stuck trumpets in our ears.

The floor show cooked up pretty hot. Angel pranced and jiggled with a Mona Lisa smile pasted on his face. Except that every so often he would catch my eye and flash a cranky face for one split second.

"She's adorable," Roberta laughed against my ear.

Angel did look terrific on stage, and didn't miss a step that I saw. He is a top go-go dancer in Newark clubs, but this performance on hardly any rehearsal brought home to me how talented he really is.

There was an intermission. Our table was comped, via Angel. On the other hand, the second bottle of champagne Cocktail Frank insisted on cost Frank a second sixty dollars.

The show was over just after eleven-thirty. The last show would start at midnight.

"We got five casinos left to hit," I told Roberta, after Cocktail Frank had left us for backstage.

"I hate to say this, but I don't think I can, Ezell. I'm bushed, just not used to this nightlife. I could *get* used to it, mind you."

"Want a nightcap somewhere?"

Roberta shook her head.

"We never got around to talking about our real estate play," I reminded her.

"Can it wait?"

"Uh-uh. A few things are going down tomorrow."

"Well, that sounds encouraging. Can't we talk in your hotel room?"

Well, I guessed we could. We walked, holding hands, down the boards to Toby's. Knowing we were heading to be alone in my room wedged some tension between us. We didn't speak riding up in the elevator.

In the room, sitting in one of the two little desk chairs, Roberta shook off a Canadian highball. I fixed one for me.

"Here's what you tell your neighbors," I said. "And they've all got to play it letter-perfect." For what seemed a long time I explained the ruse of Ernie as the Atlanta Rib King, his outrageous offer for the Utah Avenue properties, and how we hoped to shake a better offer out of the opportunists that hunt that kind of business in AC.

When I finished it was early morning and unearthly quiet in that room. My jacket and tie were off, shirt buttons loosened. Roberta still looked great in her green-and-black dress, but at this hour heavy limbed, her eyes a little puffy. She said, "I believe I'll take that drink now."

I was fishing cubes out of the little ice pail when she stepped up behind me and put her hands around on my chest.

"Your muscles feel so hard," she said. "Is that from when you were a fighter?"

I turned around inside her arms, so her hands were on my shoulder blades, breasts pressed against my chest.

"Fighting days are over," I said hoarsely. "I'm a lover now."

"Then love me, lover."

CHAPTER FIFTEEN

O

"Does this hotel have room service?"

"What do you mean? Of course, it has room service. You think I took you to the Day-Rate Motel?"

"Then let's order coffee, honey, hot, black, and plenty. I can use it."

"Well, how about I order us breakfast in bed? And the Sunday papers?"

"Sunday papers? Who has time to read on a Sunday morning?"

"Your neighborhood meeting isn't until one o'clock."

"And my four healthy boys aren't rubbing their hungry tummies right now? Yesterday I thought their Uncle Ernie could fix a meal for them, but . . ."

"But what?"

"But Ernie has strange ideas about meals, Ezell."

"Ernie is an original thinker. For instance, I'm not sure how he would take us spending the night together."

"Don't be silly. Ernie's an adult, we are adults. What are you so worried about?"

"You don't know Ernie good as I do, Roberta. You're his little sister."

"I have to be going."

"I can't talk you into breakfast?"

"Ezell, I have my boys to cook for, choir to sing in, a mess of baking and dusting before the neighborhood-association meeting this afternoon. Just coffee, please."

"Not even orange juice?"

"I'm sorry, really. Look, I'll cook you Sunday dinner, around six tonight?"

"Now I'm sorry. I'll be out hunting and dodging most of today. I'll call you tonight, though."

"It's not necessary. Really. Only if you have the time."

"I'll make the time. It was some night, wasn't it?"

Roberta was just reaching to touch my face when the spare

key scrapped around the brass lock outside. I jumped. Even Ernie would eventually zero in on the keyhole.

"Ernie!" I shouted, leaping to lean my shoulder against the door, body at a forty-five-degree angle. "Don't come in, man."

Muffled by the thick door, I heard, "What's shaking, Easy?"

I prayed for inspiration. "You need to be wearing that new suit of yours, Ernie. Go back and put it on, man."

"I'm wearing it like you told me, Easy."

"Then we need some orange juice, buddy. For rehearsing. Go get some for us, why don't you?"

"Don't this here hotel have room service?"

"It's way too expensive, man. Go down the Pork Roll House, up the Boardwalk a couple blocks. Get us some chow too."

"You got any money I could use, Easy?"

"I'll pay you back! Just go, Ernie!"

"Can't do it, behind the fact I lost every spending penny last night on them goddam cards."

"I'm slipping some money under the door," I shouted, waving at Roberta to hand me some bills. She rushed them over, thick hair down, heavily graceful and shapely, like a young Pearl Bailey.

"Here it is, Ernie. Now go get the OJ. Get coffee too. You could use some, I bet."

"You got that right, Easy. Okay."

Three minutes later, as I waved to Roberta hustling for the elevator, my neighbors stuck their light brown heads around their door frame, his a foot above hers, as if they'd rehearsed. The girl smiled at me and enthusiastically nodded her blond head. The boy glanced at Roberta's retreating backside, mouthed the word *nice*, and made half a three-ring sign at me.

I jogged the heel off my lie-guilt before Ernie galloped back. Sweating and coughing back into the room, I found Ernie a long way through the eggs and sweet rolls. "How you feeling, man?" I asked seriously, toweling off.

"I'm trimmed and brimmed and ready to skim." Ernie bowed and tipped his hat.

While I helped him polish off the rest of the coffee, we rehearsed his part over and over again. Then I showered and spruced up before I dialed D'Amato Green Grocer.

"Sure, I'm open on Sunday." Nick the Twist's voice cracked in my ear. "Atlantic City don't close just because somebody wants to make it Sunday, for Chrissake."

"When can you be here?"

"It's not convenient for me to leave right now. We got umpteen cases of romaine to ship around town. Ask your man Horton there. He understands the food business."

"Ask him yourself, he's sitting right here. What time can you come?"

"I can't leave, I told you. How about your man comes over here to meet with me?"

"Give me directions."

"Yo, Barnes, I got more class than that. My people will limo you and your boss down to my offices, *capisce*?"

"If you insist," I said. "We'll be waiting downstairs in the City by the Sea lobby."

Down at the casino carport Ernie made a point of laying a whole dollar bill on the valet in full view of Muscles Mike Marano, who chauffeured us in Nick's gleaming white stretch limo.

The Green Grocer warehouse was tucked away on Missouri Avenue back by the Venice Lagoon. Refrigerated trailers were backed into the receiving docks; smaller delivery trucks were busily taking on produce at the shipping end of the business. Looked to me as if a lot of romaine was moving in Atlantic City. The warehouse was freshly painted lime green with a forest-green trim, and was meticulously neat, like Nick's limo.

Muscles Mike mutely guided us through the stacked wooden crates to an office in the back of the tin building. Ernie roostered his way past the mostly black work crew on the loading dock. They all stopped to stare.

Without a word Mike stepped inside the frosted glass-walled office and banged shut the door.

Through the hollow door Ernie and I heard faint snatches of the conversation inside. What Mike said sounded like, "Jigs're here, Mr. D'Amato."

The door popped open and Nick the Twist hustled out, all smiles and a glad left hand for me. He was elegant in a tailored light green jumpsuit, personalized in script on the breast pocket, under which a white shirt and striped tie peeped out. Basket-weave loafers covered his stubby feet.

"I'm so honored." Nick reached for Ernie's handshake with his good left hand. I thought Ernie's eyes would pop out. "Please excuse my clothes, it gets a little messy around here at delivery times."

"So, you be the Eye-talian Scallion," Ernie said archly, examining his own hand for grease smears. Nobody calls Ernie a jig. He raised his head and peered around the warehouse like he expected it to be bigger.

Nick shot me a puzzled glance and laughed uncertainly.

"That's pretty good, Mr. Horton. Very funny." Nick ushered us into the office. It was impossibly posh for its warehouse locale, uncluttered and spotless as a museum gallery.

Nick waved us to four upholstered black wood chairs around an oval marble-topped coffee table, then opened a carved hutch and pulled out a crystal carafe with his one good paw, easy and natural as if he had two. He set the jug down on the table, then pulled out a set of pony glasses on a silver serving tray.

Ernie brightened up.

"I don't make a habit of drinking this early in the morning," Nick said ingratiatingly. He pointed his good hand vaguely in the direction of the sun. "But it is a special occasion, am I right?"

"It's twelve o'clock someplace," Ernie offered.

Nick grinned. "And it's a ritual, too, right, Mr. Horton? A seal of friendship between business partners."

"Do you no harm," Ernie said with dignity. "Start the day off with a little taste of the grape."

"Right," Nick said, a little unsure. He filled three glasses with a thick, colorless liquid, then reached into a little ceramic box and fingered three coal-black whole coffee beans into each glass. "*Con mosca.*"

Ernie picked his up, as he picks up every drink, thumb and forefinger only, pinkie slightly curled. He sniffed it. "Smell like licorice wine."

"It's the drink of my forebears," Nick said graciously.

Ernie's eyes bugged. "That's a zoo load," he observed over the rim of his glass. "Must eat you out of house and home."

"Hey, you're a riot, Mr. Horton." Ernie looked puzzled, but was too interested in his glass to care. Nick raised his pony glass on high, looked at us through it, and said, "Something special for very special people. *Salute*, gentlemen. May your children live long prosperous lives."

"Yeah, and your mother too." Ernie knocked his drink down in one gulp. It fought back.

Nick the Twist looked horrified at Ernie. "You feeling all right, Mr. Horton? It's better if you sip this particular stuff. Then crunch down on a bean to give it real bite."

Ernie's retching bazookaed out at least one of the beans. He made treading-water motions and a gagging sound like a mouth fart.

"Bittersweet." I whistled.

"Mr. Horton, I get you a glass of water, something?"

Ernie's throat was occupied with gagging, but he made a vehement refusal with his head and hands. He looked around frantically, spotted the decanter, and grabbed it.

"Like a refill, Mr. Horton?" Nick asked with a mixture of courtesy and confusion. Old Ernie was already pouring Italian hootch right from the decanter into his coffee-beaned throat.

"Try eating just the one bean at a time," Nick advised. "You're not gonna cough nearly so much, I guarantee. Hey, what was it they call you? The Ribs Nibs?"

Ernie got a grip on his convulsions and put the crystal jug back on the table. "Wash them beans from my mouf," he said by way of apology. "This is some kind of sauce," he offered respectfully, still hacking a little every few seconds. "I figured it for uptown sherry. What they call this shit?"

"That particular liqueur comes from a bottle that my father bought for the family over thirty-five years ago." Nick's dark handsome face lit up with memories and pride. "Be careful now. It's a hundred and ten proof *anesone*. We drink it slow."

"You right about that," Ernie agreed heartily. He wiped off his lips with the back of his hand. "Can we get to the talking part now? Easy be telling me how you Eye-tye gangsters want to muscle me out of the way. Be so you can steal the property off some down-and-outers. Think you at a fire sale."

Nick looked at me imploringly. "This is what you told Mr. Horton?" My eyes widened and I rubbed my chin with a shoulder.

Ernie was leaning back in his chair. He puffed out his chest, hooked the lapels of his suit jacket, and anchored thumbs under his vest.

"I'm a businessman," Nick protested. "I know no gangsters. The group I represent is interested in building a condo complex on Utah Avenue. Nothing more, nothing else."

"Then how's about we go mano-to-mano in the market-place," Ernie said haughtily. "Like the good old American way?"

"The good old American way costs everybody an arm and a leg," Nick observed, friendly. He waggled his bad wing and winked at me. I almost choked. Nick, sizing up an appreciative audience, followed with: "Nobody wins but the property owners, if we go hand to hand." He made a cartoon pirate's face and waved his twisted arm again.

Must have been the occasion and place, plus good old Ernie sitting there oblivious to the jokes, but Nick just cracked up and took me with him.

The two of us were sleeving tears from our eyes when Ernie put in, "Ernie Horton, His Nibs of Ribs, never backed out of no showdown. We got to bullfight, let's bullfight."

From me, ribs freshly aching: "What's on your mind, Nick?"

"I propose a settlement." Nick leaned forward, lengthened his face and scratched his eye. Mike Marano watched him as though he were critiquing Einstein's Special Relativity. "My business partners will make you a very handsome offer"—the goofy grin smeared Nick's face again—"to back out of the picture."

"What's handsome in your book?" Ernie asked.

"One hundred thousand dollars." Nick smiled handsomely. "More than fair, huh?"

"That offer is ugly." Ernie looked around the room as if a higher roller might drop through a trapdoor any second and put Nick in a cage.

Nick's face rouged Neapolitanly.

I put in quickly: "What Mr. Horton means is that we've received better offers than yours."

"From who?"

"Nick," I reproved. "What are we, gonna flip names around? You wouldn't want to do business with us, we do that."

"How high do I have to go?"

"Two point five," Ernie crooned, cradling his glass in his long skinny mitts. "Millions, Twist. Money talk, bullshit walk."

Inspired by events, Ernie had creatively tripled the amount we'd rehearsed.

Nick's face deflushed white.

"Too rich for your blood, scallion?" Ernie asked grandly.

"How soon do I have to let you know?" The Twist's eyes were slits—he was thinking hard.

"Give you, say, twenty-four hours," Ernie reckoned. "Come on, Easy. I got social calls to make. Time waits for no fool."

Ernie rose from his chair and weaved to the door.

"I'll get my driver to drop you off in town," Nick said to Ernie's back. He snapped his fingers at Muscles Mike.

At me he snapped, "You wait around."

When Ernie was out of sight, Nick sighed. "What moron made you an offer like that?"

"Man name of Carmine Napolitano," I said.

Nick stared. I shrugged.

"The New York mob wants in too?" His voice was coming from his breastbone.

I shrugged again. "Means nothing to us, man."

Nick grabbed me by the arm and pulled me close enough to smell his Aqua di Silva cologne.

"Your boss, Horton, he's a little *logorato*, no?" Nick's finger tapped his temple meaningfully.

"You ever meet a millionaire who wasn't? I can handle him."

"Meaning what?"

"What'd you want it to mean?"

"Well, can you choke him down on the price? There's a commission in it for you, naturally."

I shook my head. "Mr. Horton spends more money on his liquor bill each month than what you got in the bank."

"I believe it," Nick said fervently. "Talk to me, Barnes."

"How's the figure seven-five-oh sound to you? Hundred thousands."

"Terrible," Nick said. "Hundred fifty grand."

"Nick! Five hundred, then."

"All you people got mental illness, huh? Two hundred, tops."

"Three fifty, but that's absolutely it."

Nick sighed. "Two twenty-five, and you're embarrassing me, you know that?"

"Give it a rest, Nick. Three hundred."

"Two fifty, and that's the limit. I mean it."

"The check gets made out to me personally."

"*Very* reasonable request, considering." Nick beamed. "Only, make that figure stick. I don't want to look like a baboon, I go to the people I do business with."

"Stick like white on rice," I promised.

"I figured you had business smarts." Nick patted my shoulder with his one good wing. We walked out onto the warehouse floor like bosom buddies. "Here, I want you to take a box of melons with you. My gift to your family."

"I'm staying alone in a hotel room, Nick."

But he was already yelling. "Doody. Put a Jersey melon pack in the car with Mr. Barnes. Thump 'em, Doody."

To me, he said, "Green melons give you gas."

"I can't thank you enough, man."

Halfway to the warehouse door Nick called: "Slice 'em up in a dish with a scoop of lime sherbet. Outstanding."

Ernie was waiting for me in the back of the stretch Caddie. Muscles moodily opened the trunk and let Doody dump in a heavy crate. We let Muscles drive us across Atlantic City to the rear of City by the Sea.

"How'd I do, Easy?" Ernie asked when the limo was almost out of sight.

"Crazy, but convincing, Ernie." I slapped him on top of the head. "But he only offered a quarter million. We didn't juice the price up enough."

My old friend bent over and tried to pry a slat off the crate's top. "Least we scored these melons off the dude. Look good."

I smiled at Ernie until he looked up.

"What's our move, man?"

I held up both hands, like measuring a striped bass a week after the fishing trip. "I go at him again."

CHAPTER SIXTEEN

O

"And one, two, three!" A gigantic centipede stamped the wooden stage floor with its warmered legs and rippled sideways, crossing its feet and shaking its shoulders up and down. Otherwise the enormous showroom was empty. Except for the frowning choreographer and a technician fingering a tape deck behind the huge glass plate on the theatre's back wall. And me, upright in a front row seat.

On stage without makeup or costumes, but in vivid living color, was the most striking collection of women I ever laid eyes on. Tighted and stretch-suited in orange, maroon, yellow, and black, wool-legginged in gray and rose, twenty women pranced and stomped their way across the stage in a flawed unison ten times more exciting than the artfully lighted, frantically paced floor show I'd seen the night before. The noise of their feet boomed unexpectedly.

It wasn't pretty. Mostly they sweat, grimacing faces shining under the stage's white lights; armpits, crotches, and thighs dark-patched; hair flying; all rehearsal strain with nary a plastered-on smile. They flexed right legs, slid left feet, bent at the waist and snapped fingers moving forward. Angel was sandwiched in the right middle of the middle line, not a high profile spot like front-center or on a wing, where your eyes inevitably get drawn. A ponytailed blonde was right then drawing my eyes to the left wing. Angel is the best dancer I had seen until that afternoon, a good go-goer by normal club standards. But ranked with those perspiry professionals, he looked small and tentative, and almost elbowy. Angel sure has the paint-shaker hips, though.

The taped music was a mostly bass-and-percussion rendition of the show's featured song. "Legs, Legs, and More Legs," I think they called it.

The climax pounded at us, me and them, and then switched off without the final flourish. Groaning, the dancers broke formation, some flopping, others grabbing for towels or stretching legs to etch a step in memory.

The little choreographer shrieked, "I saw no-o-o excitement, la-dies! These changes are not designed to slow the show down! I've seen more exciting legs in a bucket of chicken, really! Concentrate, concentrate, concentrate!" The girls didn't seem too shook up. The dressing down was probably standard.

"Who wants to run through it again?" was greeted with another chorus of groans. The limber little man shouted, "All right, then. Remember, we're doing it tonight. Tr-y-y to be ready, please. And everybody, stage makeup no later than nine o'clock."

"Easy!" Angel bounded athletically from the stage and came to kiss my cheek. "Come here, I want you to meet my friends." His new-looking Danskins weren't very damp, and he seemed less bushed than some of the veterans.

"The show was good, yas? Angel did good too?" He took my hand and tugged me towards the stage.

"Last night's dancing was terrific, Angel." I smiled as we skipped up the side steps. "They dress you down for making faces at me from the stage?"

Angel flung his hands in the air. "Easy! How come you got to bring a stranger lady, when is Angel's night?"

"You got into trouble, didn't you?"

Angel sulked. "Bobbi Director say, you are new, Angel, and we gonna let it go this time. But if you mess up any performances again, we gonna fire you. And is this Angel's fault?"

"Well, your date was sitting at the table too."

Angel's face broke open cheerfully. "Cocktail Frank! He's so cute."

A little group of dancers was grinning at the explosion. When I smiled back at them, they swayed over to meet me.

"Well," I said loudly, "you looked great, best ever." I uncorked my most terrific smile. "All the girls were beautiful." Most of them chuckled and sized me up in a way that told me their long legs had covered a lot of rocky road in their day. So had their faces. Up close, they were more statuesque than beautiful, taut skin pulling classical features, long-legged bodies all looking sculpted in stone.

"Oh, Easy." Angel squeezed my arm hard and bounced on his toes. "This is too much like a dream, yas?"

More chuckles. Angel is irresistible to women as well as to men, but one of the dancers commented, "Peaches and cream, like in the song, cupcake. All peaches and cream. Especially the cream."

The little group broke up, first with laughter, then long-legging towards the dressing rooms.

"Who are your friends?" I asked, as we tagged after.

"Oh, that is Cassandra." Angel pointed to the blond ponytail disappearing into the dressing room door. "And the red hair is Felicia. They both very close friends of Veronica's."

"Where's Mimi?"

Angel's face darkened as it seldom does. "She miss rehearsal today. Bobbi Director is so mad! Is terrible for Mimi."

"What's the matter with her?"

Angel gave me his little Latin shoulder lift.

"Well, go get the other two for me, will you? I won't keep them but a second."

"No, come in the dressing room," Angel urged. "Is okay. Men come in there all the times."

A schoolboy's concept of heaven, maybe. Still, as I walked into that showgirl dressing room, my throat lumped up, and glands fired that had left me alone since I was nineteen.

Two dressing room doors shot right and left off the backstage corridor. The right-hand one was a rectangular space, maybe fifteen by twenty, for ten girls to change and hang out between shows: a locker for each, cheap rental-type chaises and armchairs, refrigerator and coffee machine, cigarette-burned orange carpet over a cement slab floor.

No windows, no art work on the walls except where somebody had taped a few cartoons on a mirror. All wall space not devoted to lockers was mirrored, floor to ceiling. Opposite the lockers the wall mirror was faced by a cluttered cosmetics counter and a dozen stools. Over each stool a gooseneck held a bar of makeup light bulbs.

Another mirrored wall was split horizontally by a brown dance rail. The last mirror was broken by a door to showers and toilet, through which girls kept coming and going, towel-wrapped and otherwise.

Some of the girls were showered and practically dressed for the street when Angel and I walked in. Others were taking their time, talking and smoking. Still others were obviously in no hurry at all, probably no better place to go. They sat in the armchairs, holding smokes and beer bottles or rocks glasses.

A couple of the lovelies who had come up outside smiled at me briefly; the others appeared not to notice that a man was in there while they undressed and dressed.

I set every nerve cell to keep me from gawking, and went through a cigarette-lighting to look cool. Doing okay, too, until a strapping brunette with a pixie haircut brushed by on her way to the showers. I felt the blush rise and I fumbled out an "excuse me." She stopped and commented, loudly, "I *thought* you might be playing Lucy the Elephant over here by yourself. You still need to pull out your pants pockets, though, sport." Two or three girls heehawed too roughly and too long. Angel tugged my sleeve over to the ponytailed woman at her locker, who was briskly rubbing her long tan legs with a rough-sided towel. She was wearing panties, and while we talked she pulled her bra off a hook and stood there dangling it.

"Cassie," Angel said sweetly, "could you please talk to Easy about Veronica Vallee? He had this awful crush on her."

"Lucky her," Cassandra said tonelessly. Up close the teen-aged look conferred by the ponytail was offset by a face too close to thirty, eyes close to the age of the planet.

"How long did you know Veronica, Cassie?"

"Long enough."

"Long enough to know why she was killed?"

Cassie turned and fumbled in her locker shelf. I held out my Chesterfield pack to her. She shook her head, found the Salem 100s, and unsheathed one. I did get to flick my lighter for her.

"Veronica used to be a great girl. She got strange just before she faded town."

"Faded town? You mean, got dead?"

"I mean she left town." Cassie puffed a little smoke, back on stage now. "Veronica went to Kansas City. You didn't know?"

I shook my head.

"I guess she only told me. She *said* she was clearing out for good."

I was on the receiving end of the world's phoniest smile. "What a shock when they found her dead at the marina. No one knew she was even back in town."

"You say she acted strange before she left?"

"Oh, her sugar daddy came into the picture. All of a sudden she was Little Miss Touch-Me-Not. Nothing more to do with the likes of us."

Cassie fastened on her bra.

Dry-mouthed, I asked, "That when she started hooking up with the New Yorker?"

Cassie made eyes at Angel and laughed at me.

"What's so funny?" I asked.

"Her sugar daddy wasn't no dope dealer in a top hat, Chief."

"Who then?"

"Mr. High Society. Mr. Blueblood." Cassie shook her head as if shooing flies or bad memories. "What's his name, His Lordship, Roger Trimster."

"The Casino Control Commissioner?"

"In the flesh." She laughed hoarsely. "The old fart would stop by here to pick her up from rehearsal. Real early, he'd be here, to catch himself an eyeful."

"This the man himself? Not a son or a nephew or something?"

"Unless his son is preemie gray and looks about a hundred years old."

"Thanks, Cassie. Look, can you tell me a little about Veronica and the drug supply into this casino? Strictly confidential."

Talk about a breach of social graces. Cassie's eyes turned clear and cold as a snake's.

"Not a fucking thing," she said. "How about splitting, huh? I have to get dressed."

"Thanks again."

Down the locker line at Angel's, I said to him, "What about Felicia? Can I talk to her? We'll have to go into the other dressing room to see her, I hope, I hope, I hope?"

Angel batted me with a practice slipper.

"I'm serious. I want to check on Muff Anglaise and the house drug line."

The left-side dressing room was practically emptied out, as if the girls who liked to hang out together had clumped up across the hall.

Felicia was a girl that had a home to go to. She was already completely dressed, pink shirt, strap top, and neck scarf, and was high-heeling her locker door shut when Angel and I walked in.

But she waved enthusiastically to us and seemed happy to talk. Her red hair had fooled me before. She and Angel were countrywomen.

"Easy, I have to tell you." Felicia touched my chest. "My Aunt Tilda lives on Utah Avenue. She is so thankful that you are getting lots of money for everybody on the block. That is so nice. When are they gonna get that money?"

"Working on it," I said, insides groaning. "Tell me, Felicia, Veronica died of an overdose, from the kind of packet that generally only suppliers would have, to cut and deal out. Did Veronica deal here, backstage?"

Felicia looked at Angel, who nodded reassuringly and said, "He's no narc, Lisha."

The only other girl left stalked into the showers. Felicia watched her go, nervously.

"If you tell anybody I talked to you about this, I won't work in Atlantic City again."

"You have my word."

"Veronica was Snow White for some of the girls. She sold them coke, speed. Lately I been hearing some jokes about horse riding, you know, but I never saw anybody doing it."

"Don't the casino check up on what happens down here? You'd think they'd be nervous about their license and such."

"I seen security guards in here, talking to the girls while the coke was going down." Felicia snorted. "Nobody wants to know nothing about nothing."

"How about Veronica's grandpa?"

"Mr. Nose." Felicia tapped her own, arching her black eyebrows.

"Jesus! The casino commissioner is a druggie?"

"Shssh!" Then Felicia whispered, "He's like a puppie, following Ronnie's little finger."

"Who's dealing now that Veronica is dead?"

Felicia just smiled, unhappily.

"Well, thank you, Lisha. You're a nice lady."

Outside again, I pulled Angel, still in his pink Danskins, away from the dressing rooms, down the corridor.

"The first man you saw climb on the *Polaris* had white hair, didn't he?"

"Sure, Easy." Angel dramatically sucked in his breath. "You mean?"

"Could be."

"Commissar of the casinos killed Veronica?"

"I didn't say that. Seems likely, though, that he was the first of the tag team that climbed on board the night she died."

Cassandra came out of the dressing room then, and pecked past us without a word. Tight green slacks, windbreaker, dark shades, and a babushka around her head made her look like an old fish woman.

From behind, the long thick ponytail made her look like a horse's ass.

CHAPTER SEVENTEEN

O

Angel showed me to a short staircase, then a narrow passageway to a little door under the stage that opened into the orchestra pit.

Back outside I pumped all the salt air I could fit into my chest, then jogged up the Boardwalk to the parking garage to retrieve my truck. No time to waste shaking down Commissioner Roger Trimster. No one spent more time with Veronica—he was with her the night she died. I stopped for a look at the phone book. Trimster lived at Sea View Acres, New Gretna Township, on Route Nine. That would be up the coast, about ten miles.

I cruised out of Atlantic City on the White Horse Pike, first through the back streets where restless young turks devoured casino traffic with hungry eyes, and elders looked through the passing cars as if invisible.

Across the Absecon Boulevard bridge, I breezed past Mankiller Island, where an Army Corp of Engineers barge was dredging the Intercoastal Waterway, into the marshlands surrounding Absecon Bay. The four-lane blacktop road knifed through the prairie of marsh grass, and my speeding pickup rippled the roadside reeds like yacht wake.

Tidal flats are supposed to be the richest life pools. Around Atlantic City, I had read, the salt grass flats were being tug-of-warred between the environmentalists and the money boys impatient to slap up condos. Today, sun and temperature just right, following up a good lead, I was sucking in spice from the shining marshes. The sunroof and rolled-down windows scooped in fresh salt smells. Clammers and crabbers were hunting the estuary for its hidden treasures. I had never been crabbing, but today it looked like the most fun in the world. To hell with the money boys.

The road climbed steadily out of the marshes into a scrub oak and dwarf pine area, edging the old pine barrens, a place that's always piqued my curiosity. Folks called pineys still live there without electricity or steady jobs, the way they did a hundred years ago. The acid humus topsoil they live off covers a sand and gravel underlayer that creates the finest natural filtration system. Under it is the largest underwater reservoir of pure water on the planet. If the developers get their way, how could it not end up the world's largest cesspool?

The edges of the pine barrens water the mouth of a gardening nut like myself, since it's one area that lives up to New Jersey's Garden State nickname. Truck farms, peach and blueberry orchards, endless fields of tomatoes, corn, cantaloupe melons. Wine vineyards. A couple years back Angel and I toured the two Jersey wineries outside Atlantic City and ended up buying six cases of different wines. Maybe it's not California cabernet, but it tasted great to us.

Two lanes now, the highway snaked along the coastline and through small, pretty towns. Every so often I passed a mammoth country club or a sign for a yacht club tucked out of sight behind the tall cane grasses. The town of New Gretna came up, just big enough to flash a stoplight, then disappeared in my rearview.

North of town a couple miles, an apple orchard zipped past my windows, followed by the white-board fence that marked the southernmost boundary of one big estate. Behind the horse boards stood an eight-foot chain-link affair, with spirals of barbed wire along the top. Running north beside the road for almost a mile, a six-foot fence, stuccoed a terra-cotta color that turned to honey in the bright sun, completely shielded the estate from car view.

I drove to the extreme northern boundary of the estate, where another white-board fence backed with chain link right-angled off to the west. There I graveled onto the shoulder and swung into a U-turn.

The entrance gate was scrolled with SEA VIEW ACRES across its crown, wrought-iron details of horses rearing and grazing throughout its middle. I pulled into the drive and peered through the closed gate.

Majestic cedar trees sentried either side of the gate. I caught just a peep of a thick-vined and Spanish-tiled building. The gate was electronically latched, with a service buzzer attached to its right side, in full view of the long-nosed remote-control camera mounted on its frame.

Otherwise it was unguarded, except for more closed-circuit cameras mounted on the top of ornamental iron pineapples gracing the stucco fence every hundred feet or so. Prickly red raspberry bushes were planted all along the base of the fence to discourage gate-crashers from limbo dancing underneath the electric eyes. To cover the entire fence, the cameras needed to be pivoting back and forth automatically. They weren't. It was a nice sunny day. Peaceful. Somebody forgot to turn on the electronic sweepers. Or maybe they used them only at night.

Reverse stuck on me. I eased the little pickup forward, then backed out and parked my truck alongside the fence, exactly in between two of the nonroving cameras.

Planted as intruder stoppers, in that good Jersey soil the raspberry canes were bursting with ripe fruit. Munching a handful, I hefted onto the hood of my truck, then belly-flopped onto its roof.

Over the wall and in. I followed the crushed blue stone drive curving between sycamores up a knoll to the Mediterranean villa. On its flank the old white farmhouse was now doing servant duty. Parked in the drive that circled in front was an amber Rolls-Royce. SILVER WRAITH III, said a little silver plaque on the trunk lid. That car had buff enough to dance my image off it.

A garageman or chauffeur stood by the farmhouse watching me. I paid no attention, just climbed the flagstone steps between gold-on-gold marigolds and white petunias, stepped to the oak door, and clapped the brass horsehead against the horseshoe backer. When I glanced again at the chauffeur, he hadn't twitched a muscle. Two other men now stood behind him with folded arms, staring.

From the porch the ocean blue was shockingly close. On the road you just couldn't see any of it over the cane grass.

The big door swung open on a black suit stuffed with butler. I'd never seen one before, in person.

"How did you get in?" he asked. But his eyes just said get the hell off this estate.

"Mr. Trimster will want to see me."

"He has left no instructions that a visitor is expected. The gate is locked. Kindly leave."

The butler was a tall man, and he tried his weight to shut me out. My fat foot stuck in the crack, though. Leaning with friendly confidentiality, for the outdoor workers still watching like we were the season's ending of *Dallas*, I pressed the door open again with the flat of a hand and all the beef of my shoulder and arm.

The butler barely controlled his anger. "You leave me no choice but to call someone to throw you out."

"You have another choice. Just talk to your Mr. Trimster, why don't you? Be a spot embarrassing for him if word got out he was a murderer, what?"

"You're mad," the butler snapped. But his lashless eyes had widened for a second and I pressed the advantage.

"Tell Trimster that Veronica Vallee's guardian angel is here." I smiled.

The butler nibbled his lip. But he looked to be an old fixture around the place, comfortable about using his own judgment. After a second, he motioned me to let him close the door, then scuttled off and left me on the porch. The wisteria was nice. The built-in stone seats were nice. Everything was nice. But it was an uncomfortable-feeling house. The old farmhouse a hundred feet away would slip on like a pair of worn jeans. The three men in front of it stood still with folded arms, waiting for a signal.

What they got was the spectacle of the door opening again and letting me squeeze in. The foyer was three times the size of my living room, big enough for the staircase to sweep rather than right-turn up to the second floor.

The butler stepped away from me to let Roger Trimster make his entrance, twisting his way down the grand staircase. I recognized him from the newspapers, but no photo had ever caught the full effect of his swept-back lion's mane of silver hair.

Trimster was wrapped in a red silk robe, with matching slippers. He leaned heavily on the railing, as if tired. Halfway down he stopped and sized me up.

After all I'd heard about him, I just couldn't give him a fair shake. The old man looked plain weak and foolish to me, at first sight.

"Just who are you?" Trimster's voice was frayed. A couple days' beard growth gave him the look of a man skidding down-hill fast. Ashen skin stretched tautly across his high, round forehead set off his Albert Einstein sweep of silvery hair. His eyes were red-veined bulbs glaring from dark gray pockets. The muscles of his jaw quivered into jowl whenever he spoke.

"Who are you?" he repeated, the effort coating his face with clamminess.

"Veronica Vallee hired me."

That sun-filled foyer was silent as Sunday morning.

"Why are you here?" Trimster's energyless rasp was contradicted by the prongs of his eyes.

"Somewhere private we can talk?"

Mechanically, Trimster motioned me towards one of the doors flanking the foyer, the big gold ring he wore winking in the light. He followed me into a study that also basked in full afternoon sun.

"I didn't catch your name?" he said, almost politely, looking away from me.

I studied him. Close up, Trimster's weariness was edged with restlessness. His eyes could not focus. He wandered around the room, touching his leatherbound books, his mementoes and silver-framed photos. In two minutes he would forget I was there. Four minutes and he would remember again and have me tossed out.

Trimster was fiddling with a poker in the cold summer fireplace. I refused to feel any sympathy. He was a prime bet to have snatched Veronica's videotape. Driving up there, I had figured out the one way I could know for certain.

"My name means nothing, Commissioner. But I've got something to interest you."

"Do you mind elaborating?"

"Do you mind if that film of your sexual technique floats around Atlantic City?"

Trimster dropped the poker on the polished hearthstone. A chip flew at his face, and he seemed genuinely alarmed. "What do you mean, 'floats around Atlantic City'?"

"You don't sound surprised to hear there is such a tape, Commissioner."

The old man straightened to his full five-and-a-half feet. "That tape," he said hoarsely. He cleared his throat. "My lover made that tape of us together—as a present for me. It's very private."

I laughed as nastily as a blackmailer should. "Well, that's cute. You'd give anything to have it, I suppose?"

"I would give something, not anything, for that tape. I have very little to remember Veronica by."

"Sentiment is worth something," I agreed. On the mantel Trimster was shaking hands with the current governor, who looked happier than he did. "Then there's the value of keeping it out of unscrupulous hands."

Trimster stalked haughtily behind the sofa facing mine.

"Now I understand you, young man. You are threatening blackmail. Forget it. There's no law against being a virile lover, even at my age. That film is very personal, but there is nothing in it—"

"What about the scenes of you two shooting up?" I asked blandly. "Hot stuff, Roger."

Dust motes in the sunstreams banging against the furniture were the loudest noises in that room. If there'd been a nonquartz clock, its tick would have rapped like a drumbeat.

Trimster shuffled across the room towards a large oil painting of a racing horse with all four feet in the air. His voice came to me blurred.

"How much?"

I knew then he didn't have the tape. I switched to fishing in other waters:

"It doesn't have to hurt you, man. It's only money. Your feelings have been hurt enough already."

"My feelings," Trimster repeated, wonderingly. "What on earth can you know of my feelings?"

"I knew Veronica, too, man. She was something."

Trimster turned and smiled. "Perhaps you meet women like her frequently where you come from, Mister . . . ?"

"Ezell Barnes."

"Drink, Mr. Barnes?" He wobbled to a tray of decanters. Pouring, he said, "You can hardly imagine the effect of a gay, intense, utterly sexual creature like Veronica on my tired blood."

"A man needs a breath of life sometimes."

His laugh startled me. I took the drink he held out. He had already swallowed some of his.

"How perfectly put," he said. "I think I had never taken a breath of real life before. Ever. I suppose a man like yourself has found promiscuous, accepting women since you were in high school, Mr. Barnes?"

I raised my eyebrows.

"I thought so. My situation has been otherwise, I assure you. Can you believe that in seventy heterosexual years on this earth, including thirty years of marriage, never once had a woman given herself willingly to me?"

I swallowed my drink. I tried to think what to say.

One corner of Trimster's mouth curved up. "I don't mean, of course, that I forced women to bed. Not at all. I took them on all the ceremonial occasions—the night before I shipped overseas, I remember particularly—with their calm consent. But without their interest or pleasure. My late wife occasionally answered the phone while I was swinking and swiving above her."

My hand was wet from the ice cubes in the glass on my knee. I rubbed it on my slacks.

"Nothing in this surprised me," Trimster continued. "You see, women of a certain social class are quite available to men of a certain social class. Often they fancy that a cachet is conferred by the scorning of middle-class sexual values. They're bored, frankly. The circle of men eligible to be their spouses is so narrow, and life can be a very minor whirlwind of charitable, social, and shopping enterprises."

He drained his drink, smiled benignly at me. I met his eyes, watched them drift to the side, and said nothing. He stood up and said, "How should I put this for you? Certain women value their status the way the first New Jersey Quakers valued their souls. Their very identities are subsumed in the power and affluence of their families, and of their husbands' families." His smile was pinched. "Whatever demons do exist inside them, crying for release, are small, very small. You may come inside these women, but you must never really look inside. You might discover what is missing."

"You don't think that's a little one-sided?"

"Veronica, however, possessed abundantly what I was born without." Trimster let a thin smile creep onto his bloodless face. "Blood, desire. Fresh, gay life—"

"Did you ask her to marry you?"

He looked astounded. "She was hardly a woman one marries. But what intoxication to be with such a creature! I did care for her, Mr. Barnes."

"Not everyone appreciated her, Commissioner. You know that."

"You mean my daughter."

A headful of mysteries blew into white sheets all at once. "To name just one," I bluffed. "How badly did your daughter resent Veronica?"

"She worries that I've become an old fool." Trimster hooted. "My darling young daughter is well on her way to becoming one of those fortune-cursed women I've just tried to describe for you, Mister . . . Barnes, is it?"

I nodded.

"She is losing her girlhood very rapidly now," Trimster said complacently, brushing his hand against the pale chintz of the overstuffed armchair as if grooming the printed flowers. "And, inevitably, the family name—my name—means everything to her. Put plainly, it dominates her, to a degree that I, any man, would be shamed by."

"Enough that she'd murder Veronica Vallee, to shake her off your back?"

Commissioner Trimster looked like a man opening his eyes after a long kiss.

"You." He trembled a forefinger at me. "I know who you are. A damned scoundrel. A common blackmailer. You dare to utter a word against my daughter in her own house?"

He paused, confused by the adjective he'd used.

I stood up. One way or the other the interview was over.

Before I could make for the door, Trimster, burning again with the clarity of anger, shook his silver mane and pulled himself up until he thought he looked eight feet tall.

"Get out! Damn spot!" He stretched a theatrical forefinger towards the foyer door. "Crawl back into whatever godforsaken hole you came from."

I strode quickly to the door and swung it open.

Over my shoulder Trimster kept howling, "Throw him out!"

The butler had evidently been waiting in the wings, and he had recruited a bon voyage party. I saw just a quick grin from the black chauffeur before they had clamped me all over and dragged me out the door.

CHAPTER EIGHTEEN

o

The chauffeur was barrel-big enough to pin my arms to my sides and lift my six-foot-one-inch frame off the ground.

He was the last to let go when they'd dragged me out to the driveway, and my blood was up. I jumped back from him and tried buzzing his brain with the stupidest punch I'd thrown in years, a roadhouse right designed to send him into orbit. The stocky man ducked as clean as can be, let my punch whistle over his head, and pulled me stumbling off my feet. Then he straightened, cocked a fist that would crush the bone in my undefended jaw, and waved it in my face. He dropped it, grabbed me and stood me on my balance. He swiped at my slacks a time or two and grinned in my face.

"Take the breeze, brother. Nothing in there for you."

"You move pretty good for a old turnip."

"You move like shit for a halfway decent ex-light heavy." He reached up and rumpled his grizzled gray hair, squinting into the sun at me.

"You from Newark?"

"Born on Springfield Avenue. Used to drive for Hassan Fahriq. You heard of him."

"Fahriq's an old friend of mine."

Chauffeur laughed heartily, shook his head, and urged me towards the entrance gate far away at the driveway's end.

Then the amusement dropped off his face.

"You want me to hold him for the police?" he crisply asked someone behind me. "Miss Trimster?"

I jerked my head around. Patricia Valentine stood next to the passenger door of a dark blue Mercedes station wagon, private import only. "No, that won't be necessary, Ranx," she said, clearly and flatly. "You can put him down. I know this man."

"Yes, ma'am," Ranx said. "Will that be all?" His tone was concerned and doubtful.

134

"I'm quite all right," she said. Then, with an affectionate smile, "You can go inside now and eat."

We two stood on the crushed blue stone and eye-sparred until her face unexpectedly crackled with amusement.

"Patricia Trimster," I marveled.

"Among other identities."

"We've got to talk," I said. "Your father just threw me out. Doesn't matter. Veronica Vallee's murder will come crawling after him."

"That dancer died accidentally from a self-induced overdose," Patricia said coolly. "My father had nothing to do with it."

"Then why's he squirreled himself away here, like Mister Ten Most-Wanted? Missing the hearing yesterday looked highly suspicious, ma'am."

"Don't you think he has suffered enough already? Leave him alone."

"It was you that hired me to find her," I reminded her. "You send me chasing Veronica Vallee, but only to finger her so you could peel her greedy hands off your father."

She stepped forward and stuck her face two inches from mine, jaw set as though she'd prefer to be slapping me. I grabbed both her arms just in case.

And that's where we were when the front door opened and the butler stepped onto the porch. His face was distressed with an emergency not in the butler's handbook.

He cleared his throat. "Miss Trimster. It's your father. Please come quickly."

Patricia Trimster slipped my grip and flew up the flagstone steps and into the house like a Mariah. The butler scooted after her. I caboosed them, catching just glimpses as they scurried up the staircase and through the ponderous house's corridors, secondary stairs, and connecting rooms.

Then I caught up to them. On the cold tile floor of a tiny bathroom off a sun space, Commissioner Roger Trimster, one of New Jersey's finest, sprawled like a wino.

For once Patricia acted tentatively. The butler hovered behind her, hands fluttering. I nudged them both aside, stooped and scooped up the frail body. Faint breath rattled through his parched lips. His skin felt like cold raw chicken. The blue mottled whites of his eyes rolled back in his head.

I gentled the old man's body onto a four-cushion couch.

"Call for an ambulance," I barked at the butler. "Tell them it's an overdose and he's fading fast." The well-trained butler stood in his tracks and watched Patricia Trimster. "Today, man!"

"No," Patricia said. "Call our family doctor, Hans. Ask him to come at once."

"No time for discretion, babe," I warned her. "Your father's gonna die, we don't get him to a hospital right now."

Hans had already obediently exited.

"Mind your place, Ezell," Patricia said, face tight but voice steady. "If my father is admitted to a hospital, his addiction will be front-page news tomorrow. He would rather die than suffer that disgrace."

I shrugged. This girl needed a reality dose. "Then he'll be tomorrow's obit news, lady. Heroin OD is major-league hurt."

"Can't you do something?"

"Only until the doctor shows up. Tell somebody to brew coffee—strong, black, and plenty."

I walked back to the bathroom. Steam was still rising from the tub of hot water. On the little vanity was a hypodermic spike. Scattered on the floor were four glassine packets. Each was stamped with the New Yorker's logo. They were empty.

Patricia came back on silent feet and stood next to me.

"Rich folks supposed to get their jollies from pills," I said softly. "Heroin's a poor man's escape from hell."

"My father picked up his vulgar little habit from that tramp." Patricia's sturdy body in a little skirt and blouse outfit was erect and posture perfect, but I could feel the sag of emotional fatigue in her.

"She gave him a royal screwing," she said. "Then she screwed him on to drugs. I'm sure her next step was to blackmail Father or extort money from him some way."

"So you murdered her?"

We were back to traitor in the house.

"I'd buy the whore off before I'd kill her," she declared sourly.

I turned up a card she didn't know I had: "That what you told Veronica on the boat, the night she died?"

It won me nothing but a widening of her beautiful eyes.

"Well, your daddy really bashed himself this time," I said. "If this scag is from the batch that Veronica shot up, it's over forty-percent pure heroin. Ten times normal street strength.

There's no way I can tell for sure. If it is forty-proof scag, he don't have one chance in a hundred."

"Can't you taste it and tell?"

"Only on TV, Patricia. Heroin all tastes the same. You got to snort some to judge its strength, and that test could be fatal here."

"What can we do?"

"Rummage through all the medicine cabinets in the house for some uppers," I ordered. "Bring me every pep pill you got. Diet pills, amphetamines, benzedrine, anything. No-Doze. Get that coffee up here."

She pivoted and hurried off, leaving behind the wholesome scent of citrus soap. I ran the water in the sink, rinsed out the hypodermic needle. Years back, when I was a plainclothesman prowling for purse snatchers at Penn Station on a slow Saturday afternoon, I ID'd a junkie stepping off the train from Harlem. One look at me and he was on his heels, me on his back.

By the time I laid mitts on him, the poor fool had choked down most of the dope. I slapped the cuffs on and hauled his sorry ass off, but he faded in my backseat before we reached the precinct house. I detoured to the ER at City Hospital, where a young resident took one look and stuck an intravenous tube in his arm. The doctor turned on the spigot and let a bag of juice labeled Narcan trickle into that sorry junkie's arm. He watched the clock's second hand sweep around a couple times, then announced it was time for my prisoner to rise from the dead. Within seconds the junkie jerked upright and looked around, finally fixing his hating eyes on me. The resident winked at me and spun the spigot off. Almost immediately the junkie's shoulder blades hit the table, back in heroin stupor. On with the juice again, and he popped back to life.

The Narcan took a few hours to wear off the heroin, so I passed time yakking with the doctor. He told me another way to counteract a heroin overdose was to shoot up a strong dose of uppers, to counter heroin's depressant effect. Risky, though, he said. A drug tug of war.

At my arm Patricia held a silver coffee thermos in one hand, an orange vial in the other. Benzedrine, the prescription was labeled. "I found these," she said.

"Where's that goddam doctor?" I demanded, surprised by the rasp in my voice.

"Hans left word with his answering service. But they are not sure when he will call in for his messages."

I groaned. "He don't carry a beeper?"

"Sorry," Patricia said with a very thin smile. "Please, don't waste any more time. Use those pills."

"It scares me," I told her. "I doubt your father's tired old heart can stand a roller-coaster ride like this. We pop drugs on top of drugs, chances are he'll die screaming."

She took a look at the old man. "Please," she pleaded. "Do something."

One last pitch: "Look, I strongly recommend we rush your father to a hospital. To hell with family pride."

Her jaw set. "No, absolutely not."

"Step in here." I curled a finger at faithful Hans lingering anxiously in the doorway. "We are all three witnesses of each other. Do you understand?"

Hans looked at Patricia Trimster nervously.

"If the old man rides into the sunset, remember that I advised her against doing this. She refused to take her father to a hospital or wait for the doctor."

"Is this really necessary, Ezell? You are wasting time."

"Necessary for me," I snapped. "You haven't played straight with me once yet."

"You have my word as a Trimster," she said defiantly.

"Somehow that just don't inspire confidence. Okay. Penguin, you see if he'll swallow any coffee. Raise his head and be careful not to choke him with it. Patricia, you grab a necktie from the closet and bring it over to the couch."

Trimster lay as white as the slipcovers beneath him, the ghost of an old, old mystery tale. His breath was fluttering now in a way that made me uneasy. I turned his left arm over: the underside wore more tracks than the Newark Amtrak station. Patricia handed me a simple silk tie in plain cranberry. I cinched its small end around his right arm just above the elbow and told his daughter to pump that arm back and forth until his veins blued up.

Back in the bathroom I broke open the benny capsules and poured the pink powder into the same spoon the commissioner had used as a cooker. Most of the powder dissolved in a bit of hot tap water, and the rest mixed up after I lit a couple of matches to the bottom side of the spoon. I found a bottle of rubbing alcohol under the sink and dipped the spike into it, uncertain whether that accomplished a thing. Then I cleared the plunger of air and sucked a cylinder full of the liquid benzedrine. Holding it up to the light, I thumbed the plunger until a bead of juice oozed out the needle point. Then I walked back to the couch.

Hans cleared his throat. "The coffee apparently just makes Mr. Trimster choke," he told me.

Without a word I pricked Trimster's arm with the hypo and pushed the plunger slowly, watching the blue vein bulge. I untied the tourniquet and watched.

The rush of benny juice into his system charged him almost instantly. Like a locomotive leaving the station, Trimster's breathing began to pick up; his eyelids danced about as if in a dream. Good signs. He was creeping back into the world, a breath at a time.

"It's working." Patricia searched my face to see if she should smile.

"Jump-starting him was the easy part. Tough part is keeping his heart beating while the heroin wears off."

"How long will that take?"

"Three, four hours at least." I armpit-lifted the commissioner up to a sitting position. It was like lifting Raggedy Andy. "Help me get him on his feet."

"He looks like a cadaver," his daughter murmured.

Arms around his chest, I hoisted him onto his slippers.

"Turn the shower on cold," I told Hans. "We're taking him in there."

Not until the old bird was soaking wet with icy water did I feel him grumble and squirm a little in my arms. I held him right under the freezing cold nozzle until he struggled pitifully to get free, whimpering. His silvery hair clung to his bony head.

Then we sleepwalked him. In shifts, Patricia and Hans together for ten minutes, then me. Then back under the shower, my own clothes dripping and clinging nastily to my legs and crotch. More waltzing around the sun room. After seventy-five minutes Trimster was able to keep down a sip of coffee.

Through it all the heroin kept trying to suck him under. We ended up drowning his sorrows in pots of strong black coffee, jabbing his ass with sewing needles, slapping his face over and over, first with solicitude, then with something like hatred.

The sun room was dark by the time his breathing steadied into a regular pattern. I put the narrow body on the couch, covered with a mohair comforter. When Trimster was strong enough to say his daughter's name, I let him stretch out and watched him tip immediately into deep sleep.

By then Patricia Trimster and Hans the Butler looked bedraggled enough to need the same treatment. Probably I did too. Those two watched the commissioner doze in silence. Patricia gave Hans a brief hug, which he endured with stiff shoulders but bright eyes.

We'd walked him through the poppy field, all right, I felt like telling them. But he wasn't out of the woods yet. Not hardly.

CHAPTER NINETEEN

○

Patricia whispered something to Hans, who disappeared from the room.

"It looks good for him, doesn't it?" She turned hopeful eyes to me.

I shrugged. "He'll be trying again. Suicide makes him look guilty as hell, you know?"

"I know. But thank you. You, by the way, are a mess." She ran cool blue eyes over me. "Why don't you shower up? I'll have the maid lay out a set of fresh clothes for you."

"You won't have my size."

"Oh, I think we might. Meanwhile, Hans will make sure your suit gets cleaned and pressed immediately. After you shower, we will eat in the dining room."

"Lawdy, Miz Scarlett. I disn't know how to use all them different forks and such."

"I'll fix something simple for us myself."

"I didn't think you high society women knew how to boil up a mess of ribs."

"Are you kidding?" she said, grinning with relief. She started down the hall, stopped. "I'll put them in the microwave right after I soufflé the greens."

Downstairs, decked out in wool slacks and buttoned-down shirt a size too big for me, I found pearly china and crystalware for two set out on a corner of the big dining room table. Mediterranean style, there was no tablecloth, just gleaming black wood. A candle between the settings barely took the dim off the huge room. The kitchen was off so far away that I couldn't hear Patricia humming until she walked into the dining room with a wine bottle and two glasses.

"Here's a corkscrew, Ezell. Can you manage? That's a Spanish Rioja estate wine. It is a red wine, nice and dry. Do you like wine?"

"I don't know." I scratched my woolly head, half determined to get under her skin. "One time, me 'n Rastus broke into

Massa's cellar, drilled a hole, drank all the muscatel. That count?"

"Cute."

"Hey, your tune's kind of catchy," I said, half anxious not to lose her. "What's it called?"

"*Carmina Burana,*" she said, looking like she'd rather be stirring a pot.

"What, the Latin chick with the banana hat and the conga music?"

"No." She couldn't keep a chuckle down. "It's an opera about the seasons of love, written by monks in a lonely abbey."

"Monks? Well, I guess if you're all cooped up like that, you got the time to ponder those things."

"Tell me about it." She glanced at the brocaded dining room walls as if the mansion around us were also a prison.

"Where's the cook?"

"Nervous?"

"Just curious. They were ready to slice me up like a carrot before you got here."

"Well, don't worry," she said. "I sent Hans and all the help home, except one maid who's had nursing experience, to stay with Father. They deserve it after today's disaster, and it won't hurt to be specially nice to them just now."

"You let one hired hand stick around."

"You're a hard man to please, Barnes," she said, puffing her chest out like a politician. We both laughed, but mine was still rueful.

"What about my clothes?"

"They've been dropped off at an all-night dry cleaners. They have promised delivery here by midnight."

"Well, what time is it?"

"Nine."

"Time flies, even when you're not having fun."

"Let's just drink the wine, why don't we?"

"You got a beer anyplace?"

"Of course. Would you like one? We keep all sorts of imported beer."

"Pabst'd be fine."

"Oh," she said brightly, a little hurt. "Is that brewed in Newark?"

"The giant Blue Ribbon bottle mounted on the brewery roof is what you see from my apartment window."

On her way out I noticed that she'd changed into a shiny pink sheath that slimmed out her legs and curved her hips.

After a while she came back with four bottles of Pabst and two pilsener glasses on a tray. Also on the tray was a casserole full of chicken, red, yellow, and chocolate-colored peppers, green and black olives, and chunks of tomato. There was yellow rice, too, and hot, crusty bread.

"Wheew," I whistled. "I take back my evil thoughts about your cooking. You whipped this up so quick?"

"Whipped it up?" Patricia said. "This little feast? Actually, the cook prepared it this afternoon. *Polla à la chilindron*, he calls it. It's terrific with beer."

"You got a man for a cook?"

We used up all four beers washing down the chicken pieces. The Spain Restaurant in Newark's Ironbound does it better, but who's keeping score?

After a while Patricia started telling me about her family.

"For our purposes," she said, "the story begins about two years ago. The Trimsters were your average filthy rich American snobs. Prim, proper, hunt club, charity stalwarts. Bor-ing."

"And?"

"Then, three years ago, my mother contracted cancer and wasted away in less than six months. Actually, Mother took her dying much better than my father did. I had not realized how dependent he was on her. When she died, he lost all stability. For a time he tried to throw himself into his work as Casino Control Commissioner. I think he became a fanatic. Along the way he decided to shut me out of his life, I suppose because I reminded him of my mother."

"Happens," I said.

"Oh, we all understood, his family. We were willing to wait until he came out of mourning. But Father never was really a strong man, and he was very lonely and confused. He was too vulnerable."

"Did he see other women?"

"Not at first. But then he met Veronica Vallee at one of the official functions at a casino."

"City by the Sea."

"I suppose so. That is where she worked, isn't it?"

"Go on."

"It seemed innocent enough at first," Patricia said dreamily. "I was almost glad of it. After all, my father wasn't the first man to find his fountain of youth in the arms of a younger woman. But then, of course, he began to change. He dressed peculiarly, stayed out all hours, drank more heavily. Eventually she hooked him on drugs."

"The upper class has their drug problem like the rest of the world. They just hide it better."

"Well, I tried discussing his drug dependency with him, but he claimed it made him feel brand new. And when I confronted this Veronica Vallee about their relationship, she promptly told me to mind my own sweet business, that my father was old enough to make up his own mind."

"Sounds like a plot from one of those soap operas a friend of mine watches."

"That whore was worming her way into my father's will," Patricia said. "She was turning him into a stupid schoolboy. Who knows how far she would have gotten?"

"You *are* writing yourself a soap opera," I told her. "Shame about the drugs, but his choice. Veronica Vallee was some kind of woman. I understand what your father saw in her. She could cure anybody's tired blood."

"He was insane to fall in with her!"

"Your old man's not so bad. I think he felt something for Veronica. She was worth it too."

Patricia Trimster shook her head as if with a migraine.

I tested her. "She didn't set him up with that blackmail tape, you know. The camera was hidden in a closet. She was just using the yacht, probably didn't even know the camera was there."

"Blackmail tape? What are you talking about?"

"You had to have seen it. The closet door was smashed in. Could even be, you smashed it and took the tape yourself."

Patricia stared, then gave a reasonably convincing head shake. She said carefully, as if she'd drunk too much, "What do you mean, I took it?"

"You were on the boat within an hour of me calling you that night."

Patricia was too smart to risk an answer. She poked a chicken piece with her fork, keeping her eyes down.

That made me mad. "Cut it out, lady. I know damn well you were on that boat. Was Veronica dead when you got there?"

Patricia kept her golden head lowered.

"Oh, hell," I said, exasperated. "You want help? Then don't

treat me like a servant. Was she dead when you climbed aboard that yacht?"

She glanced at me, then decided to get mad too.

"She was very much alive. I don't know if she was on drugs. I didn't see any tapes or smashed closets. I confronted the whore about her abuse of my father, and she threatened my life, then ordered me off the yacht."

"You went? Like she said?"

"She frightened me," Patricia said, with a touch of self-pity. "She was intimidating, I mean physically intimidating. I'm not used to people treating me that way."

"So you claim you don't know about the sex tape of your father on that boat?"

"No. But I'm hardly surprised. That woman was capable of anything. She screamed after me as if I'd corrupted *her* father."

I looked at her, face set.

"And now the tape is missing?" Patricia prompted.

"Your father's pretty near missing too. Wasn't any broken heart that drove him to try suicide."

"You think the blackmail frightens him?"

"Nothing else to guess. But hasn't anybody tried to sell the film back to him yet? That you know of?"

"No." She shook her head and set down the fork. "I don't think Father could keep something like that secret from me."

"Got to be any number of people in Atlantic City who would love to hold a scandal over your father's head. People that want those precious casino licenses and such."

"Can we get the tape back?"

"Last time I tried to help you, someone I liked died."

She was silent a long moment. "I didn't enjoy deceiving you, Ezell. My hands were tied. This time will be different." She stretched her hands over her head, as if to show me how clean she was. "What you see is what you get."

"Nothing's ever what it seems," I said. "Especially in Atlantic City."

"Please."

"Wait a minute." I took my time lighting a Chesterfield. "First we talk about you and Charlie Faucher."

CHAPTER TWENTY

○

Ouch, that hurt, her face said. Her mouth said: "You saw us together after the commission hearing yesterday."

"What's between you two?"

Patricia meditated for a second, perhaps mulling her chances of stonewalling me about Faucher. She bought time by inviting me into a living room where we sat in giant stuffed Victorian reproductions. Arranging her legs, she answered me carefully:

"I keep Charlie at arm's length, for reasons of my father's position. I would never try to influence Father in Charlie's favor. Charlie would never ask me to. At least I don't think he would."

"He never asked you to make a pitch for City by the Sea's second license?"

"Never."

"He ever make a pitch for you personally?"

"Ezell! Oh, damn it. I suppose it's no secret around Atlantic City that I have seen Charlie on and off for over a year." She frowned. "His idea, more than mine."

"These are his clothes I'm wearing, aren't they?"

"Listen, I enjoy being with Charlie. He is witty—and very kind. And his background is interestingly different from my own—to say the least. But for that same reason, it could never work out."

"Does Charlie know you feel that way?"

"We discuss it all the time, tiresomely."

"How's his relationship with your father?"

"Purely professional. Charlie is one of the movers and shakers in Atlantic City. He is heavily invested in City by the Sea casino. Quite naturally, he and my father have collided on the regulation and expansion of Charlie's casino, but I don't believe there is bad blood between them. In fact, I know my father is fond of Charlie."

"Charlie don't love your dad back," I said. "Not one little bit."

Patricia covered her confusion by crossing her legs, legs so bronzed and shiny they looked like stockings. She said, with a don't-press-your-luck look:

"Father has been a very difficult member of the Casino Control Commission, I believe."

"You ever suspect Charlie of setting up your old man?"

"Meaning?"

"What do you think I mean? Faucher was in financial hot water and he desperately needed a casino license your father wouldn't give him."

Patricia was shaking her head. "Charlie may have lost some money recently, but he is a self-made man, with millions."

I snorted. "That's another thing—what is this crap about Faucher's heavy investments? Charlie Faucher's an ex-Newark cop, for Chrissake."

Patricia sighed, as if forced to tell an outsider about Uncle Delby's drinking problem. "He had millions invested," she said gloomily. "He told me many times, promising me the moon."

"But you already own the moon, don't you, babe?"

"What's your point?"

"Put it together: Veronica Vallee worked at Charlie's casino, and she met your father at a casino party. After which, she enticed him into drugs and a post-graduate degree in sex. Somebody made a videotape of them; it might put enough leverage on your old man to swing a casino license. And who's more desperate for one than Charlie Faucher? Listen, Faucher makes a good salary—but millions? I don't believe it. He's in danger of losing everything. He needs that second casino to generate a fresh flow of cash. He told me if they built and managed the second one right, they could make money again."

"I hate the very idea," Patricia told me, jumping to the bottom line. "I can't believe Charlie would use that dancer to corrupt my father, much less murder her."

"I'm not so sure," I said, with fake mildness. "There's other parties interested in that damn tape. Could be they killed Veronica. Or—I'm just talking, mind you—could be that you killed her, babe. You hated like poison what was happening to your father." I shrugged. "Can't rule out your old man, either, for that matter."

Patricia's turn to snort. "He was head over heels for her!"

"And he had everything to lose by her."

She considered that for all of five seconds. "How do we prove that Charlie is behind all this?"

"We don't prove a thing, until we've got more reason to believe Charlie did kill her. You're letting your teeth show too much, kiddo."

Patricia looked half insulted, half stunned.

"You know, lady, when I saw you and Charlie together, yesterday afternoon, him mooning over you like a schoolboy, it made me wince, I got to tell you. Charlie ever regale you with why his wife left him? No? Well, every Newark cop knew the story. The Ciampelli twins, these Newark mobsters, they'd grown a mite unhappy with Charlie's constant harassment. He never gave them a night's sleep. So they started pestering Charlie's thirteen-year-old boy, forcing him into cars on his way home from school and driving him around for an hour or so. Telling him how tough they were and how much they hated his dad. They didn't dare hurt the kid, of course, but they counted on this shaking Charlie loose."

Patricia's face hadn't changed.

"When Faucher paid no mind, they went after his wife, Christine. They'd give her the evil eye at the supermarket, tail her station wagon all over East Orange in their black Gran Marquis. Christine didn't know enough not to be terrified, and she never understood why Charlie thought all this was funny. Why he wouldn't lay off the Ciampellis or have them arrested, or something. He just laughed about it, so Christine took the lad and left him, scared of what a cold bastard he'd become."

Patricia stirred. "That's terrible."

"Sure, but that's Charlie. If his family had been in any real danger, he'd have protected them like a lion. But he understood the Ciampellis better than their own mother did. He couldn't afford to blow up over something trivial. His wife never understood it. She walked out on Charlie, for good."

"Very interesting," Patricia said coolly. "Why tell me?"

"Charlie dresses like a business sharpie," I said, "but he's lost around shades of gray. For his own sanity he sticks to extremes. Something's either more important to him, or else it's less important."

"You're in love with riddles, aren't you? Are you telling me to be afraid of Charlie?"

"Leave the details to me," I said. "When all the pieces are in place, I'll let you know."

There didn't seem much left to say. "If you've got my clothes, I can drive back to town now."

"It's only ten-thirty, Ezell. Your suit won't be delivered until midnight."

"An hour and a half."

We looked at each other for a few minutes. My mind worked no more nimbly than usual. But Patricia appeared to be deciding something.

She got to her feet. It was a tricky scene to play, but I have to admit she handled herself like Lauren Bacall. With a rich tone of irony, she said: "Before you race off, let me show you one of the ways rich people relax in their leisure time."

She turned her shoulders without another look at me and strolled back through the big house, me following dumbly, through the first floor to a solarium off a room full of audio and video equipment. A small indoor pool sculpted in tile shimmered in light filtered through the glass ceiling, mimicking a cloudy greenhouse day. Patricia flicked off a sandal and dipped a toe in the water.

"Saltwater," she murmured, so low her voice graveled. "The heater makes it like swimming in a warm southern ocean."

"I got a confession to make." The words choked in my throat. Steam was rising off the rippled surface.

"You've never been skinny-dipping with a white woman before?" Patricia gave it one tiny laugh, then she undid the tie from around her neck. The pink dress slipped past her hips to her ankles.

"True, but that's not it." I could not unfasten my eyes from the sharp lines between the brown and white parts of her body.

Braless, she stepped out of the dress puddle and bent her knees to slide off her panties. I had been wrong, wrong, wrong about her. There was nothing sturdy about her body. Everything was swimmer lean, ocean-racer lean.

"Well, what then?"

"I can't swim."

"There's a shallow end."

She took a step closer. Very close. "You look like a natural breaststroker to me," she mumbled, just before she melted her taunting smile into my mouth.

The swimming part never did matter, because the closest I got to it was soaking in the hot water with Patricia Trimster's long tan legs wrapped around my waist.

CHAPTER TWENTY-ONE

O

My married friends sometimes kid me about being a stud, but believe me, sleeping with three women I barely knew was more than I usually handle in a year. I woke up in Patricia Trimster's king-sized bed, head and stomach churning like we'd split a quart of A&P bourbon.

I woke up alone too. My suit and shirt and tie lay plastic-wrapped on a bedside chair. I showered in Patricia's personal bathroom, big enough for two picture windows, one viewing the ocean, three monstrous ferns in squatty floor stands and a bowl of freshly cut flowers on the commode. A wall-sized mirror did the same work as my medicine-chest lid. The top oak drawer held half a dozen new toothbrushes still in their little boxes. I used one.

Downstairs I found Patricia in the drawing room. She had dressed up, as if for a day in Manhattan, and she stood up quickly before I could have sat down, even if I'd wanted to. She was having trouble thinking of things to say. I asked her about the commissioner.

"My father seems better this morning. He's still asleep, but breathing normally. Thank you again."

At least there would be no wriggling to get free this morning after. When I told Patricia I was late for an appointment, her relieved smile was almost insulting. But who could blame her? Picture me at her breakfast table, winking and waving a forkful of bacon at old Ranx when he came in to ask if Miss would require the Rolls this morning.

Figured I'd get at least a peck on the cheek, discreetly delivered before the door opened. And did. Only I turned the other cheek, caught the kiss in my pucker and made a little something out of it.

Patricia genuinely blushed, then hustled me out, signaling with that little Kukla wave as the door cracked close.

I hunched my shoulders, straightened my tie, then marched

down that long bluestone driveway, imaginary oglers behind every bush.

I was planning an undignified exit the way I'd come—over the fence—but just before I reached the wrought-iron gate, it buzzed and swung open of its own accord. As soon as I stepped through, head held high, it swung back with a crisp click.

My little truck was still sitting where the stucco wall would throw afternoon shade. The morning sun had soaked into the blue vinyl upholstery trim enough to burn through to my skin.

At the first gas station I reached—single bay, two pumps—I filled up and found the pay phone. Directory assistance gave me the number I wanted. When I dialed the Alpine Golf Club, a nasal voice took my name, left me hanging for a couple minutes, came back on, intoned "Eleven A.M. tee time," and hung up.

I checked my watch for the second time. It was just over forty-eight hours since the New York OC boys had skidded their warning my way. I knew a hell of a lot more now than I did then, but I still did not know where Carmine Napolitano's Easter egg was hidden. Time to beg an extension.

Long Branch was an hour's drive north, which left time to fuel up my insides at a roadside diner. The spot I pulled into, six miles up Route Nine, was a genuine truck-stop hash house in a once-silvery railroad car. Room for four little booths, with a dozen stools at the counter.

On the grill counter, everything from yesterday's grease can to today's Yankee pot roast and tomorrow's meat loaf sat in plain view of anyone sitting at the counter. I stood behind a stool and ran my eyes across the menu board behind the glass case. The short-order man wore starched white industrial pants and a clean white tee-shirt, a pack of Carletons rolled up in one sleeve. He was watching me patiently.

"You do improvisations?" I asked.

"Sure. Count Basie at the grill," he deadpanned.

"Okay, give me a fried egg platter, only make the toast a kaiser roll. And sandwich the egg in the roll. Put the potatoes on top. Coffee to go."

"Ketchup?"

"Not if it added six years to my life. Just pepper and a little salt."

"Decaf?"

"What—bad bean?"

"Kidding. For the road?"

"Uh-huh. I need the challenge," I said. "Driving with that thing in one hand ought to wake me up."

While waiting, I changed bills for silver and made two phone calls.

The first was to Roberta.

"Sorry I couldn't call you last night," I said ahead of her hello. "I know I promised."

"It's all right," Roberta said, not exactly cheerful, but not hurt either. "I'm glad you called, though. We were wondering how to get hold of you."

"Something happen over there?" I snapped, alarm jumping in my voice.

"Nothing new," Roberta said. "But with Junior's van totaled, we have no transportation for our grocery shopping. Would it be all right if we borrowed your truck some time soon?"

"Of course. Whew! Funny, I feel a little let down."

"Well, sorry about that. People get on with their lives when you're not there, Ezell."

"What'd I do to deserve that?"

"You didn't do a thing."

"I been playing high-and-mighty hero with you?"

"Oh, a little, maybe. You do seem to think you are sent by heaven to rescue the poor and helpless."

"Well, I like that! Your neighbors can't help themselves too much, can they? The other day you all were begging me to help. Now you want me to lay off?"

"Not at all. Keep on trying to help them, please. It's just that you should know everybody's life doesn't revolve around you."

I shut my eyes and let my breath vibrate against the back of my throat. "Listen good, Roberta. Goons're going to come snooping around your neighborhood soon. No matter what, the offer from Ernie is a rock solid $120,000 per house. Every last man, woman, and child has got to hold fast to that story or all our gooses are cooked."

"Strangers have been in the neighborhood already," Roberta told me. "Yesterday. They could be back this morning too."

"You think everybody stuck to the story?"

"I'm sure they did," Roberta said without conviction.

"I'm worried about that paralyzed neighbor of yours. His wife's determined to take the lowball offer. They're our Achilles heel."

"They're not the only ones getting nervous," Roberta said gloomily.

"Oh, God. Try to buck them up, will you?"

"I will. And Ezell?"

"Yeah?"

"I do appreciate what you are doing for us."

"Okay."

The second call went to D'Amato Green Grocer. Monday morning, business hours. A professional woman's voice answered, then tortured me on hold with a Muzak rendition of "Come Back to Sorrento," before Nick came on the line.

"Nick, it's Barnes. We need to talk. About money."

"Oh no, we don't," Nick said fervently. "Hang up, Barnes, call me back, tell me about this new Ukrainian restaurant you found or say you want to order a case of cello tomatoes."

"Nick, this deal's important to me, but it doesn't have to break your back."

"I talked to my people yesterday," Nick said as if that ended discussion.

"It'll be no joke maneuvering Horton out of the picture," I said. "The old crackpot loves New Jersey— can you believe it?"

"I believe anything you could tell me about that guy."

"To take him out I'll have to trick him, flat out, Nick, and he'll see through it in no time. He'll come after me with lawyers, and muscle, and anything else he can think of. I need more money, Nick. Lots more."

"The people I work with are gonna hate this, Barnes."

"One million even, Nick. Nothing less, or the deal's off. Not worth the risk to me."

Nick's little groan actually cracked into falsetto.

"Get off it," I said. "That condo deal'll have receipts of six hundred million. You can't tell me a million bucks more or less makes a hair of difference to them."

Nick was still moaning softly. "You don't know thing one about it, buster, believe me. You don't know shit. You're squeezing me up the middle."

"You'll look great, fixing a giant deal like this. Do it, make it happen, Nick."

"Oh, Christ," said the Twist. "Where do I reach you?"

"That a boy! Call my hotel room. I should be in late tonight or tomorrow morning."

"My day's a wreck now," Nick said. "Thanks to you. Bet those melons were good, huh?"

"I like them when they're properly thumped," I said, but Nick had hung up.

The Alpine Golf Club was set back from Route Nine, connected by a winding double lane that split the front and back nines of the course. The flattish green fairways were groomed like pooltable felt, and even the bright morning sun had not burned the dew off the darker greens yet.

At the head of the road a big colonial brick structure was tricked out as a clubhouse. None of the trees was more than a generation old, planted maybe twenty-five years ago when these farm pastures had been landscaped into a golf course.

I knew what I was looking at. Like a lot of Americans, the second-generation Italians had believed that money talked in American society. They washed their faces, combed their hair, and stepped up to join the world of Manhattan offices and high-toned suburban clubs. Which would not have them on a platter.

So they built their own idea of high-toned clubs. The underworld types in particular went in big for them. Pool for the kiddies, tennis, and bridge for the wives, and for the men, a man's game: swinging at a little teeny ball, then riding around in go-karts.

I eased the pickup into one of the last open spots in the parking lot, walked past the caddy shack and into the pro shop. A couple of caddies, hanging around for work, looked at each other, grinned, and laid a little "brother" shit on me.

The club pro, a tubby man with a face like Lee Trevino's but without the laughing mouth, also greeted me: "You a member here?"

I started to explain, but a cold voice broke in over my shoulder: "He's with us."

Curly-head Al was just golf-spiking his way in from the locker room, all in pastels. He looked down his hooked nose at both the golf pro and me.

"He's gonna golf in a suit, Al?" the pro said, eyes dancing with amusement.

"Golf is not my game," I said.

"No kidding! If it's got no running or jumping, then you spooks are no damn good at it."

"Cal Peete, he's surviving." I grinned. "Earned half a million on the pro tour this year, didn't he?"

"Al? I wouldn't mind showing this dirt bag the door." The pro eased his bulk from behind the counter.

"Of course," I said, gesturing at a smeary oil portrait above the pro's counter. "Old Champagne Tony could swing a club himself."

"Tony Lema don't need your ding-dong compliments," the pro rasped, jowls purpling.

"Billy," Al said, imperious as Caesar. "Cut the nonsense, all right? This fellow and me and Mr. Carmine are business associates. We are trying to reach an understanding."

I nodded.

"Who you going out with today, Al?" the pro asked. "Mr. Carmine coming up?"

"No, nobody," Al said. "Give me a box of Top-Flites and a bag of tees. I want Chester to caddy me around, and Barnes here is going to drive the cart."

Al looked at the face of his wristwatch and strode fast out the door towards the first tee, me scooting behind him.

"Need an extension, man," I huffed, as soon as I caught up. On the cart path a black caddy was throwing Al's bag into the back of a two-seater cart.

"You get in," Al head-motioned at me. "And drive, Barnes. Chester, you tag along, handle my clubs."

Not knowing what else to do, I stepped down on the accelerator and we spit turf towards the first tee, where a foursome was duffing away. Not one hit a respectable drive, all slices or hooked balls into the woods.

"Extensions are terrible, Barnes," Al commented, almost incidentally. "Terrible for business. No, not the driver, Chester. Give me, let's see, the three wood."

Chester pulled the blue-and-white ski hat off the club and handed it to Al.

"You see, control is the key," Al said, swinging his head vaguely towards the first tee. He took a couple practice swipes at an imaginary ball. "Look, if I give *you* an extension, how's that gonna look to the other people I do business with? Pretty soon everybody's asking for extensions, and before you know it, I've got no control."

We waited and watched while the middle-aged group in front played their second shots.

The first two golfers both sprayed wildly out of the rough, diagonally across the fairway and back into the rough.

"See my point?" Al's Roman nostrils flared. "Control. Capital K."

"Get off it," I told him. "If control's all you want, hit everything with your putter. Take you about a hundred swings to reach each green, of course, but every last shot'd go right where you aimed it. That's not the answer. It's power—used with judgment. You got to pick your spots for using muscle. Those duffers ahead all hit drivers; way too much wood for this narrow fairway. That's why they all four need compasses to find the green. The right club is the three wood, because it's got power with some finesse, gets the job done, without losing the ball."

Al looked at me with interest. "Where'd you learn the golf patter, kid?"

"Used to caddy—as a *kid*, Weequahic Golf Course in Newark. But like I said, it ain't my game."

"So, surprise, surprise, you don't think I should come down hard on you." Al was bent over, teeing his ball.

"No, because I'm close," I said. "Very close. But what's left has got to be handled with finesse. I try and bull my way through this thing, I could lose more than a ball in the rough. Two more days, I should be holding what you need."

"I don't hear any humor coming out of you." Al drove a nice shot down the left-middle of the fairway, though only about a hundred eighty yards. "You lose that sense of humor of yours? Because I better have what I want in my hands in two days. Or I'm gonna tee off on you, Barnes. Drive, for Chrissake, what are you waiting for?"

On the way to Al's ball, I said: "There's a couple loose ends I need tied, to get you what you want. Answer me just this: Was it your people that wasted Veronica Vallee?"

Al cock-eyed me. "You must have eggplant puree between your ears." He climbed out to stroke his second shot, shaking off the one iron and calling for the three, which I took as a good sign, don't ask me why. He hit it, straight and short again, still a nine iron from the flag. "We were the ones that found Ronnie in Kansas City after she took a hike last week. If we were looking to kill her, we'd have done it in a corn field."

"Why'd she leave town on you?"

He motioned me to the cart, but you could see Al thinking. He waited until we pulled up and he wedged his third shot over the front trap and into the frog hair. Al smiled. He handed the iron back to Chester and told me, "She was getting a little nervous, maybe. About a job she was doing for us."

I waited until we were set to drive after Al's shot for par. I said, "She scared you would shut her up anyways, soon as she did what you wanted?"

"Drive, Chester," Al ordered. He tough-eyed me out of the cart. He took out a Benson & Hedges, lit up, staring at me, flicked the match overboard. Chester swung in with a little chuckle only I could hear.

Just before they jerked away, Al ran a hand through his thinning gray locks and said, very calmly, "You want to hear something funny, Barnes? Two days from now is the final deadline. Eleven o'clock in the morning. No further extensions."

"Smell my exhaust, turkey," Chester added. He grinned and powered them away towards the green.

CHAPTER TWENTY-TWO

O

Back in AC I stowed my truck in the Kinney lot and walked without joy to my hotel room. All I had on my agenda was, one, trapping an old hero into a murder rap and, two, setting up an old friend as the human decoy. What I really craved was just sitting and studying the ocean for about ten hours, learn some of the secrets my life experience seemed to have left out. I would have to settle for a couple of mixed drinks and a steak dinner. Maybe later spend some time with an honest woman like Roberta.

I knocked on Angel's door—no answer. The hotel corridor was empty, the only sign of my young Wisconsin neighbors being a green foil heart they had taped under their room number. In my own room I dialed the switchboard at City by the Sea casino. *I'm sorry, sir. I cannot connect you with the rehearsal studios. Yes, I can tell you if a rehearsal is going on, and one is going on this afternoon.*

I called Charlie Faucher.

"Hey, fella," he said easily. "You still in Atlantic City?"

"That's right, Charlie. How about that dinner? Where do you suggest?"

"The Salt Summer Air Room at City by the Sea, of course. Prime steaks, fresh seafood, best decor in town."

"How about someplace else? I'm staying at Toby's Royale. They got a spot?"

"Got half a dozen. There's Randy's Deli—"

"No thanks."

"Eva's, which is sort of continental and French, Le Buffet, which is a glorified smorgasbord, Gianni's, which does lobsters and steaks, and the Manhat Lounge, which is pretty much a twenty-four-hour snack bar."

"Gianni's okay? On me. Seven o'clock?"

"Sounds good. Better make it eight."

I showered for half an hour, changed into my light gray suit, and strolled down the chockful Boardwalk, picking my way

158

through Hawaiian-shirted dads balancing three custards in each hand for the family, and thick-legged women window-shopping the garish little shops. I needed my third shower of the day by the time I ducked into the coolness of City by the Sea and threaded through the gambling maze to the show-room. The doorman recognized me from the day before and let me in to watch the girls.

They were wrapping up rehearsal. Angel spotted me almost at once, and in ten minutes was free to come prancing up to me at the back of the showroom.

"Come to the dressing room, say hello to the girls."

I was tempted. A dancer in purple tights whom yesterday I had seen toweling her way from the shower was halfway off the stage when she noticed me, slowed, and smiled. I flapped her a little wave, and she moved on.

"I can't. Listen to me carefully, Angel. I need you to do a job for me tonight."

"Angel got to dance tonight, Easy."

"Before you have to dance. At eight o'clock I'm meeting a man for dinner at Gianni's. At the hotel where we're staying?"

Cassie, in yellow gym shorts and leg warmers, blond ponytail bobbing, trotted past as if we didn't exist.

Angel nodded up and down. "Oh good! Angel go to dinner there yesterday. Cocktail Frank take me. He's *so* cute."

"What I need is for you to look carefully at this man's face and tell me if he's the one you saw climb on board Veronica Vallee's boat, the first night we were here. Can you do that? He'll be sitting at a table with me. Come by sometime after eight o'clock."

"Papi?"

"What?"

"Why don't Angel come go to dinner with you and this nasty? Could eat the Jumbo Killer Lobster and look very carefully at the McNasty's face for you."

"Listen good, amigo. I don't want him noticing you. Don't stop at the table and talk to me, or anything like that. If he's been playing the part I figure for him, this is one dangerous dude."

The other dancers had all wandered into the dressing rooms. I noticed the little director, Bobbi, standing in the wings, nervously watching me and Angel.

"You got everything straight?"

"Sí. Sure thing, Easy."

"After you ID him one way or the other, I need a signal from you. How about you scratch your left foot like a horse counting, if you make the guy?"

"Eas-y! Angel will tug her left ear if this is the right man. Right ear if not the right man."

"Left ear if you did see him on the boat."

"Right."

"Angel, please don't do comedy. There's nothing funny about the hole I'm chasing these rats into."

"Okay. Left ear, on the boat. Right ear, was not afloat."

"Be careful, man, will you? I'll check in with you when I can."

"Good-bye, Easy."

I spent the next hour and a half wandering on the Boardwalk, mapping out what I knew, what I didn't know, and what my moves might be two jumps down the line. Above all, I needed to find Veronica's videotape. Next important was the situation with Roberta's neighbors, also eating away at me. All those people trusting me to bring home their bacon. Forget that it was Ernie's fault for setting me up as an Afro-American Superman. These folks didn't appreciate subtleties like that. Besides, they had nobody else to turn to.

I exercised my brain cells until my painful skull needed three aspirin, until I had six minutes to be on time to meet Charlie Faucher, then I sighed and tucked what I couldn't cure back in my mind and walked back to Toby's Royale to meet my problem number one.

Gianni's was off Toby's main lobby. Inside, Charlie had already set up camp at the best table and was stirring a pitcher of Manhattans he'd mixed himself from a tray.

"I like a drop of bitters," he explained. "Nine parts Old Fitzgerald, two parts sweet vermouth, one part dry. And a drop of bitters."

"What do we eat, Charlie?"

"Steak is very special here. But I always stick to the broiled lobster. They serve a two-and-a-half pounder here."

"You having that too?" When Charlie nodded, I looked around for a waiter. "I already ordered," Charlie said. "You don't mind, do you, Barnes? They know me here and all."

"I think it's great, Charlie. Is this a good place to talk?"

"Good as any in this goddam Peyton Place." He sampled his Manhattan and looked pleased. "I hear you and the Rib King are looking to burn the town down. What's the status of that?"

"His offer's genuine," I said, with a shrug. "But anything could happen to hex the deal."

"What's that mean? You claiming pressure?"

"Everything's going okay, Charlie, calm down. I just mean that Mr. Horton's got his fingers in a lot of pies. It's possible, just possible, he'll get called out of town on urgent business before this land deal gets wrapped up."

"Jesus, I hope so. Keep me posted, will you, Easy? Nothing out of line, you understand, just don't let me, and my casino, be the last to know?"

"Got some info right here for you, on a different matter."

Faucher looked at me sharply.

"Veronica Valentine and your pal, Commissioner Roger Trimster, were a serious item," I said.

"Oh? What makes you say so?"

"All manner of hints. What do you think?"

"I think I knew it already."

"How'd they hook up, do you suppose?"

"Who knows? Any old way the OC brain could devise."

"She had recent mob contacts?"

"I had Newark PD telex their file on her. Ronnie Valentine kept in real close touch with her late boyfriend's old hood friends."

"What'd be the OC stake?"

The restaurant was the kind that spaces out tables for privacy, and a good buzz level filled the air, but Charlie looked carefully in all directions before he answered:

"The New York mob is horny as hell for a toehold in Atlantic City. They haven't had a stake here since that Jew accountant of theirs sold them down the river ten years ago. Remember? We handled that case too."

I shook my head. "You did, Charlie, not me. I remember it all right, though. Cat's name was Jules Goldstone, wasn't it?"

Charlie looked pleased that I remembered a big case he had handled.

"Jeez, those things stick with you?"

"Well, I've been thinking a lot about old times lately, Charlie."

"Me too," he said shortly, pinching the linen napkin between his fingertips. "Never stopped."

"Goldstone was the New York OC rep that turned up in a trunk around the time our boy Cricket Finnochio did likewise, right? Best you could figure, he got whacked for walking off with money earmarked for a lend-lease arrangement with the Philly outfit?"

"Exactly. Not much it could have been but a deal to let the New Yorkers grab a piece of Atlantic City. When Goldstone got taken out, the deal went down the toilet. They've wanted in on the action for the last ten years."

"What'd they want with Ronnie Valentine?"

"Well, I knew something was in the air. In a position like mine you live and breathe by unofficial news currents. It didn't take me long to pick up that Trimster was involved with one of the girls."

"But why?"

"What else but blackmail?" Charlie said, looking straight at me. "Drag Trimster into a scandal he could be threatened with, force him to swing the Casino Commission towards their license application."

"They have much chance for a license without him?"

"Not a Chinese prayer. Less than we have."

"Blackmail for what?"

Charlie shook his head. "For anything they could think of. The usual: sex, drugs, maybe gambling."

From a couple tables over floated the chant, "Cigars, cigarettes, Tiparillos? Cigars? Cigarettes? Tiparillos?"

"Mainly sex, I would guess," Charlie said. "Ronnie Valentine must have been a lousy screw, or else she didn't collect good evidence. The mob doesn't tolerate a fool gladly. They offed her as soon as they saw it wouldn't work."

"OC thugs wasted Veronica? Ain't their style two bullets behind the ear? I never heard of them serving somebody an OD."

"Maybe they're getting creative in their old age," Charlie said casually. He refilled his stemmed glass. "All the signs point towards them killing Valentine."

"Police see it that way?"

"Last I heard, they were definitely leaning that way."

Our lobster platters arrived then, giant oval metal plates with healthy lobsters on them, also a thick coating of oily breadcrumbs and undersized thimbles of drawn butter.

Not to mention, we had to let the waiter fasten bibs with grinning cartoon lobsters around our necks.

Cracking my first claw, I asked: "Why do you suppose old Trimster missed the commission hearing yesterday? Smells like low tide, no?"

Charlie shrugged. "Broken heart?"

"No. Somebody's leaning on him, Charlie. If the New York mob gave up, who's doing the leaning?"

I was sitting facing a wall muraled with bulls and lobsters somehow rubbing shoulders. His back to it, Charlie looked over my shoulder and grinned.

"Cigars, cigarettes, Tiparillos, gents? After-dinner mints, gummy bears, Rolaids?"

Charlie shook his head, choked with laughter. "We're just starting our meal, honey."

I knew I shouldn't turn around, but I just had to. Angel wore the full regalia: net stockings, nonexistent skirt with tiny ruffle, mock-tuxedo shirt and bow tie, and a suspender tray of cigarettes, cigars, and yes, gummy bears.

"Excuse me," Angel said with a winning expression. "How you enjoying your dinners, sirs? You having the black-and-blue fish?"

Charlie hooted. "You mean the blackened redfish, miss? Can't you see the lobsters on our plates?"

"Is that the house giraffe?"

"What? Oh, you mean the wine."

"Sure. Well, I got to scratch my left ear," Angel said deliberately. He did. "Don't you want no cigars, señors? Hershey bars?"

Booming, Charlie extended a droopy dollar bill to Angel. "Nothing. But thanks for stopping, honey."

Angel curtseyed, stage-winked, then sailed off, not forgetting to hit another table or two before he exited for his show. He'd be cutting the time close, and I appreciated the effort.

Charlie tucked into his lobster again, still chuckling. But my appetite had fled, though I made a show of giving my critter a tussle.

Charlie looked up from his plate. "You don't like lobster?"

"No, I do," I said. "Ate lunch too late, I guess."

I watched him eat, a big, trim, shrewd ex-cop that I'd heard tales about for years. I had no stomach for taking Faucher on. I thought how reassuring it would feel to stay on his good side. But all I knew to do was flip over a last unplayed card.

"That dead drug dealer—the New Yorker? They were going to lock me up for it? Police ever figure who killed him?"

"Gimme your claw?" Charlie asked, smiling.

"What?"

"You going to crack that claw? Let me?"

"Yeah." I passed it over and repeated: "Any idea who killed him?"

Charlie was peeling a little piece of shell off his lip. "Barry Wenhome called me; they figured a junkie for it." He shrugged. "The usual. What else?"

"You see it that way?"

Faucher stabbed the air in front of us with his shell pick. "Either that or our OC friends again."

"Strains my sense of coincidence, you know? I hook up with Veronica and the New Yorker, same night both get dead."

"Well, you are the connecting link, aren't you, friend?" Faucher said, grinning ever so slightly. It wasn't a pleasant sight. "Worried?"

"Yeah, I am worried," I said truthfully.

"Well, you should be. I can't believe you. Here you are, investigating an Atlantic City murder—after the AC homicide cops tell you to stay clear. You know how the game's played, Easy, you were a cop once. I got four words for you: Keep your nose clean. Babysit the Atlanta Rib King, lose the grocery money in my casino. But stay the hell clear of an ongoing homicide investigation in which you're already half a suspect."

Charlie looked down at his plate, realized he was sermonizing, and broke out a grin. "This is your old friend talking, Eefus. My well done ran dry with the AC po-lice. You sprint up their alley again, I can't run interference for you."

Charlie winked at me until I cracked a tight smile back at him. Then he resumed his methodical destruction of the giant lobster. I watched his powerful hands make short work of cracking, digging, and dipping. His manner was nonchalant, hands deft and relaxed. If the man was a murderer, then he had one hell of a peaceful conscience.

Damn it, I'd gone into this dinner morally sure that Charlie's hands were red. So, all I get from him is free and open talk about the case and a well-deserved lecture for my own good.

I stopped eating and watched him. Without trying, Charlie was transmitting the confidence he'd been famous for back in Newark. Competent, knowing, and cool. And incorruptible to the point of a sort of craziness. Made me wish to God I was teaming up with him again, instead of lining up against him.

But Angel's ear tug had put an end to that wishful thinking.

CHAPTER TWENTY-THREE

○

Swinging down from the Boardwalk to the Club Harlem, I laid all the pieces out in my mind. Here's what I had:

Fact: Commissioner Trimster, his daughter Patricia, and Charlie Faucher had all gone on board the *Polaris* the night Veronica was murdered. Plus two other men, very probably Curly Al and a Long Branch golfing crony.

Fact: Judging from the assignment they'd shoved at me, the OC boys had set up the old commissioner for a spot of blackmail via a videotape of the romantic duo engaged in rank sex and ranker narcotics.

Fact: New York OC for certain did not now have that tape.

Fact: New York OC very much wanted that tape.

Fact: Veronica Vallee had sensed that something was about to fly hinky. Scrounging refuge funds, she hired me to scout outside money for her, then bolted to Kansas City—of all places. Maybe she had relatives there. No matter: her OC friends found her flash-fast and hauled her back to finish the job on Trimster. Whatever her role was.

I shook my head over that. I was not ready to admit to myself that Veronica had willingly set up Trimster. I wanted to believe that her hand had been forced.

Very strong hunch: New York OC was hungry for a piece of AC action; they'd been shut out since an accountant named Jules Goldstone betrayed them and got stuffed into an automobile trunk for his pains.

Middling strong hunch: Roger Trimster didn't kill Veronica. No doubt he was one weak-willed victim of second childhood, fell hard for a sexy woman and puppy-dogged her into every vice known to the human race. Maybe developed a taste for cocaine, then "just one time for a thrill," let her drill horse into both their veins. Probably it got to be a routine part of all their big nights together.

Then, when Veronica disappeared for nearly a week, Trimster was hooked enough to sweat purple with the hit-

need. Soon as she got hauled back to AC, she hunted up the New Yorker, phoned Trimster, and he trotted over for some quick sky. He'd have been more than ready.

But Trimster's part added up to an old fool with a ring in his nose, not to a murderer. He might have come to resent what Veronica had done to him, but he needed her dope too much to kill her. And I was convinced that he had really cared about her. Besides, how would that old white turkey lay hands on forty-percent pure heroin?

With that background singing, you could hum the tune any of three ways.

One: Patricia Trimster killed Veronica Vallee, furious and fierce at what'd been done to her father. Then she pocketed the tape. As for Faucher, either he just tailed Patricia to the boat, or else he had parlayed his old acquaintance with Veronica into a piece of the action. He climbed aboard, found her dead, and blew off. Curly Al and friend came on, looking to pick up their tape, found both Veronica and the tape gone, and went looking to make trouble for everybody. Me included.

The motives sounded right, but there was the same trouble about Patricia laying hands on wholesale-quality smack. It's not something you stumble on in the suburbs, believe me.

Second version: Patricia had bearded Veronica on the yacht and been bullied off it, just as she claimed. Charlie Faucher came aboard next, wanting that tape to slam an advantage against the Casino Commission. Maybe he and Veronica had worked out a deal whereby she would two-time the New York mob.

Maybe it was the double cross that scared Veronica finally. She reckoned that if Al and company didn't pull her plug, Faucher probably would do the job. She fled town. When she got dragged back, she knew her only hope was to play square with the mob. When she told Faucher he was cut out of the deal, he fed her a killer eightball of H and scouted up the tape for himself.

An old street cop like Charlie would have a much better idea where to score that kind of dope than any suburbanites, I figured.

But it was dirtier pool than I had ever figured Charlie capable of. And besides, why kill Veronica when all he really wanted was that damn tape?

Because he knew that, first thing, Veronica would blow his cover to the OC lads, deal or no deal. If so, they'd take him down in a matter of hours. From his angle, Veronica had to be shut down.

Third: Either Patricia Trimster or Charlie Faucher snatched the dirty tape—Patricia to protect her father, Charlie to menace him. Either way, when the mob peeked in and found Veronica sans-a-tape, they punished her foul-up with death. This was the weakest version, but not impossible. The main problem was that whoever took the tape could not afford to leave Veronica alive. And if Patricia was too uptown to realize that point, her faithful lover, tailing behind her, surely would never miss it.

Stepping into the Club Harlem's smoky bar, I shook my head. Hard to keep it all straight, harder yet to peel truth from guesses.

I did have one lead left to follow up, though. Whoever killed Veronica Vallee had acquired a large dose of superexpensive dope, and the New Yorker, whatever he'd disclaimed to me, was Mr. Pipeline in AC. If you bought drugs to overdose Veronica, you'd probably want to silence the New Yorker but good.

The piano man was Morse-coding the keys in the outer bar. Half a dozen shot-and-chaser drinkers sat on stools. Otherwise the place was empty. The sunrise show wouldn't even start for another six hours.

Behind the bar Mocha Joe had his barrel-shaped head buried in the stainless cooler, laying in a few cases of beer bottles.

I circled the bar until I was standing just across from him.

"Got a minute, Joe? I got to have a word with you."

"Hmmph." Mocha Joe growled his head up, then ducked back down at the sight of me. "Only word I got for you is no."

"We do this the hard way, Joe? Or the pleasant way? Your call, man."

"We do it my way." Mocha Joe's voice was muffled inside the cooler. "My way don't include you."

He straightened up, let me see all six-and-a-half feet of stocky body and thin legs. His cold face knew exactly why I'd come, without me telling a word of it. He slid the cooler top shut, punched the cash register, and eased a 9mm automatic out of it. Concealing it against his big belly, he waggled the gun at me before he tucked it in his waistband under the tent-like red dress shirt he wore outside his slacks. Then he stalky-legged away, an empty cardboard case dangling from each hand, stranding me against the bar without even a drink, nye and dry.

I was humped. Mocha Joe knew it; so did I. No way I would ever call in the cops—it'd be my well they pumped dry, not his. I was the living-breathing common thread between the New Yorker and Veronica Vallee: both got dead the minute I poked my fat nose around them.

I didn't figure to muscle a cat like Mocha Joe either. He was no overweight dandy or punk goombah. He was big, and his pocked face had seen everything there was to see in this life. To my eyes he had ex-con branded on his forehead.

With no better idea, I parked at that bar for forty minutes. Mocha Joe never did come back. One by one the barflies fluttered out; only one or two hung on, glumly nursing the last sips. Even the piano man faded. Through the street windows I watched the searing city cool and quiet. Finally a big light-skinned mama strutted behind the bar, wheeled her eyes around, then set the regulars up with fresh drinks. Me, she ignored.

I didn't care. A way to loosen Mocha Joe's tongue had finally bubbled to my surface. It meant calling Newark. I found a pay phone in the showroom lobby.

I talked to a woman I never met, then a man I didn't know, until finally a familiar voice chuckled at the end of the line.

"Brother Ezell! I bet you need a favor. I got that right? What do I do? For you, Brother Boo?"

"Been a while, Hassan, no? I heard you were building a shopping center, in the lily-white suburbs, for crying out loud. Any truth to it?"

Hassan Fahriq hooted. "Ain't it the best! We looking for a name right now. What you think, the Jesse Jackson Mall?"

"Better make it Jesse James, if I know you. You got those ring fingers stuck in every pie worth slicing up and down the eastern seaboard."

Fahriq howled. I could picture his eyes flashing, his greyhound's body coiling to his own wit.

"Hey, time's money." He changed gears and throttled up the indignation. "Lay your shit on me."

"Got somebody here needs leaning on."

"Well, hot damn! I always enjoy helping a fellow traveler find his way." Fahriq loved the give and take of business, street style. "Life is such a lonely journey, and we must lean on one another for comfort. Am I right?"

"Here's what it is," I said. "Got to know who iced a dope dealer down here that called himself the New Yorker. Only place I got to start is this large-size at the Club Harlem." I laid out the rest of what Fahriq needed to know, keeping the names to myself, except for the New Yorker and Mocha Joe.

When I was finished, Fahriq said quietly, "On your best days you still nothing but a bad dream, brother. You the only chump in Atlantic City got to make big trouble instead of big green."

"Save the zoom," I said wearily. "You got any pull down this way?"

"Cost you five grand," Fahriq said, probably lighting a thin cigar while he said it.

"Hassan, man. Remember? It's me, Brother Bad Dream."

"Oh, shit. A grand. You got a piss-ant grand, ain't you, Brother Bad?"

I snorted. Fahriq needed another thousand bucks like a third pinkie ring. But his code forbade doing things on a friendship basis.

"You got it. You need the number of the Club Harlem, so you can pitch to this dude?"

Fahriq didn't chuckle so much as let his lungs knock together and the sound ooze out his mouth. "Only Mocha Joe I ever heard of is Joe McCoy. You're in luck, babe. I did hard time with his brother. Ten years back, the income tax thing. Trenton State prison."

That the Iroquois McCoy you told me about? That behaved like an animal? This bartender is his brother?"

"Sounds like it. He about six foot, one million?"

"That's him."

"Shoot, I know the man, personal-like. Need speed?"

"Bet your ass. How do I know when you've fixed him?"

"Skies will part," Fahriq said dreamily. "And a voice will intone to you." His tone changed: "And I do expect when you drag your hopeless ass back here to Newark, your first stop will be my office, where you will personally lay one thousand smiling George Washingtons in my hand."

"Cash on the old bucket head. Or is that barrel head?"

"Just so it ain't your head the cash price is on."

We let a little silence grow in the dark.

Fahriq whispered so I could barely hear, just as he hung up: "You in the big leagues, chump. Play like it."

Back in the red-velveted bar business was picking up. The

piano man was back at the keys. I bellied up at the same spot. Three women were now serving the cocktails. The youngest one consented to bring me a BV highball, when I flashed my teeth.

Five identical piano tunes later she arrived with my refill. Scrawled at the bottom of the little square napkin was my answer: *Hackney's Pavilion. 2 o'clock.*

piano man was back at the keys. I bellied up at the same spo
Three women were now serving the cocktails. The younge
one conversan

CHAPTER TWENTY-FOUR

○

The old Hackney's restaurant stood by itself on the deserted northeast stretch of Boardwalk that Faucher and I had jogged along. Stubbing toes down Atlantic Avenue, close to breaking my fool neck on the heaved and cratered sidewalk, I ached for a flashlight. The few street lamps had been smashed with rocks, finally switched off for good. Old Absecon Lighthouse was most all you could see. A decorative beacon simulated the old fog cutter, flashing warm yellow, but just bouncing off the fog rolling in off the ocean. I kept hoping to pass some kind of all-night store, pick up a penlight or something, but probably they'd legislated light out of that junked neighborhood. At long last I cut left onto Maine, then half a block on Pitney and up to the Boardwalk ramp.

Two-by-fours were nailed across the dilapidated rampway. When the light swung by, they flashed bright yellow. The houses for blocks around were burned-out shells, lurking like ghosts in the gray sea night. The roof and walls of an old concrete rest room had crumbled away, for all the world like a battered pillbox that once guarded the city from somebody's invasion.

At this northern end, far from the casinos, the hurricane had ripped great chunks of the Boardwalk into a roller-coaster ride. Most of the desolate stretch was closed to a public that could not care less, anyway.

I hopped the barway and squeaked up the ramp to the Boardwalk. Hackney's restaurant, giant fading lobster festooned across the side, was on my left. Its flimsily boarded-up windows flexed in the sea gusts. A small dock and pavilion shot off just south of the old landmark. The iron railing around the pavilion had lost its top rail and been eaten by the salt wind until it looked like an old comb with most of its teeth gone. The only lights, other than old Ab, were blinking on top of the channel buoys marking the inlet. As I toed down to the pavilion to size things up, a bell clapped hollowly on the green blinker.

The usual sign warned trespassers to stay off the pavilion dock, but the plastic bait cups and Schaefer cans declared that fishermen sometimes traipsed out there.

North, past Hackney's, an additional five hundred yards of Boardwalk stretched, thirty years more ancient, gapped and splintery. It finally collapsed at the inlet, where a gigantic shape was moored—an Army Corps dredger, maybe; too dark to tell.

The abandoned Boardwalk to my right and left added up to about a mile of open space, without a stitch of cover, other than the restaurant building. I did a neck circle to ease the tension. The pavilion, where the note sent me, had no emergency exit except onto the black rocks and exploding surf fifty feet below it. A great place to pass on information—or pass away without a trace. Not this mama's child.

I backtracked to the ramp, rehopped the crossed two-by-fours, and banged feet back down to street level. There, I Drifted under the Boardwalk, down by the sea, which had pulled far back to low tide. I felt, but couldn't see, the scabby pilings that run for miles down the beach, like a swamp forest. Creosote and dead clam smells skittered me along the sand, crouched to save a head thumping, until I figured I was approximately beneath the pavilion entrance.

Unlike the loose street-side sand, the under-Boardwalk variety was packed hard as a landing strip. The small waves broke ten yards from the pilings where I shadowed myself. I waited a long time without burning tobacco. Every so often the overcast night sky opened, and the moon pin-striped the underworld beach through the Boardwalk slats.

It pumped my pulse, standing in the dark so close to the ocean. Before long the waves began sounding closer and more aimful. Then the willies came and knocked on my stomach. I fished for a cigarette and lit it with shaky cupped hands. Smoking didn't make the situation calm, just routine.

A quarter pack later the boom and drag of the surf was punctured by the sharp taps of somebody walking north, up the Boardwalk, towards me. Steady as nighttime faucet drip, the taps grew louder until I could identify them as a woman's high heels. She tapped right over my head, then stopped.

I let her shift her feet for a couple minutes. I heard two clicks as she opened her handbag, then flicked a lighter to her cigarette. I let her smoke the whole thing. That flame could be a signal to any backup she had waiting for me. I was not about to stick my fool neck above board like a shooting-gallery turkey.

I moved closer and peeked up her skirt instead.

"Sorry to keep you waiting," I called up.

"Sweet Christ!" she shrieked, jumping. "Where the devil are you?"

"Down here, where the fishes swim. Told me you got information for me?"

"Who are you?" Suspicion and fright choked the words in her throat.

"You don't want to know," I said. "And what's more, you don't want me knowing you either. Am I right?"

"You got that right." She picked up the thread. "I'm just a crooner in the night."

"Nice and safe that way, baby. What you got?"

"You looking for something on the New Yorker, right? Well, I only know what I seen, night he got killed. Behind the fact that I weren't with him before he seen me, or after he took a ride with that white dude."

"What time was this?"

"I don't carry no stopwatch around with me, see. It were just after my third trick that night. New Yorker come staggering into my place, looking like he stuck his face in a Osterizer. He just about done washing the blood off his fat face when whitey knock on my door and ask to see him outside."

"And?"

"And next time I seen him, he was just a picture in the newspaper."

"What'd the other man look like?"

"Like the same-old same. Like a cop." She paused to pick her words. "They all look the same, no matter what."

"You been hooking in this town for a while?"

"Six years, baby. Don't I know your voice from sometime?"

"That's long enough to know the locals," I said, ignoring her question. "This white dude an Atlantic City cop?"

"Naw, he weren't no AC police."

In the long silence that followed, I listened to the waves grind away at the beach. On this stretch they were busy hauling the sand away, and somewhere down shore they were just as busy building the beach back up.

"Hey, mister," the prostitute whispered through the cracks. "You still there?"

"Yeah. I was just thinking."

"Well, don't be wasting too much thinking on it," she said. "That fat man weren't worth it. He treated everybody rotten. He was a bum fuck."

"I know," I said. "Listen, I'm poking something up at you."

When she unfolded the bill and flickered the lighter to see it was a hundred, she added: "Maybe you could come see me some night, make something sweet together."

"Only I don't know who you are, kid, right?"

"That's the damn truth," she said fiercely. "And if you ever tell somebody what I just told you, I'll swear you're a lying pig, mister."

"Cool out, sugar. My lips are sealed."

"I be kissing off then," she said. I heard her taps for a long way down the Boardwalk.

Playing big-league ball, I scurried like a sand crab down the beach, along the pilings, and didn't pop to the surface until the very marina end of the wooden walkway. Then I slunk to my hotel in the dark, the long way back. My head hurt, and I needed it. To set a trap.

CHAPTER TWENTY-FIVE

○

The reason the New Yorker died was somebody covering up buying the overdose that killed Veronica Vallee. Charlie Faucher killed the New Yorker. Charlie Faucher killed Veronica.

I didn't like it one bit.

As I prowled up the four A.M. corridor of my hotel, the door next to mine opened and my teenaged neighbor stuck her beribboned head out to beam at me.

"Hi! Did you know your phone's been ringing for hours and hours?"

I thanked her until her door closed again. I tugged the .22 automatic out of my jacket pocket, hugged the wall left of the doorknob while I snuck in my key, then booted the door wide open. It crashed against the inside wall. I counted to ten, then tensed my leg muscles to the trembling point before I burst around the jamb and covered every direction in the empty room.

Letting down my shaking arms, I leaned my head back into the corridor. Four golf-ball sized eyes stared without a blink from the neighboring door frame. The boy held his hand over his mouth.

I grinned at them, at my little pistol, back at them, and flicked a merchant seaman's salute. I stepped back inside, kicked the door shut, locked it, even hung up the futile chain. I padded into the closet, found a wooden hanger permanently fixed to the closet pole, unpermanented it by yanking downwards with all my weight, and carried it over to the table and chairs. With the thin steel gardening knife I always carry in my hip pocket, I whittled two little wedges from the hanger and pounded them into the crack under the door, holding a boot by the toe for hammer. Then I rasped the entire queen-sized bed, frame, headboard, and all, across the room. I didn't stop until it stood in the one inside corner not on a beeline from a gun outside the door.

I took off my sticky clothes, lay down, and dreamed the kind of cinematic perversions usually brought on by jury verdicts, death-row nights, or bad clams.

I woke at seven, forced my body to soak up two more hours of bed rest by turning the pages of my Atlantic City book, finally called room service to send up coffee and sweet rolls. I showered long and hard, scrubbing my skin with the rough side of the cloth until it stung. I switched off the water, stepped onto the mat, heard pounding at the door.

"Mr. Barnes! Your room service is here! The waiter didn't want to wait—we told him to leave it."

I tried yanking the door open, discovered the wedges, still thoughtfully crammed, and told my guardian angels: "Thanks. Leave it outside. Help yourself to coffee."

When I heard their steps turn away, I pressed against the door and listened until they faded. Then I pulled the wedges and went through my whole entry routine in reverse, relieved that no civilians were passing to catch my revolver on the lips.

I drank the good coffee, sopped the rolls, dressed carefully in my cream suit, new socks, new shoes. When it was ten o'clock I tapped out the Trimster phone number at Sea View Acres.

"I'm sorry, sir," answered Hans the butler. "Miss Trimster is with company at the pool and cannot come to the phone."

"Garbage, Mr. Penguin," I said in my mocking best. "You know me. If the lady of the house don't get off her chaise longue and flip-flop to a phone, I'll be there in an hour to belly flop into the pool party."

"I'll see what can be arranged, sir." Hans put down the phone. I pictured him decked out in a formal black tank suit and bow tie while working poolside.

"Ezell, this is a surprise." Her voice was low and cozy into the receiver. Less for my benefit than that of her pool guests, I bet.

In the background a child shrieked.

"Ezell?"

I imagined her gold hair slicked back, like in a shampoo commercial, her head tilted to keep from dripping saltwater on the phone.

"This thing ends tonight," I said. I felt curt and sour, a repairman. "Nice and quiet, if everything works perfectly. Maybe a little noisy, otherwise."

"Then you know who the murderer is?"

Her intensity almost jumped through the phone.

"How's your father doing?"

"Better. I've asked him to stay in his room. He needs the rest."

"He squirmy for dope?"

"Our family doctor has been here on and off since you left. My father seems to be doing all right."

"I bet. You figure Dr. Feelgood can hype the old man for the rest of his life?"

"It's a medical condition. I'm not the best judge."

"Yeah? Well, I got a detective condition for you. Just do what you're told, let me be the judge. Agreed?"

"What do I have to do?"

"Trap your boyfriend into tipping off his guilt for the Vallee killing."

The phone line was filled with the sound of Patricia Trimster's rich playmates having a ball in the pool.

"You all right?"

"How can you know it was Charlie?"

"Have to turn my back on a mountain of evidence to deny it."

"I don't believe you. Are you jealous because he is my lover?"

"I'm sorry," I said. "I've admired Charlie for years. He was a legend way back when, the straightest arrow in the quiver. I'm giving him every chance."

"I won't help you trap him. How could you even ask a thing like that?"

"Call it a fair trial then. Phone Charlie at his office. Tell him I was at your house and bragged to you how I'd solved Veronica Vallee's murder. And say that I am convinced that he killed both her and a black dope dealer called the New Yorker."

Patricia said nothing. I wished I could see her face.

"Here's the important part. Tell him I bragged that I have an eyewitness to Veronica's murder, but I've been hiding the witness until I could figure out all the angles. That I've been afraid to go to the AC police, because I think they're stooges for the casino, but now I've decided to spill it to the Feds."

"Is this all true?"

"Some is. Most. The witness part is God's honest truth."

"Who is your witness?"

"She's a dancer in the *Peaches and Cream Revue* at Charlie's casino. A hot Latin number."

"What's her name?"

"Names are beside the point. Faucher has the contacts to find out who I'm talking about. One phone call downstairs and he'll have it. We feed him too much info, it'll smell like a setup."

"You can tell me, can't you?"

"Patty, I need you to swing this end of the deal for me. Don't mean I trust you as far as I can kick you, babe."

"You don't need to be insulting."

"Today, somehow, I think I do. One last thing. Tell Faucher that I'm dragging this witness to the Feds right after the second show tonight. She refuses to miss a show and risk her job. He'll understand."

"Do you think Charlie has the videotape of my father and that revolting whore?" Her voice sounded the way ground limestone feels under your fingernails.

"Likely so. I can't see why else he would kill Veronica, except to keep her from tipping his ass to the mob."

A long pause, then Patricia said, "It's all so vulgar. Makes you want to lock the door and never step outside again."

"Days I tried that," I said, "the phone kept on ringing, and the mailman shoved the bills through the door slot at me. Don't work, just bottoms you out. Got to stick your neck out if you want to see the light."

That was about that. We hung up. Or, really, I hung up after a time, with her voice still pleading me to call her immediately anything happened.

I looked at the phone for a couple of minutes. I picked it up and dialed Angel's room.

CHAPTER TWENTY-SIX

O

When Angel didn't pick up his phone, I switchboarded him a message. Then I reached for the button to redial the reservations number at City by the Sea and reserve tables for both shows of the *Peaches and Cream Revue* that night. But while my finger was still pressing the receiver button, the phone rang.

I let my thumb up and heard, "Let me talk to Barnes, will you?"

"Nick?"

"The very same. How you doing?"

"How's it look?"

"Looks like showers later."

"Our deal, Nick."

"Looks terrible, like I predicted."

"What happened?"

"The people I conduct business with blew up when I passed on what you wanted. They claim you are a chiseler and an Indian giver. They don't want any part of the deal anymore."

"You can't let it happen, Nick!"

"Yeah, I got a good chance of telling these people what to do, right?"

"What's the big deal over a measly million bucks?"

Nick hesitated. Then he said, "They think the whole condo story's starting to smell like old Brussels sprouts. They want out, that's all."

"Don't hang up, Nick! Come on, man. I committed myself. I got to shake something fast. Can't you tell me what they don't like about the deal?"

Nick paused again. He said thoughtfully: "This won't bruise anything, I guess. I think it's you and that old cop, Faucher, from the casino. The two of you are paisans, my people know that. They don't like the way your piece of the rock gets bigger and bigger."

I was too stunned to get a genuine word out.

"That's a banana groan, I can tell," Nick told me.

"What?"

"Banana groan. Things been going wrong for you in bunches, am I right? We got to eat dinner again some time, couple years from now. You wanna run into each other again in Abe's?"

"Nick," I said, but the line was dead.

With so many things going down the cesspool for me, the merely poor land deal with Nick had been practically the brightest star on my horizon. Damn.

I made the showroom reservation call, stepped outside and locked my door. Then, on second thought, I unlocked again, grabbed something from my bureau, pushed the room service cart into the hall, and hung the doorknob with a cartoon of someone sleeping. I relocked, looked both ways quickly, slipped off a loafer, and hammered the two little wooden wedges above the doorjamb, exactly my hand's breadth apart.

I straightened up and dusted my hands. Then I hustled downstairs to search for Angel.

No luck at any of Toby's Royale coffee shoppes or the shopping arcade, but in the casino, freshly reopened for the new day, Angel was bumping rumps with a hairnetted woman who had staked claims to two side-by-side dollar slot machines. A damply smoldering cigarette was clamped in the slot-hog's jaw as both her fists pumped the one-armed bandits. Angel darted back and forth behind her, squawking like a chicken muscled out at the barnyard trough.

Every time the woman dropped a hand to fish another dollar token out of her plastic cup, Angel would lunge for the slot handle, only to catch a perfectly launched haunch in the rib cage, blocking him from reaching.

"There is a law against you, you pig," Angel fumed. He aimed his beaded purse at the fat woman's backside, but she paid no notice.

"Let it go, Angel." I had to pull him aside. "She hasn't scored on either of those machines yet."

"Papi, Angel played both them machines all night, last night. Until the casino close. Didn't win nothing."

"So you're fighting to get them back? Shrewd figuring, Angel."

"That means," Angel said with cosmetic patience, "that good luck is due. Them machines are primed for the big payoff."

"Chump change's the most you ever win out of those

things," I scolded. "Got the worst odds in the house, by far. Only losers play them. Look at that slot-hog's hands—they're lathered gray with tarnish from all the coins she's lost."

Angel glared at the woman. "Yes, loser," he snapped. Just then a bell alarmed and one red dome light flashed a jackpot. Dollar tokens began to rattle in the trough like pennies from heaven. They just didn't stop. Pretty soon half the slot players in nearby rows were clustered, greedily watching the shrieking fat woman run blue-veined hands through the silver pieces and scoop them into a half-dozen coin buckets.

"Oh no," moaned Angel. "Here comes the cashiers too."

A dark-suited, broad-chested young man accompanied the miniskirted cashier to the still-ringing slot. With a key, he turned off the bell. Then he watched impassively as the cashier stripped bill after twenty-dollar bill off a roll and into the woman's outstretched palm.

Angel looked up indignantly at me. His eyes smoldered.

"Who knew they had slot jackpots that big?" was all I could manage.

"They got them for a million dollars!" Angel retorted. "I hope that money makes you sick," he told the eye-glazed woman. "Gives you malaria. Your husband, too, if you got a husband."

I pulled Angel off and shook him a little. "Settle down, amigo. Why so much aggravation? Not worth it."

"Easy, sometime you got to stand up for something." Angel glared around for the woman, but she had disappeared, along with her treasure. "Principle."

"Well, those machines're free now, anyway."

Angel's look turned to scorn.

"I never saw you so greedy for money, man," I said quietly to him.

Behind us the bank of slot machines clattered and brrred. All except the jackpot machines—they were bare of players, scrupulously avoided.

"Angel does nothing for just money." My friend's voice held pity for my slow comprehension. "Don't love somebody for money and don't gamble for just money. Angel plays for the thrills."

"Glad to hear it. Amigo, my man, I got a proposition that's gonna frost your cake with excitement. Buy you lunch, and I'll lay it all out for you."

We weaved our way through the thickening morning crowd

that, on a casino floor, always sounds like an orchestra tuning up. The highs and lows on the scale of noises were anchored by the regular percussion clatter of the slots and wheels and rhythmic patter of the dealers.

I steered Angel out the door and then, to his surprise, all the way around the casino to the Kinney garage. "You tired of eating Dip-Stix on the Boardwalk, Easy?"

"It's better that we go out of town, buddy. You like combo sandwiches? I know a spot."

As we drove south on Atlantic Avenue the sky darkened from white to charcoal gray. By the time we crossed out of Atlantic City—maybe five minutes—a light, persistent rain was flecking windshields and high spirits. Soon as we were in Margate, I wrenched us through a sudden U-turn and ran a red light—standard tail-shakers. Angel's eyes lit up like Fourth of July. Not a sign of anything.

After a while we saw Lucy the Elephant looming six stories above Atlantic Avenue, Margate. The old real estate promo was once again in pristine condition, all one million wood bits restored and coated with gray skin paint and bright colors for the howdah. The signboard declared that Lucy had been built in 1881 and was now a National Historical Landmark.

Angel was a thousand oohs and aahs, rolling down his window to gawk in spite of the chilly, small rain.

Next door to Lucy was a fern bar that had changed names five times in the ten years I'd known it.

A hostess sat us at a table looking out through rain-splattered glass at Lucy's profile. Spider plants tentacled down the window like hair locks blown into your eyes. Nobody much was in the place so early. Even out on the gray main drag only a few cars whooshed and sprayed along. Inside, on the walls, faded rotogravures showed early beach fans of both sexes, clad to the neck, all stiff and tinted violet.

"So, Mr. Thrill and Chill."

"Hmmm?"

"What excitement you got planned for little Angel?"

"A death-defying act," I said, more light-hearted than I felt. "You're going to help me catch a murderer."

"Yas! Like Nick and Norma!"

"All you have to do is dance in the show. Tonight you'll be the star attraction. The killer will show up just to see you."

Angel's big smile dripped off his face like melting ice cream. His lower lip trembled.

"Papi, what did you do?"

"Charlie Faucher knows you saw him go aboard the boat the night Muff was murdered. If he fed her the overdose, he'll be wanting to shut you up but good."

"And while Angel is on stage shaking her feathers, what exactly you be doing to catch this murder man?"

"I'll be there watching," I said. "I'll collar him before he shoots the tail feathers off your costume."

But it wasn't funny to Angel. You can never make enough allowance for the vividness of his imagination. He stopped shaking his head long enough to ask, "How come you don't just tell the police on mother-Faucher? Why does Angel got to be some duck in a shooting gallery for?"

"Not the police, Angel. In this town they're Faucher's bosom buddies. If he's the killer, we go to the Feds."

"Why don't we go to some Feds now? I know, because this mother-Faucher is your friend?" Angel's face was set.

I eased my neck. "I do respect Charlie, enough that I want to be absolutely sure before I blow the whistle on him. Look, Charlie is mixed up in a couple other things that I don't care about, but that the Feds would love to crucify him for. If I turned him over, they'd have him nailed up plenty quick, whether he killed Muff or not."

The waitress arrived. "I'm gonna have the Eggplantic City combo," Angel said thoughtfully. "The one that comes with eggplant Farmer John, fried peppers and tangy tomato sauce, on Italian roll." Menus fascinate Angel.

"I know, I know," the waitress said.

"Ice tea," Angel returned.

"Okay. You?"

"Think I'll have the Eydie Gorme. Side of fries and a Diet Coke."

"You like to eatie gourmet, huh?" the waitress said to me.

"What?"

"That's a joke we always say."

"How about that."

After the waitress bustled off, Angel said, "After these sangwiches come and go, Angel will catch the bus back to Nowork."

"You don't mean that," I soothed. "Trust me. Look it, Angel, I could have set this rolling without even telling you. But I got too much respect."

"That's the worst thing you done," Angel said indignantly.

"How come you got to tell Angel, anyhow? If I don't know is a bad man coming to kill me, I got nothing to worry about."

I sighed. "I know you feel that way, Angel, but it's not my decision to make. I'm tired of dealing with you like you were a six-year-old."

Angel stuck out his lower lip. "Is very simple, Mr. Smarty. Danger do not bother Angel. *Worry* bothers her."

"Remember, I'll be out there with you."

"Oh yas? How many eyes you got, Easy?" Angel pressed all ten bright red nails against his cheekbones and made as if to rip scars in his own cheeks. "The showroom is too big for two eyes."

"How about I get somebody to help me cover the place?"

"Suppose something happen to you?" Angel said. "Then Angel's got his tushy in a wringer, no?"

"Have I ever let you down before?"

"Oh? Angel needs skin grafts, been in so many close scrapes with you, Easy."

But at my big grin, Angel flashed me back his white-toothed smile.

"We always beat the odds, don't we? You got to admit, we've had thrills galore."

"Yas," Angel sighed.

"Like Bette Davis and Cary Grant?" I prompted.

"No," Angel said decisively. "Not Bette. Ingrid and Bogey. To do or die, like love and gory."

"That's it," I said.

"The fun and mental things apply as times go by."

"Ingrid Bergman didn't say it better. I knew you would answer the call, Angel. Thanks."

Our sandwiches arrived, and we chowed down. After a bit Angel dabbed at the corners of his mouth and slipped a Virginia Slims menthol-light from his pack.

I flicked my lighter under his nose.

"One more thing you got to remember, Angel. After I drop you off, don't go back to your room. And don't go anywhere near Toby's or City by the Sea until makeup time. Then I want you to get Felicia and a couple other girls to walk into the dressing rooms with you. You'll be all right once you're in there. Just stay where there's lots of people milling around."

"And what is Angel suppose to do until nine o'clock tonight?"

I stood up and laid a ten-spot on the bill. "You ever catch the Lucy the Elephant tour?"

"Can I go to any other casinos?"

"How about reading a book?"

Angel's face twisted with doubt. "Could maybe try a wood unit," he volunteered unenthusiastically.

"What?"

"Wo-od u-nit. A book."

"Spell it."

"Double you, Aitch. Oh, Dee. You, En, I, Tee."

"Whodunit?" I started chuckling. "Try one, Angel. You might learn something about Who-ods."

"Just you stop laughing, Easy. Stop it! I'm going to a casino, for sure."

I thought it over.

"Tell you what. I'll drop you at Trump's Castle. Over by the marina? Call Felicia from there, set up where you're going to meet her. When it's about time, call a cab to come pick you up. Don't use one from the taxi stand. Understand?"

I held out one of Patricia Trimster's hundred dollar bills to my old friend. "Have fun, man. And don't worry. We'll get the skin off this thing yet."

CHAPTER TWENTY-SEVEN

O

Just before two o'clock I parted company with Angel until showtime. Watching him waggle through the rain into Trump's Castle and turn to blow me a kiss, my belly cramped with apprehension. I jiggled in the truck seat, stubbed out my smoke, and sucked in a few fresh chestfuls.

I needed to recruit Ernie for the showroom showdown. So I swung across town, through the Monopolyland shadow world the tourist bureau discreetly never mentions, to Utah Avenue. And face it: sooner or later I needed to tip off Roberta that the land deal's propeller was busted. I did not relish facing her, apologetic hat in hand.

I thought briefly about phoning first, decided it was quicker just to drop in, and pulled into a metered spot down the block, near where Junior Evans's ride had been torched. Somebody had towed the old van away, but the scorch marks were plain.

I should have felt something was flying funny from the unusual quiet of the street, but I just chalked it up to the summer rain.

Which is why I just knocked once, pulled Roberta's door open, and walked in on a thunderous meeting of the neighborhood association. Apparently me, myself, and I was the major order of emergency business.

The minute I walked in, the jabbering and bickering lost its bubbles. I kept my face cheerful, but every eye in the place locked on me. Two seats were arranged facing the rows of chairs. In one, Ernie sat in glum disgrace, even his loose vocal cords shut down. His new suit was nowhere in sight. In fact, he was sitting in knee socks, tee-shirt, and light blue boxer shorts. Filling the other, Roberta, bare-shouldered in a green two-piece sunsuit, looked at me with a mixture of surprise and entreaty.

"How are you all doing?" I managed, mildly.

Nobody yelled at me—nobody broke the silence. I figured things were *really* bad. "Hi, babe," I said to Roberta with a little smile. She tried returning it, but didn't have much oomph.

"You might as well tell me," I said, still easy as cornflakes.

"Our good neighbors here," Roberta said slowly, "have all just voted to accept the offer from Short Line Enterprises, of ten thousand dollars each."

"Why, for crying out loud?" I turned an angry face at them. "That's still peanuts. We're angling to scoop you all much, much more."

You could have heard a cigarette ash hit the carpet.

"They got no faith in us, Easy," Ernie snorted finally. "Don't think you and me know which end to stick on the toilet seat."

"I know all of you are getting nervous," I said reasonably. "But we need a little more time, is all. You can't sell for ten; most of you will end up living in the godforsaken projects."

"Where we gonna live, we listen to you? Casino penthouses?" growled the lone white woman, who today wore skimpy orange shorts over bruised, but still handsome legs. "You and this worthless piece of dog dirt over here," motioning at Ernie, "that you brought with you."

"Wait a minute," I warned everybody. "Ernie's a friend of mine. He's a good friend, and a good man too."

To Ernie, though, I shot a look that accused: "What'd you do, borrow cash off the whole block?"

"Where is our money?" Junior Evans asked politely. He sat on a folding chair in the corner, wearing his brown sheriff's-style security uniform.

"I'm working on it," I began.

But the woman with brillo hair cut in with: "*How*'re you working on it, on our money?"

"I'd rather not say."

"Hmmph," said ten voices around the room.

"What I mean is, if I tell you, my plan will be jeopardized. There's a lot of secrecy and deception involved." I turned to the old disabled sailor for backup. "Loose lips sink ships, right?" The old salt avoided my eye miserably and sat slumped in his chair, the wind gone from his sails.

"You got that right! And the damn ship is sinking!" The white woman jumped in my face. "We're fed up having you fast-talk us and then do nothing!"

It was open mutiny, the racket level rising like an onrushing locomotive, until the old navy wife hollered: "You the greediest bunch of fools I ever laid eyes on."

Her husband sat in his strap tee-shirt and colorless wool trousers, his head bowed.

She looked hard, first at the brillo-haired lady, then at the white woman, who recrossed her bare legs. "Just a couple days ago you was singing 'Something Over the Rainbow.' Now you crying the blues and blaming it on this poor man." She motioned at me. "He ain't no salvation, and he ain't your damnation, neither."

"But we ain't heard nothing about nothing from him," the white woman protested. "Hard to sit still when you don't know what's going on."

"It's harder yet for Ezra and me to sit still when we been offered the moon." She put her hand on her husband's shoulder.

"You've been offered more than ten thousand dollars?" Roberta asked.

She nodded with dignity. "But I promised Mr. Barnes a couple days for him work things out for everybody. And I'm sticking to *my* word."

"What kind of money?" somebody yelled at me.

"Three quarters of a million at least."

"You got them to guarantee that kind of money?" The white woman shook her straight white hair, which curved under her chin. "Or's this offer a figment of your wishful imagination?"

"More than a figment, ma'am," I said respectfully, but without eloquence.

"Well, my future don't take one hell of a lot of imagination," she responded sternly. "The end of this month the city's gonna condemn my house, move me right on out, along with everybody in this room. Except *you*. What're we gonna do then, without no money or nothing?"

"Bird in the hand's worth three-quarter million up the bush," shrilled a thin woman whose feathered hat looked older than me. The crowd responded noisily to that brand of wisdom.

The navy wife was still standing. Roberta stepped up next to her: "Is it smarter to grab at not-enough money and doom yourself to a miserable life? Or to give Ezell and Ernie a chance to help us? Whatever the rest of you do, I for one am waiting until Ezell tells me to sell."

"You promised, Roberty!" The feather-hatted woman shuddered with indignation. "Just like everybody else did, you promised we'd sell or wait together, as a group. You can't go back on it."

"I can, if it means acting like a fool." Roberta faced them coolly. "Go ahead and sell without me. When my property's the only one left, they'll offer me the moon for it. A million dollars, maybe."

That set the crowd's greed to boiling again, and their noisemakers to rattling. You couldn't hear the words, but it sounded like everybody craved being the last to sell his property and get offered the moon for it.

The navy wife whispered in my ear, "It looks like they gone hold ranks for you—for a while." She sat back down next to her husband and bellowed up at me: "But you better be quick."

When the neighbors showed no sign of letting up, I grabbed Ernie by the arm and steered him out into the kitchen. Roberta followed.

"What's gonna go down, you think?" Ernie said, eyes hopeful, when I let go of him.

I looked at Roberta.

"It may take a couple more hours of persuading," she said softly, "but they remember again how badly they crave the extra money."

"Give us a minute, Ernie, will you?"

When my old friend winked and sidled out the front door, I took Roberta by the shoulders and said: "You turned the tide, you know. You are a piece of work.."

"Will you come to dinner tonight?"

"I just can't, tonight. Give me a rain check?"

"Of course. Some other time, then."

"Roberta, things are worse than your neighbors even think."

The brown-uniformed bulk of Junior Evans came clambering out the living room door. He stooped to kiss Roberta's cheek, showed me the palm of his fist, by way of encouragement, and said soberly, "Going to work now.'

Roberta smiled at Junior. But when the boy was out the back door, her hand flew to her mouth. She pulled it down again. "What are you saying?"

"That Ernie and I had the buyers moving up the scale towards three-quarter million, like I told you. Except, a couple hours ago, the whole deal fell through. Right now, you and your neighbors may not have even ten thousand each."

"Oh. Well. It could be worse," Roberta said bravely, straw

clutched firmly in hand. "We all still hold our properties. We just need another developer to buy it from us."

"I'll be working on that, I promise."

I started to call Ernie back, but Roberta put her fingers on my forearm.

"Can't you even tell me why?"

"Why what?"

"Why you want to turn me down. I'm not trying to start a big deal with you, Ezell. I just thought we enjoyed each other's company, that's all."

"Oh, Roberta. I'm ear-deep in trouble right now. Not something I want to drag you into."

"I realize there's a lot I don't know," Roberta said determinedly. "I don't go on many dates. But I want you to teach me."

"Did you think I was disappointed? We got a winning streak going, don't we?"

Not meeting my eyes, Roberta changed the subject: "Will City by the Sea purchase our property itself, now that Short Line Enterprises has pulled out?"

"Very, very unlikely, would be my guess. In this town nobody makes a deal like that except through the proper underworld channels."

"Well," she said, and raised her bare shoulders, "then you will just have to find us another buyer."

I kissed her on the lips. "Try to coax everybody into keeping up the story about Ernie's offer. It might get some buyer's juices flowing, who knows?"

Just as Roberta nodded, a blast of indignation shook the wall between us and the living room.

"You better get back to settling them down. Send Ernie out, will you?"

Sitting in the truck with Ernie, I could see that his nearly unsinkable ego had taken some heavy torpedo fire from Roberta's neighbors. He said not a word, just sat crestfallen. Hating to see him feel so bad, I didn't tighten the screws by scolding him for spooking Roberta's whole neighborhood.

Instead I laid out what I needed him to do that night at the City by the Sea showroom. Ernie perked right up on hearing that I needed his help. We rehearsed his role. He would walk to the Atlantic City *Press* offices, pay a fee to search their files for photos of Charlie Faucher, and then study the pictures until he could recognize the man. Then he would meet me extra early at our reserved table in the City by the Sea showroom.

I know Ernie well. I made him repeat everything to me three times. "You show up at eight o'clock, right?"

"That's it, Easy."

"You certain you got everything?"

"One-hunerd percent."

"Good. Catch you later, man."

"When is that?"

"Ernie!"

"Just pulling your hind leg, Easy."

CHAPTER TWENTY-EIGHT

○

By the time I pulled back into the parking garage, it was after four o'clock. I went up to my room to make preparations for the night's work. No sign of my neighbors. The wedges were in place, a hand's breadth apart. I was beginning to feel a little foolish about them.

The skittish rain had dampened my clothes, and the cold humidity drew clamminess out of my skin. First thing I did was reshower, shave, drape on my second suit hanging freshly dry-cleaned in the laundry exchange door. Crisp starchy shirt, newly shined shoes, lucky parrot tie. Over all that I strung my old beat-up shoulder holster. I made sure my wallet, with money and licenses—investigator's and concealed weapon carry—was buttoned into my right hip pocket.

I cleaned, oiled, and loaded my guns. I keep a separate cleaning kit for each. First the little pearl-handled Colt .22; it loads with six rounds. I thumbed the safety on, slipped the little gun into my right-side jacket pocket. Then the Police Special Smith & Wesson .38, cleaned and loaded, went into the shoulder holster. Most old habits I just can't break. Shoulder straps are one. They're not cool these days, my cop friends kid me. Too easy to spot, and the gun's too damn hard to pull out from under a jacket. Nowadays plainclothes cops clip weapons to their belts or strap on ankle holsters. Me, I keep on doing it the way I was taught.

I also swabbed and loaded my largest piece of firepower, a Charter Arms .44 Bulldog. But I left it under my pillow. You can't conceal a pistol that huge any more than a ballpark vendor can hide that box he's toting.

When I was dressed and armed, I phoned Charlie Faucher's office to establish his whereabouts. His secretary primly told me that Mr. Faucher was in conference and was not taking calls. No, he had not informed her when the conference would be finished.

Hot damn. If she was to be believed, then I had a little drop on Faucher. I took a last mirror peek, stepped outside and buttoned my door with the wedges.

When I looked up, two rapt teenaged faces were studying me from the neighboring door.

"Going out," I mouthed elaborately, pointing at the door, then the wedges. "Won't be needing it till later."

The girl and boy smiled uncritically, but made no move to leave the protection of their door frame.

I hunched my shoulders and stalked off to make some fur fly.

"Have a wonderful evening!" the girl's voice followed me.

It was just after five-thirty when I hit the service alley connecting the Boardwalk and Atlantic Avenue, along the side of the City by the Sea casino. No way I could tail Faucher all the way from his offices, which were crawling with his own security people. But to get into the showroom or to go backstage, Faucher would have to take one of two possible routes. The main showroom entrance was set off the rear of the casino floor so that, like everything else in Atlantic City, you had to thread through the gambling pits and tables to reach the show. The backstage entrance led off the service alley. Three gigantic steel double doors were lined up above a loading dock where a D'Amato Green Grocer truck was off-loading its romaine through the left-hand door. I caught myself checking the truck for a flat front tire. The middle door was blocked by numberless enormous bags of laundry, waiting for Giuseppe Linen Service, no doubt. Backstage access was through the right-hand door. Directly in front of it a little cement staircase led down into the alley.

When I had asked Angel about it, he told me the door was spring key-locked both inside and outside. Just the opposite of a fire door, it was designed to keep people *in* as well as out.

Angel had told me that a couple of security guards held the doors open from seven until ten P.M. and identified the girls going in, along with the customers, musicians, crew techies, agents, VIP's, and so on—anybody they had instructions to let pass. After ten, nobody but nobody got through that door until the end of the final show.

Needing a vantage point, I scoured that service alley. Little concrete seats and benches were built into a central land-scaped area between the truck lanes. The walls of both neighboring casinos were festooned with loading docks, hand-railinged ramps, fire ladders, underground parking ramps, architecturally utilitarian zigs and zags.

About one hundred feet down the alley from the backstage door, I found what I needed: a niche chiseled into the ten-story wall, for God knows what reason. It threw a plenty dark shadow, and let a head peeping around its edge observe the backstage door well enough.

Foot and truck traffic arriving from Atlantic Avenue would catch me in full view, however. There wasn't much of it yet, and I could only hope that not too much would develop later. No matter, whoever did come my way would see a man leaning casually against a wall to light a cigarette.

My wristwatch said six-ten. I might be waiting until midnight or past. I scooted back up to the Boardwalk, braked at the first cart I saw, bought three hot dogs, three bags of chips, and six containers of coffee: four black, to drink first, then two with cream and sugar, in case it got really late.

Chips stuffed into my suit pockets, everything else on a little collapsible cardboard tray, I lugged it all back to my post and methodically ate dog after dog, stoking up for a long night if need be.

At six-fifty the backstage door opened and a large uniformed man kicked down the little leg to hold it open. He and a clone exchanged laughs, lit cigarettes, shot the breeze. Always, though, the first man remained outside the big door, the second man inside it.

Damn, I should have picked up the little mustard-to-go packets instead of pumping on the Gulden's from the gallon jug. Now I had mustard stains on my new shirt.

At seven-twenty the girls started dripping in. Watching them made the waiting go better. At ten to eight Angel, Felicia, and two other girls walked up to the door, chattering like four machine guns, and disappeared inside.

By 8:45 all the girls, musicians, and crew had scooted inside, because the security guards relaxed, even pulled out folding chairs to sprawl on. If all was working right, by now Ernie would be scanning the showroom entrance for Charlie Faucher.

Just before ten o'clock the guards stretched, kicked up the door's retaining leg, pulled the door locked shut.

I broke from cover, hustled up the alley, onto the Boardwalk, and around the corner through the City by the Sea casino door. Ernie and I would have just enough time to claim our reserved table for the *Peaches and Cream Revue*.

The casino floor was slippery with gamblers as I squirmed through towards the gaudily decorated showroom entrance.

Just beyond the baccarat tables an arm hooked my right elbow and a hard hand landed on my left shoulder. Before I could turn, a pair of heavyset bodies pressed me from both sides.

"Barnes," said a voice I had heard before. "You're under arrest. I'll reintroduce us: I'm Lieutenant Detective Wenhome of Atlantic City Homicide. This is my partner, Sergeant Devine. We're taking you in for questioning on the Veronica Vallee murder." Their tightened grips told me they weren't buying any woofing tickets.

"You and an accessory were seen boarding the *Polaris* just before Vallee was found dead," Wenhome said. He patted me down, slipped out my .38 revolver matter-of-factly, raised his eyebrows when he found the little Colt .22.

Most of the gamblers ignored us, but three blue-haired old ladies gathered to watch. I tried playing to the audience.

"Where's your damn warrant?"

The ladies clucked disapprovingly.

Wenhome's partner put in: "Do I understand that the perp wants to see a warrant, Barry?" He grinned and cracked wise: "We don't have to show you any stinking warrant, creep."

I turned to look inquiringly at Wenhome.

"This is my town, Barnes," Wenhome said quietly. He nodded at the younger detective, and they started to pull me off the casino floor. The little ladies scattered like scratching hens.

I thought as fast as my mind allows: "Did Charlie Faucher sic you on to me? Something real dirty is stinking the place up, you know?"

"Save your breath," the younger cop gloated. "You'll have plenty of opportunity to talk, believe you me."

"Rubberhose treatment? Or you boys gonna hook my balls up to telephone wires and dial long distance?"

"Us?" Wenhome's understudy sneered. "We're only small city cops. Hicks. We'll just put you on ice for a while. Keep being an asshole, and it could be dry ice we sit your butt on."

"Shut up, Andy," Wenhome said, impatient, not angry. "Come on, Barnes, move."

As I looked longingly at the showroom door, they tussled me across the casino floor like a thief caught red-handed by security. No sign whatever of Ernie. I hoped that meant he'd gone in without me. But how much good could Ernie do alone? My only play was to cooperate and tell my story fast—get the cops hooked on it so they'd go in and at least protect Angel.

Before I could do much cooperating, though, two uniformed casino guards in neomilitary uniforms joined the posse, and they all muscled me fast towards the first-floor security office. I caught glimpses of rooms to either side, crammed full of video monitors and recorders for all the casino camera eyes. Brain-dead technicians glued unblinking eyes to the screens and didn't even notice the passing mob. Uniformed guards as well as plainclothes operatives ignored us on their way out to the casino floor.

At the end of the hall I got tossed into a holding room and handcuffed to the solitary steel chair.

A recessed fluorescent light and a silvered window were the only fixtures in the tan-walled room. No windows to the outside. The knobless steel door hushed closed.

I stared at the one-way viewing mirror. Somebody would be looking at me. Those things are built so witnesses can look in on suspects. But at cop stations there are always one or two gawkers who can't resist peeping through them, whether on business or not. On the far side of the door I could hear Andy grumbling about me, Wenhome murmuring answers. But I didn't care what kind of a hard time they were cooking up for me. All I wanted now was a chance to spill the setup and buy Angel some protection. I wished to hell they would hurry up and interrogate me.

That they had dragged me into a casino security holding tank instead of the police station was no big surprise. The law says that once a suspect gets picked up, cops get only a "reasonable" amount of interrogation time before they have to charge him formally before a magistrate or else release him. Anywhere from two or three hours to half a day constitutes "reasonable" time. It's a court rule linked with due process. Cops all groan about it, but it keeps them from bearing down on a suspect day after day until he'd confess to eating small children. Courts in most states of this fair land call that coercion with a capital Undue.

To circumvent the rule of reasonableness, cops sometimes lie about when they actually picked up a suspect like me. They stash him some place like this interrogation room and work him over until he's ready to cough it up. *Then* they take him downtown, book him, and start the clock running. Reasonable time doesn't run out that way, and the confession won't be suppressed in court.

Handwriting on the wall was big enough for Stevie Wonder to read. Wenhome and Andy were fixing to sweat me for a confession to Veronica's murder. Meanwhile Charlie Faucher would be taking Angel out easily, with me on ice.

My skin felt itchy all over, I couldn't move much, the chair being bolted to the floor. By twisting my neck like taffy, I could see my watch saying 10:33. Damn it, hurry up and interrogate me.

What happened, instead, was that the mumbling on the far side of the door faded out of earshot. I was left stewing in my own juices. Felt painful taking a good deep breath. The room seemed unventilated. Sticky perspiration beads began dribbling down my ribs. Probably Faucher would wait for the second show at midnight. Or maybe he'd hold his move until after both shows, when the girls were leaving for the night.

Hell, I'd be out long before then.

If only it wasn't so damned quiet in here.

CHAPTER TWENTY-NINE

O

In every story I read, at some point the author tries to convey how slowly time crept along. No problem. You want to suffer from stand-still time, try sitting locked up while a friend that you promised to protect gets stalked by a killer you turned loose on him.

I watched the hands crawl around my watch dial, minute after minute. Every five minutes on the dot I yelled the same words, to the one mirrored wall: *An innocent person's going to be murdered tonight unless you people prevent it; just give me a chance to explain it to you!* Nary a response. By eleven-thirty it dawned on me that the detectives didn't mean to come back. I let loose a stream of language calculated to make even a whore blush. What a chump: I was nobody's suspect. Faucher had simply called in a favor, asked these friendly AC cops to freeze me for the night. Could be Wenhome and Andy had even gone home to their wives and kiddies. Nobody would disturb me until morning, too late, too late.

I strained my ears for sounds outside my door, guessing that if anything had gone down, like a dancer being shot on stage, there'd be some kind of racket in the security offices. Everything stayed steely silent, thank God.

My watch showed 12:05. The second show had started. Angel was back out under the bright stage lights, where he couldn't even see the audience sitting in the dark in front of him. His beaming Latin face would line up in its appointed place for every choreographed movement. Easiest target in the world for a gunman sitting in the dark, silencer screwed on. All the while, the electrified band would be banging out the decibels. There'd be pandemonium when Angel fell. But nobody would understand exactly what had happened until much later. If they ever figured it out.

Burning with frustration, I yanked on the cuffs, but only bruised my wrist. Sometimes, in Newark, I think to carry a handcuff key along with my other gear, but I'd packed light for this trip to Atlantic City. No matter, that steel door looked four inches thick and was locked tight.

My arm and chest skin was prickly as a salted cut. But I tried not to stop thinking altogether. At the next every-five-minutes spiel, I yelled how fiercely I needed to use the toilet. *I been drinking a lot of coffee*, I bellowed.

For ten minutes nothing happened. Then keys jingled in the outside lock, and my pulse blew through my arteries. The door cracked open, slowly.

"Mr. Barnes?" a young man's voice whispered.

"Yeah." My whisper trembled.

"It's me, Junior Evans." His head popped through the crack; his big earnest eyes studied me.

No face ever looked better. "You got your keys, Junior?" I clanked my shackles for emphasis.

"Sure do." Junior looked around once, then stepped in and closed the door behind him. He was holding a big key ring. "I'm gonna uncuff you, all right?"

"Yeah, that'd be okay."

Junior bent over me, neatly dressed in his gray City by the Sea security uniform. He thick-thumbed the handcuff key until finally it twisted in the cuff and freed my wrist.

I rubbed it but good. "Mr. Barnes," Junior barely whispered. "Why you locked up?"

"How'd you know I was here, Junior?"

"Just luck," the boy said. "I always fetch coffee around about midnight. I took one to the guard on the one-way. I took a look myself, and it was you. What kind of jam you in? You been screaming about a murder."

"Where's the guard now?"

"He's out getting a sandwich. I told him I'd watch the window for him. He figured you was safe enough, locked up and handcuffed and all."

"ACPD leave?"

Junior nodded his big solemn face. "Couple hours ago."

"I got to move fast, man. I was not kidding about a murder going down tonight. Can I get down that corridor all right?"

Junior nodded again. "Sure, if you look like you know your business. Mostly it's a different shift out there, from when you came in. Besides, I'll be escorting you. Look official."

"Not on your life. They'll fry your ass."

"It's only a job, Mr. Barnes," Junior said. "You stuck your

neck out to help my mama and all our friends. I can always find myself another job."

I shook my head. "Job hunting's tough from a jail cell. Listen, did you and the guard both hear me yell I had to use the toilet?"

Junior's head bobbed up and down.

"Then that'll be the story. You were just helping out this other guard. After he left, I began screaming pitifully about my bladder. You couldn't stand it anymore and you uncuffed me to walk down the hall to the men's room, then I jumped you and knocked you out long enough to blow this joint."

Junior's calf's eyes were unsure. "Suppose they check, see if I'm really hurt?"

"Not to worry. I'll take care of that." I winked just before I kneed Junior in the stomach and then clipped him under the chin as his head wobbled down. Disbelief flashed in his big browns just before he went under. I caught him in my arms and laid him gently on the tile floor.

"Thanks, man," I said. I stuck his keys back in his hand and straightened my aching back. Twelve-twenty, said my fiendish watch. I poked my nose around the door and slipped out.

CHAPTER THIRTY

O

Exiting the security offices, I was paid no mind by the technicians behind their glass walls. I passed only two or three floorwalkers going on or off duty. I looked so sure of what I was doing that none of them gave me more than a first glance. Most of the security force was out on the floor anyway.

I don't know how many mustard-stained black men my size go in and out of a casino every night, but when your business involves plenty of surveillance, as mine does, you learn to melt into a crowd, make yourself look smaller and different. Dummying in front of a slot machine, I stripped off my suit jacket, shoulder strap balled up under it, unlooped my necktie, rolled up my shirt-sleeves for good measure, then glided off, looking nobody in the eyes, moving slowly but purposefully.

The hostess at the showroom entrance was kicking back for the night, chatting about the high cost of money with the cloakroom girl. After all, the last show was nearly half over.

When I asked her about my reserved table, she flashed annoyance in my face. The nerve of some people—what did I mean showing up this late, after I failed to honor my reservation for the first show?

Nobody asked for my reserved table for the first show?

Nobody that could pay the cover, she snapped.

Was there a table where I could sit for this second show?

She glared at me some more, but finally admitted that the same gentleman had returned with enough money to pay the cover for the second show. She wasn't sure she should allow me to join him while the show was in progress. She scowled meaningfully.

I sighed and held out a twenty-dollar bill to her. I never saw a piece of paper disappear so fast.

Inside, the stage was ablaze for the featured singer, and the walls were shaking with the bass and organ. With the house lights off I couldn't spot Faucher while I was being led through the tables to where Ernie was sitting. Well, with luck Faucher couldn't spot me either.

"Holy shit! Where the hell you been, Easy?" Ernie screamed into my ear. "What's shaking?" He was wearing his new suit and an anxious expression.

"Is Angel all right, man?"

Ernie nodded vigorously. "I never knew Angel could dance that good," he said. "Dance girls come back out after the comedians do some more jokes."

"You see the man we're looking for?"

Mournfully, Ernie shook his head. "Been hanging around this joint since eight o'clock," he yelled. "Waiting for you. I went down to the newspaper and looked at the pictures and everything, like you said. Then I come down here. You didn't say I be needing money to slide in here, Easy." Ernie pulled his mouth from my ear and looked at me accusingly. "You know I be stony, man. They give me the bum's rush first time, then I find a dollar and parlay it into eighty bucks at the big wheel. Cost me fifty-five just for this crummy little table."

I didn't ask Ernie where he "found" the "dollar." "Thanks, man," I told him. "You keep looking. I'm going to scout this joint."

Ernie poked my arm with something metallic hard. Far from the stage lights as we were, I could still see it was a cheap Italian automatic.

"Get rid of that," I shouted in Ernie's ear. "You crazy, man? Where'd you get that thing? You don't even know how to use it."

Ernie got dignified on me. "Roberta loaned me some bread, buy my suit out of hock. And I pick up this little rooty-tooty at the pawnshop. Don't you worry: I learned all about guns in the service, sonny boy."

"That was World War Two," I reminded him. "I think they used M-1's then? Gimme that thing. Remember, keep those eyeballs twitching."

I made no friends sidling in the dark down the narrow service aisles in front of the tables, bumping knees and rocking drinks. Almost everybody yelled at me to sit down, and one drunk stood up and shoved until he realized he couldn't budge me.

The comedian's amplified voice was mock-complaining: "That's some approach to social problems, ladies and gentle-men: we got violence in the ghettos, we join hands across

Utah; we want to stamp out poverty, we throw a rock concert."
The well-oiled audience howled.

The tables half ringing the stage rose in steep tiers. Ernie, even in his new suit, had drawn the second-to-last row. The aisle along the right end of the row was empty of waitresses or security guards. I peered uphill. Behind the last row, high on the back wall, a ten-by-ten plate of glass let the lighting crew direct the spotlights and project the special effects on the stage over the audience's heads.

I headed for that booth. Twenty feet from the right aisle a windowed door, velvet-papered to match the wall, swung open when I fingered it for a knob.

The little cinder-block hall I stood in was unlit except by reflections, and smelled of plastic and burnt oil. Three cement steps led up to another metal door. It swung open when I twisted the knob and leaned my weight on it. I stepped in and closed up soundlessly, but there was no need. The sealed room hummed only faintly with the showroom noise, but the single man in the projection booth wore headphones and stared out at the stage.

This control room might have been twenty by twenty but was stuffed floor to ceiling with heavy metal shelving dropped seemingly at random, and crammed with cans of film, enormous racks of video and audio tapes, wiring and electronic parts, and stacks of script books and scores.

I hesitated, not anxious to jostle the man's necessary concentration on the show. But I sorely wanted to scope the audience through that big observation window. Without a clue as to what I'd say, I shuffled a few feet towards him and the window through all the rubble.

Behind me I heard the booth door creak open. I turned quickly enough to snap off my neck.

Charlie Faucher stepped into the room.

If I gawked at seeing him, his eyes practically bulged out of their sockets at the sight of me.

"Jesus Christ," was all Charlie said. He was wearing an expensive-looking charcoal suit, white dress shirt, dark red tie. His arms dangled by his sides.

"Don't try nothing, Charlie," I said. I slipped Ernie's little gun from under my belt buckle and showed it to him.

He grinned crookedly. "You order off the top shelf, old buddy?"

"Save it, man. You're under arrest."

"The hell are you talking about?" His voice flirted with hilarity, but the air between us crackled. "I heard *you* were under arrest, Easy. What's it got to do with me?"

By now the lighting technician had taken his headphones off and was watching us with big young eyes.

I jerked my thumb at him. "I said save it, Charlie. You want me to spell it out in front of a third party?"

"Let's take it outside, Easy," Charlie said, no longer chuckling, but still not very serious. He walked over to the observation window and glanced at something before he walked outside.

I found a switch for the bare light bulb in the six-by-four hall.

"Hurry it up, Barnes," Faucher said. He reached into his pockets, showed me his lighter and cigarettes, and offered me one. I took it. When we were both puffing, I said:

"I'm sorry about this, man. You killed Ronnie Valentine. And you capped the New Yorker. I can't prove the New Yorker, but I think I can pin you with the Valentine hit. You proved it yourself, by showing up here to waste the informant that saw you that night.

That got Faucher's attention. "This is my casino," he argued seriously. "I'm head of security here, for God's sake."

I shook my head. "You don't spend your nights haunting the showroom, Charlie."

Charlie snorted with exasperation. "I thought you were eighty-percent slicker, Easy. Did you really think I wouldn't smell a setup when Pat Trimster called with this eyewitness crap? When you bait a trap, you use Velveeta, don't you, buddy?"

"You had your AC cop buddies cool my tail, didn't you, man? Get me out of your way? And now I find you skulking around Angel's show. No way you can shake off all that evidence."

"For Chrissake, I'm not even packing, Easy. Did you forget to check?" I stepped forward and patted him down. He didn't move. Nothing. That shook me some.

"We're wasting time," Faucher said, irritation rising. "Let me out of here, and everything'll get explained later."

"You're out of your head, Charlie. Long as I got you covered, Angel's in no danger. When he's through dancing, I'm steering you to the FBI. Tonight."

Charlie gave it full urgency: "Just look out the goddam observation glass, will you? You'll see what I mean."

I motioned him back up the cement stairs and into the projection booth. I followed him over to behind the technician's back. Through the plate glass you could see the entire showroom, the stage and every table, though it was too dark in the house to make out more than shapes in the seats.

The projectionist looked up questioningly at Faucher. Charlie gestured him to lift up an earphone. "Throw on the house lights, Bernie, just for a count of three."

"Give me a break, Mr. Faucher," the young man moaned. "That'll be my job."

"No, it won't," Charlie said, with more than a touch of the old assurance. "Switch them on when I tell you."

To me he said, "Second row, table all the way on the left aisle." Then he tapped the kid on the shoulder.

The house lights shocked the magic darkness into white glare, then cut off again.

Even through the insulated glass you could hear indignant murmurs. The projectionist, listening through his headphones, winced.

"See it?" Faucher asked me.

I saw it. The little man with the silver lion's mane, hunched at the stage-side table, was all too familiar.

CHAPTER THIRTY-ONE

O

Fighting our way across the back aisle and down towards the stage gave Faucher and me a mother of a time. The comedian was finished, and the band was riffing before the girls came back on, stalling to give the waitresses one last chance at drink orders. The aisles were crowded with them and their trays; the lights stayed low. Sometimes I felt I was wrestling Charlie as we butted and tugged and stubbed our way towards Roger Trimster's table.

"How about calling in your security people," I gasped. "We're making pitiful progress."

"Not a chance," Faucher snapped, pushing a waitress against the wall and edging past her. She started to complain, then recognized him.

"Why the hell not?"

Charlie turned and grabbed me by my shirt collar. His breath was scented with mint. "You rug head! That's Pat's father! I'm here to keep the lid on. I won't have her humiliated. This is a small town, Barnes. You bring my people in and there'll be a leak."

I was wising up, though: "You're not even sure Trimster did kill Ronnie Valentine, are you? You think just maybe he's here cleaning up Patricia's mess. That it?"

Faucher's breath exploded from his chest as he kept kicking a path down the long aisle.

I pressed after him. Four or five rows from the front I heard Charlie swear. He turned angrily. "Bolted."

"Goddam. What do we do?"

"You look backstage. I'll search out here. If you find him, bring him to me. And for God's sake, Barnes, keep it quiet."

Faucher bulled down to Trimster's empty table, and while I hesitated, disappeared in the dim lights.

As I stood there, the *Peaches and Cream Revue* pranced back on stage. That set my feet to moving. Cutting down through the band pit, I collected a bundle of scowls and head shakes, but basically the musicians were too busy to bother about me. The amplified racket was terrific. At the little door penetrating under the stage, I yanked the handle and kept right on trotting down the crude, skinny hallway, up the concrete stairs, until I was stage level. I eased towards the stage wing, fake-beaming and nodding at everybody I passed.

Lots of people back there, a few watching the show with headsets on, but most skittering to and fro. One crew hand recognized me from my rehearsal visit and gave me a little thumbs-up gesture. I repeated it heartily and made like I was laughing. He slapped me on the back and pounded by.

Peering around official-like, I cased the backstage area, poked my head into both dressing rooms, came up empty-handed and more panicky.

I propped against a wing curtain and stared out at the glaring stage and the glowing, straining, shiny-toothed dancers, Angel among them. They looked seven feet tall with their slick-stockinged legs and their shiny skullcaps fluffy with colored plumes.

I studied the sets, the backdrops, the facing wing, the darkened house. From where I stood: empty, not a sign of trouble. My eyeballs felt coated with something gummy. The lights were too bright; I felt dazed and in slow motion. All at once I heard voices over my shoulder gasping, then giggling and calling to others to come look. Someone jostled up beside me, pointing with outstretched arm at the middle of the stage.

I refocused my eyes on the bouncing showgirls. Everything looked normal for a second. Then I spotted the commotion's cause.

Out in the back row, middle, under the revolving magenta floods, Angel was ruckusing around, feet in perfect step, but arms and head waggling in some weird dance all his own. While the other dancers pretended to be waltzing Christmas trees, on tiptoes, arms angled out sharply, wrists stiff, Angel was rubber-dolling his shoulders in what I took for an imitation of Egyptian hieroglyphics or maybe a fishing flamingo. Angel's head kept swiveling vehemently, from the wing where I stood to the stage's opposite side.

Most of the backstage techies were bent over, flabbergasted. The little choreographer was quivering with rage. The audience's astonished tipsy delight registered even through the electronic musical buzz.

The showgirls had joined hands and were sweeping forward

in a line, swiveling one knee across the other. Angel, his hands clutched firmly by the girls on either side, was still trying to make like a walking Egyptian. I wasn't sure he could see me, but his face kept flicking from where I stood to across the stage.

The scene suddenly crystallized: Angel was signaling. His mechanically smiling face looked stricken.

I squinted hard into the blinding stage lights: the Egyptian walk was Angel's attempt to keep dancing and at the same time flag me towards the opposite wing.

I wheeled, pillowed into a muffling curtain, punched loose, and dashed around the wing into the corridor behind the backdrop. It looked to shuttle all the way cross-stage to the opposite wing.

I plunged in. That curtain-lined tunnel stretched on for miles. Not a soul followed me or passed traveling the opposite direction.

Spilling out the other end, like a plane tunneling out of clouds, at first I could focus on nothing, just piles of dusty storage cases and trunks, built-in and portable, cables and boxes of lights, stacks of lumber and sawhorses.

Only one stagehand stood back there, watching the performers and handling big-knobbed switches on his cues. He flashed me one sharp, questioning look, then trained his full attention back on the performance. I remembered that this was a newish number; the techies didn't have it on automatic pilot yet.

Smiling and waving to him, I crab-wised around his switch panel and towards the parallel rows of narrower and narrower curtains that framed the stage wing.

I felt the short hairs prickle on my neck.

Slipping Ernie's pistol from under my belt, I rose onto my toes, bent over, and crept forward. No real need for stealth, with electronic "I Write the Songs" clogging the air like fuzz, but instincts were twitching me along.

I couldn't even feel my feet touch, but I know I looked like the Hunchback of Notre Dame until I stiffened outside the innermost wing curtain for a count of three.

The cheap pistol handle was slippery with nervous sweat. I dried my right hand off on my chest, fitted it back around the grip and found the trigger. With my left hand I grabbed the wrist of my gun hand and powered my body around the curtain, arms extended straight out, forefinger trembling on the trigger.

Roger Trimster stood, in dinner suit, gaping at the sequined and feathered girls thumping their feet on the stage. His left arm hung along his side; his right was partly extended towards the stage, elbow bent under the weight of the long-barreled revolver.

Not a long barrel, my brain corrected: a quick-connect silencer, clicked onto a walnut-grip Colt .38.

Over Trimster's head the stage lights made the girls seem larger than life and right on top of us. Other than Angel, they showed no signs of noticing either of us, not even ponytailed Cassie, shaking her tail just six feet away. I saw Felicia, smeared with makeup, working hard. Only Angel stared directly at us, stumbling, slender brown body unaccustomedly wooden and shiny with sweat, face frozen in a frightened Howdy-Doody mask.

I edged closer.

No way Trimster could hear me; he must have felt my presence. He cranked just his head around, without a flicker of his wild-eyed, Einstein-haired face. Then his entire body followed, twisting in slow motion, to face me.

His gun hand carouseled around, not really re-aiming. Quick as slapping a fly, I jerked the pistol from his hand by the silencer.

He coiled his arms and upper body backwards, like a man catching a piano.

For a second I thought he didn't even recognize me, so bewildered were his eyes. Then he mouthed my name.

Over Trimster's coal-red eyes I saw the brightly illuminated showgirls again, bouncing and shaking, glistening with sweat, forming and reforming their lines. Under their glittering headdresses their faces were stretched in bored or ironical, earnest or icy smiles.

The whole scene reached me as if through the grease lenses Hollywood uses to blur flashbacks. The music was momentarily muddled at a murmur. Angel, eyes no longer glued to Trimster and me, looked shaky-legged enough to collapse. From the audience a drunk howled hoarse appreciation.

Sticking both pistols in my belt, I squeezed Trimster's bicep and muscled him back into the crew area. He didn't resist. The commissioner zombied past the confused stagehand and stumbled down the backdrop tunnel in front of me without protest.

When we popped out the other side, Charlie Faucher was standing among the performance crew, suit jacket unbuttoned, tie loosened. His eyes lit up when he spotted us.

Motioning with his head, he led the way from the stage, past the dressing rooms, to a relatively quiet little landing next to the one outside door.

I showed Faucher the commissioner's silenced revolver.

"Wheew," he whistled. "Anybody else see the old idiot with that thing?"

I shook my head.

"Christ," Faucher said, rubbing his scalp with his fingers. "Let's get him the hell out of here, up to my office."

"Why your office, Charlie?"

"Because the commissioner and I need to have a long heart-to-heart that can't wait. Hold him while I round up a guard with a key for this door."

Faucher disappeared. Trimster suddenly came to life. He fixed bright, hard pupils on me. "What happens now?" There was lionlike dignity in his baritone.

I let my breath out and heard a disappointed wheeze in it. "My guess is, now Faucher blackmails your ass, Commissioner. Seems to me that's why he's been so concerned about keeping this fool stunt of yours hushed up."

"What about you?" Trimster demanded. "Have you thrown in with Faucher?"

"Not exactly, but I don't know that I can stop him, man. And now that you tried to kill my friend Angel, I don't know as I much want to."

"Do you still possess the videotape?" Trimster's hoarse whisper had a wild edge. The hand he raised to clutch my sleeve trembled. "We can do business. Cut Faucher out and I will make it more than worth your while."

"Listen, man," I whispered back. "Forget that shit. I was bluffing. I'm no blackmailer."

The old man's mixed look of terror and scorn could have blistered my black skin.

I said, almost resentfully, "Your daughter didn't tell you I saved your godforsaken life?"

"Very convenient for you," Trimster scoffed, "to keep your victim alive and therefore still lucrative to you."

Behind our backs, at the corridor's far end, Faucher rounded the corner, tailed closely by a uniformed flunky, maybe thirty feet from us.

Before I could get another word out, the outside security door squeaked and opened inwards.

"Oops, sorry!" said the outside guard, still untwisting his key. He stepped inside. "I didn't know anybody was—"

Darting between the guard's arm and the door, Trimster brushed the man loose from the key ring. His wrinkled white hand found the doorknob, and the force of his dash yanked it thunderously shut and spring-locked, the keys now dangling outside.

Before I could twitch a muscle, Faucher had pounced down the hall, pulled at the unmovable steel door, and turned to shout at the other guard.

By the time Tweedledee dropped his key ring, shook out the right key with fumbling fingers, and twisted the door unlocked, Trimster had been free in the salt summer air for at least a full minute.

Faucher and I crowded shoulders bursting out after him, but the old man had vanished from the service alley. Charlie snarled at me, with rage in his face and also a dose of despair that shook me: "Find him, Barnes! You work the Boardwalk—I know the streets better."

"There's only ten thousand places to disappear into on the Boardwalk," I yelled back.

"Just fucking find him!"

Without another word Faucher and I split up and flew in opposite directions, like mirror-image bats out of hell.

CHAPTER THIRTY-TWO

○

Diving into the river of bodies flowing north on the Boardwalk, I didn't break stride.

The three A.M. crowd was scattery thick, mostly casino and hotel traffic. A few of the fast-food joints kept their lights on and their pizza ovens working, but not much else was open.

Dogtrotting fast on the boards, I peered up every avenue as I passed it, and quickly eyeballed the clientele in every calzone palace. The late-late-night summer air was so thick with humidity, the streetlamps sprayed light like mist from a showerhead.

Trimster had squirmed like a baitfish out the backstage door, fueled by nervous energy and adrenaline. I hoped to hell he wasn't one of those wiry, athletic little old men. Relax, I told myself, a junkie is not going to keep up the track feats for long.

Outside the darkened Ocean One Mall I stopped and stared in all directions. By now Trimster might be blending with the crowds in any of a dozen casinos, or maybe even checking into any of a hundred-thousand hotel rooms.

My mouth made motorboat sounds. Enough with playing chump to everybody. If finding old Roger Trimster was so urgent to Charlie Faucher, then I sorely wanted to find him first myself. I shuffled farther north up the Boardwalk, past the statue of baby Caesar, past a line of bible addicts protesting everything their foggy minds could think of, past Bally's purple-striped pointy tents, past the tacky old Garden Terrace Buffet, past Frozen Custard, Imports of the World, Charlie's #1 in Fashion—Hoods and Tee-shirts.

At Park Place I scratched my head, then leaned on the railing, sucking in humid air and staring wistfully at Bally's, the Sands, and the Claridge glowing above their fountained park—at night, the most exciting panorama in Atlantic City. Trimster could be slipping into any one of them right this minute.

Back to moving my feet. The crowd was thinner at this end,

just a scattering of couples, and all the shops were locked for the night. Hyperaware, my eyes took in the darkened doorways: Tiffany's Smor-Gasbord, the Cash for Gold Emporium, Lady Luck Discount Shoes, Family Fun Video Arcade, Readings by Mdm. Ruth, $.99—Everything In Store. Three Brothers from Italy Pizza, Frozen Custard, Old Tymes Tobacco and Cigar Shoppe, Steele's Fudge, Miss Sharon Phrenologist, Pier 21 Gifts, All Shoes $11.90 Salon.

The salt air, soaked with dampness, felt charged with electricity. Prestorm gusts of wind began flapping my jacket from random directions. My skin itched; the tibia I cracked in high school began to ache.

I kept walking and concentrating, trying to notice everything and everybody. Palmer House Smorgasbord. Jaymes's Original Salt Water Taffy: Cut to Fit the Mouth. Teepee Town. Mdm. Latrina Readings—a crystal ball emporium every hundred feet, all standard Gypsy-issue signs and prices. Most likely, whoever isn't cooking Gypsy dinner that night goes down and plays Mdm. Latrina.

A lightning bolt shaped like the frayed end of a whip silently splayed over the ocean. The open construction framework of Atlantic Palace condos flashed on and off like a big mouth opening and swallowing. All the time in the world passed before the thunder rolled out its distant grumble.

A city block ahead, the Boardwalk ran out of casinos, construction, shops, and streetlamps. I stopped in front of the locked-up entry to the old Central Pier and debated pushing farther north without light. Across the Boardwalk were only darkened tee-shirt factories and abandoned 1940s bars and movie marquees.

An enormous grinning clown face loomed over the Central Pier entrance, colors faded enough to look a hundred years old. AMUSEMENTS OCEAN END OF PIER. HAVE FUN. SEAQUARIUM. NO ADMISSION CHARGE. SKY TOWER ENTRANCE. A chain-link fence topped with barbed wire kept the curious well off that defunct Have-Fun pier.

Inside the chain link, a little mall was filled with old-timey clip-joint paraphernalia. The seaquarium's display windows offered dioramas: sea horses, whales, and octopi, Oddities of the Deep—hilarious papier mâché sprayed turquoise. All the old wonder makers lay about in cobwebbed boxes. At the end of the old arcade mall, a hangar-style glass door two stories high was open a torso's worth.

Behind the mall, on practically the last of the carnival-style piers, the famous Sky Needle spired over one hundred feet into the thundering night. It had been closed to the public for years, now just the world's tallest lightning rod. As I turned my eyes back to the Boardwalk, the storm exploded above like a concussion grenade.

The pier's old pilings creaked, with the wind and surf swirling and pounding at them.

Right of the chain link a rickety set of steps led off the Boardwalk to the beach. I slid along the fence and looked out towards the growling ocean. The dark beach seemed barely wide enough.

Another flash of lightning sneered the smile on the giant clown's puss and momentarily picked out a black clot at the edge of land and water. The thunder rumbled closer. Eyes fastened on where the black shape had been, my feet automatically propelled me down the steps and out onto the beach.

The fluffy sand trapped my haste, twisted my ankles, squeezed out forehead drops of effort and anxiety. I stumbled towards the nightmare black water, watching it pelt, shatter, reshape. My city ears could hear only menace in it. Not many downtown kids ever learn to swim. Believe me, nobody knew how to float in the foster homes I grew up in around Newark. I never even laid eyes on the ocean until I was fifteen; I remember standing with my friends on the Asbury Park beach as if in church. I still love to see it. Old ocean's in my blood, draws me like a snake—just so long as it doesn't touch me.

Ten yards from the sea edge the sand was packed harder and my foot speed picked up. I still could see nothing but that grim black mother, wavy edges bursting and creaming even in the dark.

But the wind blew at me bursts of human noises—someone sobbing. I followed the sound. Thirty yards down the beach a man's shape was barely visible, thigh deep, undulating like a wand with every changing wave.

I ran along where the sand was wet and firm. The man had walked out just twenty feet or so. Pulling up at the wave spill, I had no doubts who it was, though it was too dim to make out the silver of Roger Trimster's mop.

Unmoving, as if penetrating secrets of the deep, Trimster didn't notice my presence even when I yelled into the wind at him. I raked at the sand until I touched a stone and I hit the dark shape with it, then another, until his head turned. Trimster's voice floated clearly on a gust: "You!" He dismissed me with one hand.

I took a step towards him, and he shuddered forward, as if towing a great weight.

The freezing seawater hit my anklebones.

"Don't move another inch," I shouted.

The wind amplified his whisper: "Another ghastly attempt to keep your golden goose alive—"

"Take it easy, Commissioner. Don't get crazy on me."

Trimster snorted derisively.

Through cupped hands I shouted, "You haven't hurt nobody yet." Trimster shook his head, maybe because he could not hear. Then the wind shifted and blew my voice at him: "You only went after Angel to protect your daughter, isn't that it? You're out there now, still trying to protect her."

Trimster's words were mostly stripped away from me. "Nonsense . . . disgrace . . . bear them." He turned back to look at the sea.

I edged forward as retreating water momentarily left open sand. The waves seemed to have doubled in height, towering like a moving prison wall. Thickish raindrops began to batter my head and shoulders.

I shouted, hasty and fearful in my own ears: "The drug dealer that sold Patricia that overdose she fed Veronica—he's dead, man! Nobody can prove a thing. Police believe it's all mob killings. They're dragging their heels, looking for how to quit on it!"

"Patricia?" the old man said, wondering. "*I* killed her." He took another step into the pimpled waves and immediately got knocked onto his back. His head bobbed just above the water. As the wave retreated, he staggered dripping to his feet.

I inched out towards him until an incoming wave shocked against my knees. My underpinnings shook; my breathing flew away from me.

My eyes closed and opened. "To hell with disgrace," I gasped. "You got enough money that you'll never lack for friends. Go off to that horse farm of yours, screw the world."

The Commissioner turned his head once more. He was close enough now for me to study his smeary face. A lightning flash let me see his jaw working, but silently, as if words were kidney stones.

Water swirled suddenly up around my waist, terrifyingly.

Skin crawling, I convulsed backwards, kicking until my knees were free again.

I stretched an arm in Trimster's direction, but he was looking out to sea again. His head was very steady.

I wanted to move closer to him; almost lost my balance; couldn't command my leg muscles.

With a jerk, Trimster surged a yard farther into the waves, and was knocked off his feet again.

This time he disappeared totally in the charcoal waves and gloom.

Sweeping my brain clear of fear, I churned three strides into the waves the way a dog soldier charges a machine gun.

Cold saltwater slapped me in the face and clutched at my waist. I howled to the skies, in fear and self-pity. I was a lost child, and shivering, and nobody loved me.

My knees shuddered me willy-nilly back to where the sand was dry. I yelled for Trimster, but in the wind, thunder, and furious water rushing and blasting at my feet, my voice was small. I swept laterally up and down the beach. I was all alone. Nothing but lunatic water.

The clouds emptied lashing ropes. I stalked among them howling his name, disgusted with my cowardice.

After a time five early-adolescent boys came up on my back.

"Mister," one shouted at me. His MEN AT WORK tee-shirt was pasted to his narrow chest. "Did somebody go in the water? Should we go in after him?"

I shook my head, started stalking towards the beach steps.

The boy caught my arm, tugged at it, and pointed out at the waves. "Maybe he's still floating out there," he screamed, his voice wind-torn. "We're going to dive in for him."

I grabbed the boy by both arms. He had a mop of nicely barbered hair over clear-looking eyes.

"Don't be a jerk, kid," I said, a hundred times too harshly. "The waves are six feet high. He's dead. Just stay on the beach until the police come. You want to do something more, say prayers."

A little raincoated crowd pressed against the board fence near the beach steps—only in Atlantic City would folks be up and looking for trouble in a four A.M. storm. No cops yet. "Was it the diving horse?" somebody yelled, and was rewarded with a multithroated hoot of laughter.

I clambered up, shoved myself a space through the grudging rubberneckers. "You better wait here for the police," one threatened. I shoved him with my self-disgust; his back hit the railing, hard. He whimpered, then shut his mouth. Nobody else said a word as I stomped off, across the Boardwalk and down Tennessee to Pacific Avenue and the wet anonymity of Atlantic City streets.

The storm that had blown up so quickly already showed signs of wishing to quit. The rumbling sky flashed behind me like a distant air strike. In Atlantic City things had blown over.

CHAPTER THIRTY-THREE

O

It's a mere twelve-block walk from Tennessee Avenue to the lights of Utah Avenue. It can take near an hour, though, when your mind is straining like a moped motor and you let your feet wander.

Just a skeleton crew manned the City by the Sea executive offices at four-thirty A.M. As I brushed by it, the scale model of City by the Sea's ultraluxury resort gleamed palely from within, impossibly distant, like an exit sign in a dream. The receptionist Faucher had introduced days before as Loretta sat guarding the VP gates. Only tonight she just stared across the hallway, blinking not an eye as I quiet-stepped past her to the door of Charlie's private office.

From the threshold the long space was suffused with the pink, violet, and black tints of something Art Deco. The far wall, all glass and purple morning sky, framed the solitary chair centered in the huge room into a sharp black shadow.

The smell was unspeakable: plastics and chemicals smoldering in a dump burn.

I stopped fifteen feet from the chair and cleared my throat. "Trimster's dead. It's over, Charlie."

"Word spreads fast." Charlie's voice was calm from the shadows. "I know he's dead. Everything's over." His smooth-shadowed profile hung motionless above the armchair.

"I was there with him. Before he disappeared, he told me he killed Ronnie Valentine. Don't sound right to me, Charlie."

"He was in over his head."

"Patri ia tipped him that Angel was a threat?"

"I don't think so. He probably overheard her feeding me your line on the phone." For the first time, Charlie's body shifted, slowly revolving the chair to face me. "She's a good woman, Easy. She played it straight with the both of us."

"But you weren't sure until Trimster showed tonight?"

Faucher shrugged. "She adored that flea-brained father of hers. She has the gumption to kill for him."

"Then why didn't she?"

Charlie shook his head. "Believe me, I've studied everything about Patricia. The only things she's guilty of is loving one damn fool too much and another one not enough."

I wanted to step closer to him, couldn't. "You're still covering for her, Charlie. You killed the New Yorker for her, didn't you? You knew an overdose that big would get traced PDQ to the dealer. She didn't. You put the New Yorker down to cover her traces."

I braced for anger or worse, but Charlie's voice was full of strange pride. "As much as she loved her old man, I loved her more. I asked for nothing more than to love her for the rest of my life." He added with no particular tone, "You know, sometimes I think she could barely stand to look at me?"

"Women," I said.

"What do you know about it?" Charlie's face tightened in almost boyish resentment. "You never got married. You never found your one great love."

"Tell me about it," I said.

He grunted. "You'd be the Prince Galahad of any woman in Newark."

I shook my head, tired of it. "Everybody sees himself taking the romantic lead in a sad movie, Charlie." I nodded at his smoldering wastebasket. "You didn't have to burn that videocassette. Kind of dramatic, no?"

"There were things on that tape that I couldn't allow anyone to see—ever."

"You mean, like Patricia feeding Veronica the heroin hot shot?"

"You're nuts. Drop it, will you?" Charlie stared grimly at the wall of concealed files.

"Puts my butt in the wringer, but good, man. New York OC gave me the job of tracking it down."

"Don't be a chump, Easy. That tape was worthless the minute Trimster pushed the foolproof antiblackmail button: he swallowed seawater. Won't let you off the hook, though. New York OC will want your ass, I hate to say it. You better think of a way to make them smile."

"Wish to God I was back home."

Faucher snorted a nasty laugh. "Yeah, all the players from Newark in this game got their asses kicked. Didn't we?"

"How about you and me team up, like old times, see what we can salvage?"

Faucher stirred. He said, not without a touch of the needle: "I'm not available for teamwork, buddy. You have to unstick your Johnson all by yourself."

I shook my head, but the cobwebs clung. "I don't get the Madame Butterfly routine, man. You tried your best to save Trimster—he was a loser. And his suicide shakes Patricia clear. Cops can't prove you hit the New Yorker, and they won't try. Nobody gives a shit about that. I sure the hell don't."

I wished Charlie would smile or frown, or anything.

"You admired this big office, remember? Know how a mere security man gets the best office in the joint? He has to own forty-five percent of the house stock, at least technically."

"I heard you had money."

Charlie's head shake was small and private. "I don't have shit, old buddy. Except a limited life expectancy."

I stared at him.

"Oh, I *had* some money, eight years ago. I rolled down AC way after my retirement, met the right people, or maybe the wrong ones, got offered the chance to invest in a casino development plan. I pledged everything I had, almost a million, and agreed to sign an informal note with my partners for about eight million more. Then, holy moly, out of a couple dozen proposals, ours gets approved and we are off on a greased skid. We're gonna be instant jet-setters."

"Where'd a retired cop get a million dollars, Charlie?"

Faucher ignored me. "Except we built the wrong kind of casino. People don't want to gamble in our casino. We didn't plan for enough hotel space to make up the difference. Operating expenses are in the red a couple hundred grand every month."

"Sell out, then. You can still work—you're a hell of a cop, Charlie."

Faucher sighed. "My partners have been advancing my share of the operating debits against my initial investment in stock. It's been all theirs for over a year. Plus a couple million on top of that. Interest is piling up like Topsy."

"Jesus, man. Don't tell me your partners are Philly OC?"

"I've been staying cool," Charlie said to the wall. "Things go bad, you think your way around them. Three opportunities I had lined up—any one of them goes right and I'm back on top."

"One of them was blackmailing the commissioner so you'd get your second hotel."

"Worked out great, huh? Second was the Utah Avenue condo development. *That* I figured for a sure thing. Only, the night before last, my partners pulled out. I have you to thank for that, old buddy. You told me you were representing Horton, and I stayed off your back, didn't I? But when you tried to sell them Horton's action, my ex-partners figured I had put you up to it."

"Oh, Jesus, Charlie. I had no idea."

"Just the last straw. They already didn't trust me a damn."

"Can we do something yet with your third plan?"

Charlie shrugged. He said, thick-tongued:

"Not a plan. Everything I ever wanted. If I could get Patricia to agree to marry me, her money could tide us over until we were showing a profit again."

"You're a complicated man, Charlie."

"Fuck you."

"Ronnie Valentine tip you to the New York mob blackmailing the commissioner?"

"Well, I used to see her, you know. I knew her from years ago in Newark, and I wasn't getting far with Patricia. I smelled something and pushed a bit. But old Ronnie, she was a-willing to cut me in."

"Why?" It mattered to me.

"I don't know. Either she figured she'd double her profits, double her fun. Or she'd gotten in for more than she could handle and was hoping I could protect her."

"Why'd she hire me? She wasn't really looking for Cricket Finnochio's insurance money, was she?"

Faucher's voice was dry and tired. "I think she knew you and I used to work together, in my better days. By the end she didn't trust me either anymore. Bringing up the old Jimmy the Cricket story to you was her way of fingering me."

"I been dumb, huh? Cops don't ever save a million dollars. You killed Finnochio, that right? Along with that crooked accountant for New York OC?"

"Goldstone," Faucher reminded me, his voice dead. "Jimmy the Cricket was my informant. I had him eight ways to Sunday, and he needed to do me a big favor, fast. He tipped me that Goldstone would be carrying cash to buy a piece of Atlantic City for a New York family. So I showed up to surprise Goldstone before the seller arrived. I made Jimmy come with me. Goldstone jumped funny, and both of them wound up dead. And here were these cardboard boxes of U.S. currency scattered over somebody's kitchen table."

"You put their bodies in the car trunks?"

"They were scumbags, Easy. Bottom of the cesspool."

"I'm not crying for them, Charlie."

Faucher sighed. "It's goddam morning. Look."

I hadn't noticed the violet light wash away in overcast gray. Facing away from it, Faucher's face was mottled with canyons of shadow. I could guess that from where Charlie sat, my face was lit up with morning light like a choirboy's.

"I've forgotten what it feels like," he said wearily, "to sit here talking to somebody you don't think is gonna back-knife you. Intentionally, anyways. First time you blew into town, I daydreamed about working with you again, somebody I trusted."

"Trust? I don't know you anymore, Charlie. You don't know me."

"Don't kid yourself. You never change, Easy. I doubt you know how to. You just keep at it and at it. Look, I'm going to offer you a deal, pal: raw meat to feed your New York OC friends."

My pulse rippled. "What's my end?"

Faucher's shadowed face was a theatrical mask—comedy, tragedy, I couldn't say which. Maybe the one where the face is split and is the most knowing of all.

"I want you to lay off Patricia," he said. "She's worth it, no matter what happened."

I guess I nodded. Anyway, he started talking.

Charlie Faucher had spent his career springing nasty jokes on organized crime. Only he could have explained how I could poison the New York mob on what the Philly mob had vomited. My mind tacked to and fro like a sailboat in the gigantic ocean prowling outside Charlie's window.

When he was finished and sat fixing me with that small smile of his, I said, "You're not gonna do something crazy, are you, man?"

The smile widened a rueful half inch. "You mean, pull my own plug? Don't be a schoolboy. They don't answer my calls. They don't extend me any more credit. All I have to do is sit still. They'll come get me when they're ready."

Finally, I understood. "Put your coat on, Charlie. My ride is parked a block away. I got a fair chunk of cash on me, and I got savings I can mail you. We can be at Newark Airport in two hours. Go anywhere you want to. Keep it a secret even from me. But don't sit and wait for it."

Faucher rubbed his cheek and the side of his nose hard. "Get the hell out of here, Barnes. I don't have to listen to crap. You don't understand one goddam thing about these people, do you? I just hope you're up to saving your own ass."

"Charlie, it's the goddam mob. You've been pushing them around for twenty years. The Ciampelli brothers—"

"It's not the same, Easy." The shadows were now blotching most of Charlie's face. They hid his expression. "Those days, I knew what they were, I could handle them. Hasn't been the same since I started wanting the same piece of action as them. There's no difference between us."

"Why don't you let me help you, man?" Maybe someday I won't be ashamed of the way my voice wavered.

"For the last time: because there is no fucking help for the cancer I caught. And because you're too nice and dumb a guy to take the fall with me."

I held my hand out to him and let it drop when he didn't move.

"Don't forget what I told you." His lips barely bent. "Do it fast."

From the corridor by the shining condo model, through his unclosed door, I took my last look at Charlie Faucher. He'd swung his chair back so that I saw his profile. He was watching the dawn. After a second his shoulders slumped.

CHAPTER THIRTY-FOUR

○

A few people I know blame me for walking away from a way-back friend in trouble and going about my business. But those people probably read the kind of books where civilians tell organized crime where to jump off, and live to grin over it. Me, I live in New Jersey, and I know it doesn't happen that way. Besides, I had a variety of other folks depending on me that morning.

Make it fast, Charlie had said, but I hardly needed the advice. By the time I shuffled into Toby's Royale hotel, my clothes had nearly dried, crusting on my skin. The Wisconsin boy from the neighboring room was waiting for the elevator as I stepped off. A carry-on bag was strapped on one shoulder, and he clutched a suit bag in his other hand. His downcast eyes lit up when he saw me, and he started to say something.

In my urgency, I brushed him off and raced to my room. I phoned Roberta, woke her up, and told her what she needed to do.

Roberta, big-minded and competent, listened carefully, asked questions, took notes, said she thought she could get it all done in time.

Next I dialed the 201 area code and my lawyer's Newark number.

"It's Easy, Marty. I got a neighborhood association," I said before his sleepy hello, "that wants to sell their properties as one parcel. You can set that up, can't you?"

"It's too early!"

"Out to catch a big worm."

"An incorporated group?"

"Nothing like that. Just forty poor souls that need to sell all at the same time and plenty damned fast."

"How fast?"

"This morning."

"Plain to see you've been wasting your life on the streets instead of in the legal chambers of this great land." Marty yawned. "The wheels of the law turn slowly, my friend. Besides, you know I do only criminal work."

"You have contract whiz kids at your firm?"

"Maybe."

"Well, roust 'em out of bed, Marty. You got a nine A.M. meeting."

Marty laughed like I'd told a campy joke.

"Double fees."

His voice firmed up: "We do contract work on a negotiated commission basis."

"Gonna be two to three million dollars changing hands."

"We'll take ten percent."

"You'll take five percent and count it a high-profit item. Call in your youth with the thick glasses. Oh, and bring a secretary and a legal typewriter, Marty."

"We use word processors now," Marty said mildly. "By nine o'clock? Where?"

"Well, I'm in Atlantic City. Your people'll never drive here in time. How about they meet the neighborhood's representative in the Parkway Service Area at Brick Town? Nine sharp. Plan on having the papers drawn up by ten."

"Atlantic City. That should explain plenty. What, I don't know."

"Any delay, the whole deal goes under, Marty."

My long-suffering attorney chuckled.

I called Roberta back, got an encouraging progress report, and told her where and when to meet Marty's contract-law wunderkind.

When I hung up, my watch read 6:45. I changed clothes, went down to the Kinney lot, and retrieved my little pickup truck. I had two or three longish errands to run before I picked up the contract at ten A.M. Just barely enough time. Good thing I didn't have to bother phoning ahead for an appointment with the buyers. They were already expecting me.

At ten past ten my truck grumbled down the coffee-shop parking row at the Garden State Parkway Service Area between exits 122 and 126.

Inside HoJo's Marty had somehow taken over a third of the restaurant. He and Roberta sat talking a blue streak and carving dramatic strokes in the air with their hands, while one woman and one man in dark suits, both younger, held

forefingers on passages in thick books and scribbled on yellow
pads. Two telephones sat on their tables, strung by hundred-
foot cords from somewhere. Coffee mugs and bitten Danish
were strewn everywhere.

At a separate table a motherly woman in a gray skirt and
sweater sat with a sweet smile, coaxing what sounded like
three hundred clickety-clacks a minute from an IBM portable
computer.

Roberta spotted me first and was betrayed by nerves into a
startled face that did nothing for the prickles along my spine.

Marty pulled me into the seat beside him and pushed a
penciled yellow sheet in front of me.

"Okay, we're running approximately twenty minutes behind
schedule. But Roberta did a beautiful job anticipating what we
would need. These are dummies of the contracts."

"Marty, can you add a clause specifying a finder's fee for me?
I'll fill in the amount."

Marty looked startled, then said, "Good for you, Easy.
Everybody should get a little piece of the action."

"I'm going to ignore that remark."

For the next fifteen minutes he filled me in, rapid fire, on
some technical details.

"Blah, blah, blah," I said. "Where do I get them to sign?"

By then the word-processing lady had finished printing the
triplicate forms and was table-smacking their edges level. I
tucked everything into a manila envelope that folded to fit a
breast pocket.

"It's 10:38," Marty told me.

"Thanks, everybody. Got to run." Check your car trunks.

The little group was back to business before I even cleared
the door.

By the time I U-turned back south on the Parkway, shot off
the Long Branch exit, and drove to the Alpine Country Club,
the hot sun had dried last night's rain from the fairways, and
foursomes were carting all about. When I climbed out, it was
close to eleven-thirty, and my stomach ached as though
somebody'd been standing on it.

In the pro shop Billy the wiseass pro kept his mouth shut
this time, except to disappear into his back room for a quick
phone call. He dodged looking at me the way some people
avoid the eyes of beggars. Or lepers. Or death row inmates, I
guess.

In three minutes Al and two chums strutted in, dressed as always for golf.

"You're late, Barnes. We were just having a laugh about you."

"Not my fault. I'm here now."

"Take it outside," Al said, eyeing me out to the warm-up tees. None of the three wasted even a glance on Billy the golf pro.

In the breeze by the practice tees Al wasted no time.

"You bring the item, funny man?"

I held both hands as if doing a push-up standing up. "That tape has been destroyed, Al. Not by me either."

Al grinned mischievously at his goombahs and said, "Well, that's terrible for you, huh, Barnes?"

"Why? It's useless to you—Commissioner Trimster committed suicide early this morning. He's blackmail-proof."

Al crinkled his black eyes. "That tape cost us a fortune. We set the whore up on the biggest yacht in New Jersey, for Chrissake. You were told to find the tape, Barnes. Be a man: you fucked up. It happens."

None of the three had moved a muscle, but I found myself talking faster. "Listen, Al. I did what you told me, busted my ass tracking down that damn tape. Not my fault it got torched before I found it."

"Who said it was your fault?" Al grinned. "Who's asking? How about you go have coffee with my friends here? There's a good diner down the road."

Before anybody could move, I said: "I brought you something else, Al. You'll like it."

"A present? For me? You are an entertaining guy, Barnes."

Hawked by eight eyes, I pulled my jacket wide open, reached carefully for the manila envelope tucked into the inside breast pocket.

"What do you got, a gigantic Christmas card? Peace on earth?"

"No," I said. "A piece of Atlantic City."

It took Al about an hour to kick me upstairs to Mr. Carmine Napolitano. Al didn't fancy making a fool of himself, but he was an educated man and not stupid. The forms looked legal, and they offered a block of Atlantic City just off the Boardwalk.

In the clubhouse we sat in Mr. Carmine's private suite,

around a conference table. What appeared to be his entire family, men and women, sat at the table and on chairs along the walls. Everybody wore golfing clothes or colorful sunsuits, like a clothesline in a Puerto Rican neighborhood.

Mr. Carmine looked more like Gabby Hayes than Marlon Brando. His shiny cannonball dome and black-rimmed glasses framed his droopy nose into a Halloween witch's. Every time he pursed out a word like "no," I thought his lower lip would kiss his nose tip. When I leaned to shake his hand, I caught a whiff of provolone cheese.

After he scanned the contracts, he had a hundred thousand questions for me. Nobody else butted in a word.

"What do I want with a street in Atlantic City? I ain't gonna build no Monopoly hotels, am I?" That drew appreciative chuckles from everyone but me. I handed him the classy development prospectus paid for by City by the Sea: the architects' drawings, the builders' estimates, the marketing consultant's figures. He studied them in silence.

"I got the scale model in the bed of my truck," I threw in after a minute.

"Get it." Mr. Carmine head-motioned a couple goombahs. I tossed them my keys. I'd be the only Japanese pickup truck in that lot, I was morally certain.

"So maybe I do build a hotel," Mr. Carmine gap-toothed at me, spraying foam flecks like fireworks. "Here it tells me I'll make twenty million bucks. So why do *you* give it away?"

"Well, I don't personally have access to the purchase price."

"You work for a man that does."

This took me aback, wondering just how much the old fox did know.

"That's true," I admitted. "In fact, Mr. Ernie Horton made an offer of one hundred and twenty thousand dollars apiece for these properties."

"He sells spareribs," Mr. Carmine explained to his people, and arranged a curly lasagna smile on his lips.

"He's been called away suddenly on business," I said. "The people on Utah Avenue have been given to understand that his offer's been withdrawn."

"You did that?" Mr. Carmine said, half mocking, half admiring. "What for?"

"Well, I didn't want to come here this morning empty-handed."

"You cheat the man you work for?"

"I don't think of it as cheating. Mr. Horton's best interests lie in Atlanta, Georgia, not New Jersey."

Two youngish men in red, white, and black golf outfits were arranging the luxury-condo scale model on a separate table. They found the plug to light it up from inside. The room erupted in oohs and ahs.

"You don't like him," Mr. Carmine prompted me. "He's not generous to you?"

I waved a hand so it landed palm up.

"What's your price?"

I passed the contract, penciled with ninety thousand per property, times forty, to Mr. Carmine.

He read every word, twice. "What's the hidden costs?"

"Nothing. Just a finder's fee, of course, for me."

"What kind of fee?"

I passed along my last piece of paper.

"One million dollars." He grinned. "You got a pair like a donkey, huh?"

We looked each other in the eyes for a few seconds. Everyone else was humming and buzzing about the condo model.

"You ask too much," Mr. Carmine said loudly. "Take it and get out of here."

The buzzing stopped.

The chair fabric felt like sandpaper between my shoulder blades. "There may be a little flex in the asking price," I ventured. "We'd be willing to come down to eighty grand, for example."

Mr. Carmine burned his black eyes into me for a few seconds more. He motioned Al to his chair, and they whispered a little into each other's ear.

"Wait outside," Al told me.

Sitting in Mr. Carmine's living room with Al's three goons, I figured my odds. Mr. Carmine's family wanted the condo like a suburban kid wants a pony. What Mr. Carmine himself wanted was hard to sniff. Charlie Faucher had told me that New York OC had a long-term yen for Atlantic City action. I just hoped that was true enough.

I was summoned back. As we filed into the conference room, the shining eyes of some of the crowd gave me a positive hint.

"Sit down, Barnes," Mr. Carmine said. He adjusted a corner of the contract papers and pushed his glasses up his nose with a middle finger. Then he smiled. "I got good news and bad. Good news for your property holders. Bad news for you personally."

My stomach muscles hurt.

CHAPTER THIRTY-FIVE

O

Mr. Carmine laid out his offer: "We are agreed that this condo development is worth looking into and all that. Of course, if we do business with the people that own City by the Sea, it would be different than if we can't do business with them."

I nodded.

"You know the people that own City by the Sea?"

"Not personally."

"You better not, sonny boy."

"I don't, I promise you."

"We are gonna give you sixty thousand per lot. I like a fifty-percent discount."

I cleared my throat. "That'll be acceptable."

"We don't feel you personally should get a dime. Your finder's fee is *niente*—we ought to make you pay us for screwing up the work we give you to do."

"Hold on, Mr. Carmine—"

"Shut up, unless you're canceling the deal."

I looked around the room. Al smiled at me significantly.

"This isn't right, Mr. Carmine. It's not just."

Carmine enjoyed the moment. "You little creep. You gonna tell me what's just? You're a thief. You steal from your friends." To Al he said, "Get him the fuck out of my sight."

Out in the living room again, Al's boys and I killed enough time with gin rummy to have played eighteen holes of golf.

People came and left the conference room in tidal waves. Some of them carried attorneys' briefcases. Maybe some of the others that didn't look Italian were accountants.

At last Mr. Carmine entouraged out of the conference room without so much as a glance for me. A skinny man with a dancing Adam's apple lingered behind to hand me copies of the signed and sealed contracts. One of them was a receipt for a check deposit of $2,400,000.

"As Mr. Napolitano's business attorney, I will act as guarantor of the payment," he told me. "I'm driving to the bank now."

He also didn't offer to shake hands with me. Nobody else did either as they escorted me to my truck and watched me climb in. Neither Mr. Carmine nor Al made a farewell appearance.

I actually felt a little lonely finding my own way out and connecting with the wide desert places of the Garden State Parkway.

An hour and a half later, back on Utah Avenue, Atlantic City, New Jersey, an anxious bunch crowded the sidewalk and tiny lawn outside Roberta's house.

"Come on in," I told them, and led the neighbors to a final meeting in Roberta's living room.

After Marty Kranz's fee was deducted, the pot divvied up to almost fifty-seven thousand dollars each. The room exploded when I spelled that out. Maybe a few grumbles were mixed in—you put big ideas in some people's heads and they can't enjoy much anymore—but enough goodwill flowed my way.

Roberta explained to them pretty well what the optional trustor scheme Marty drew up was all about. Anybody that wanted to leave their money in could join a mutual-fund investment group made up solely of former Utah Rangers. It would disburse monthly payments, either of interest plus some principal or of interest only, with a calculated amount of capital growth. Access to the principal was guaranteed, with financial counsel available gratis to all members from an investment house Marty knew well.

Roberta and I were hoping most everybody would sign up, but of course, since these folks had never had a dime to their names, more than a few just grabbed the money and ran. Still in all, twenty-three of forty neighbors joined in the mutual investment group.

When the last neighbor had left, Roberta took me by the hand, put a finger to her lips, and led me into her bedroom.

As I stepped out of the shower later, just a towel wrapped around my middle, she sprang a last surprise on me from her bed.

"Everyone voted to award you a five-thousand-dollar bonus, out of sale money, Ezell. They all agree that you earned it. I personally feel that you earned a *lot* more. And right now I am thinking of other, more creative ways to reward you."

I managed a short laugh, but said, "I don't want money out of this, Roberta. I told you that."

"Oh, I know. I think it's terrific the way you bluffed those gangsters with a finder's fee request so they would gloat over taking advantage of you. We decided on our fee to you before you even pulled that trick. Don't worry, just sit back and enjoy it. You've earned it, mister."

"Well, Ernie gets a chunk of it for helping me. So does Angel, poor soul."

"Now, at long last, how about having dinner with me to celebrate?"

I winced, and smiled ruefully. "Hate like hell to say this, Roberta, but I was looking forward to getting back to Newark tonight."

Roberta's face and shoulders, all that I could see of her, flushed dark. "I don't know what to say—didn't we go through this before? Or was I dreaming a bad dream?"

I rubbed my face with my palm. "I'll be back, Roberta. You couldn't keep me away. You're something special, baby. You deserve better than the evil mood I'm in right now."

"I'm not just your holiday piece, then?"

"More than that, and I suspect you know it."

"I suppose we still have a winning streak going, don't we? Better than finishing one."

I smiled and at the same time started shaking my head. "I can't hang around Atlantic City while Charlie Faucher is sitting in his office, waiting to be hit." I squeezed my eyes at the image. "I've had enough of this town for a while."

Thoughts of Charlie Faucher wouldn't have left me alone even if the first newspaper box I passed hadn't featured him. Front page of a five-star Atlantic City *Press*: Charlie's photo, banner headline. I hustled past. Then I forced myself to walk back and buy the paper. My old hero fell into a casino elevator shaft opened for maintenance. Possible foul play under investigation. Don't make me laugh.

I still needed to round up Ernie and Angel, see if they were staying or leaving with me. Roberta had promised to root up Ernie. Angel I found watching Oprah Winfrey in his hotel room. He jumped fast for the idea of going home, actually leaping in the air, with little cries. He didn't even seem worried about running out on that night's performance; no doubt one of the understudies could cover, and would be overjoyed at the chance.

When I opened my own door to pack up, the phone was ringing and ringing, like a distance runner.

"I've been calling you since the wee hours this morning," said Patricia Trimster's tremulous voice.

"I feel bad about your father."

"You did all that you could to help him. He was an awfully weak man, wasn't he, Ezell?"

My aching stomach muscles cramped again. "He was physically brave." My voice sounded thickened. "He just wasn't a gambler, that's all. He was past taking any more risks."

"Just what does that mean?"

"Charlie Faucher's dead too. Happened early this afternoon."

Patricia let out a God-honest shriek that bounced my ear right off the receiver.

"Oh, my God! Why, Ezell?"

"Those two men cared about you more than most people deserve. Charlie would have done anything for you—he did."

"More riddles!"

I looked at the receiver, then said, "He killed that drug dealer, the New Yorker. He was worried that maybe you had bought Veronica's overdose; he thought he could cover for you."

Someone in the hallway knocked timidly on my door.

"Just one dial on Charlie's control panel, you know? On or off."

"Well, that's not love," Patricia said coldly. "To suspect me of a murder? And then he went and killed an innocent man? Not for *me*—I don't accept that."

"Not an innocent soul in sight," I said dryly. "And how far was your father capable of going for you, Patricia?"

"What are you implying? Ezell, are you deranged? Stop talking to me like this. I called because you went through so much for my father and me. You deserve much better than you got. I've made out a check for five thousand dollars. Will you come out for it? Or shall I send it to your office?"

"Send it to your trash can," I told her. "People've been poking bills around me since I got to Atlantic City. I won't take money from you. Not now."

"Let me get this straight. Are you actually accusing me of murdering that dancer? Because if you are, you are out of your mind."

I emptied my lungs in one angry whoosh. "Charlie thought so—and he loved you. Everything fits."

"Charlie was obsessed!" Then in a quieter voice: "Doesn't everything also fit if I was only trying, futilely, to help my father?"

I tried to think why she was wrong. My mind slipped on it like wet rocks at the sea end of a jetty.

"Ezell? Can't we talk this through? Please? When can I see you?"

There was more knocking on my door, louder.

"I'm leaving Atlantic City tonight," I told her. "Packing right this minute."

"What will you do?"

"Nothing for me to do." I laughed, very shortly. "Enjoy your life, Patricia."

That's all either of us said. She heard the receiver click in her ear.

Head buzzing, I pulled the room door open and said hello to the teenaged Wisconsin girl from next door. She wore tight jeans and a long tee-shirt. Her light brown hair was severely tied back—her entire face looked rumpled and sad.

She stepped gingerly into my room and peered around to see if I was alone.

"Something come up?" I asked her. My patience was not good. "Give you a hand with anything?"

"I saw you come in. Jeff left to go home this morning," she said.

"Saw him leaving."

She nodded, then smiled lamely. "Isn't this awful? I come barging in here with my troubles. You hardly know me."

"Happens all the time. You know nobody, away from home, need somebody to talk to. We've said hello a few times. It's enough."

"You are a sweet man."

"You all right?"

She shrugged thin shoulders. "For three days Atlantic City was our paradise. We gambled, and swam, and held each other every night. On our fourth morning Jeff wakes up and says he's sorry but he has to go back to Stone Lake, to his wife." The last word came out the way out-of-staters say "New Jersey."

I let my face show my sympathy.

The girl forced a smile, meant to reassure me. "Oh well, we

knew running off was a long shot. It's just—I just wish I didn't always take the wrong chances."

"Nobody beats the house edge in Atlantic City. You must have noticed that. My own luck's been mixed down here, believe me. Taking chances is fine—only in AC the game's usually different than what you expected."

"Oh, I like Atlantic City, very much. I was thinking about looking for a job here."

I just looked at her. Against her thin, girl's face her eyes were movie-sea dark blue. Not the color of New Jersey's ocean at all. My own brown eyes probably shone like a Raritan mud.

The girl looked uncomfortable. She said, uncertainly, "That's one of the things I wanted to ask you about—where I should start job hunting. I was thinking about waitressing. There are so many food places in this city, and the girls must come and go like crazy, don't you think?"

"You out of money? How about I loan you the price of a airplane ticket to Wisconsin? Pay me back when you're able."

"No, thank you," she said with quick politeness. At my expression, she said, "I didn't mean—it's an awfully nice offer. But Stone Lake is out for me." Her laugh ended as quickly as it began. "My family knows every other family in our town. Just think, this week I trashed a marriage with the president of last year's senior class!" She shivered. "There's more for me here, I can feel it. What do you think, am I crazy?"

"Girls who hang around Atlantic City," I said carefully. "They meet some peculiar people, date men with no visible means of support. Most wind up with boyfriends they wouldn't care to explain in their letters home."

"Oh," she said, as if to a child, "don't you think waitresses work too many hours to get into much trouble, except their feet hurt? And the tips must be great in a city like this."

"There's nothing else you've wanted to do?"

"Well-l-l." She bit her lower lip as if humoring me with thoughtfulness. "My grampa had a clock repair shop when I was a kid. I always loved to hang around while he was working. But I don't think the money would be good."

"Why not this? Call every watch and clock repair place in the shore area, offer to work cheap as an apprentice until you see if you really like it?"

"That's a good idea," she said, relieved to close the subject. "Maybe I'll try it."

"The plane ticket offer still holds."

"You *are* a dear," she told me, twisting the doorknob. Then she stepped back and stretched on tiptoes to brush my cheek with her lips. "And you don't even know me."

"I know you," I said. "You like trying your luck, and you don't moan if you lose. I've been running into women like you lately." The pretty smile froze on her face. "Listen," I said quickly, "I admire you. I've been liking these women I meet in AC."

"But you want me to go back to Stone Lake!" Her voice was tense; her body unconsciously leaned away from me. I realized that my smile had fallen off.

I put it back on. "Don't mind me. I'm just a worrier from way back. You got a different outlook. You can't be guided by me."

She nodded, puzzled, then stepped again to the door.

"Wait a minute." I reached an arm to the bureau and opened my wallet. Her frown dropped when I handed her my business card. She glanced at it, smiled at my funny name, and stuffed the card into a jeans pocket.

"Hang on to it," I told her. "Helping people is how I make my living."

Her grin was at least half amused. "I'm not surprised." She lifted a hand, then slipped out. The door thumped softly behind her.

I had crammed a soft bag full and was tucking my two new suits into the suit bag when I realized that I had not gotten her name. For a second I thought about knocking on her door. But she had my card. I decided to mind my own business.

CHAPTER THIRTY-SIX

○

"Okay, Mr. Crabcake. Why you got to be sad? How come you don't drink no champagne?"

"I'm driving," I told Angel. He and Ernie were most of the way through a magnum of New Jersey champagne, Renault Vineyards, that Angel had scrounged for the celebratory truck-ride home. Ernie was passed out in the rear jump seat, snoring.

"That never could stop you before, Easy."

"You know, you surprise me, celebrating like this after the director canned you. I know they warned you and all, about disrupting performances, but don't it upset you? Don't tell me you're happy about coming back to dirty old Newark? I mean, Ernie was busted so flat by Atlantic City you could spin him on a turntable, but this was your big chance. Or am I missing something?"

"You are missing Nowork," Angel informed me. "And Angel is missing Nowork too. I don't like to be far away from my friends."

"You were making friends among the showgirls, no?"

"Too much drugs in the showgirls." Angel shuddered. "I don't like it."

"They were nice girls, though."

"They know to have fun," Angel admitted. "Some is nice, Felicia is nice. Some is not at all. Papi, what you laughing for?"

"You're coming back to Newark because it's *nicer*? I don't think anybody ever put it that way before."

"They rehearsing this new number, sí? *Pieces of Cream* is gonna be finish next week. They say everybody got to audition all over again. They are not friends to the dancers. Phooey on that."

"You really do surprise me, Angel."

My friend shone his smile of wisdom on me. "Atlanty City is, ooh, pretty much excitement. If they don't fire me, Angel probably don't go. But now is time for going home."

"Well, you probably are better off in Newark. Less shifty than along the ocean."

By the time we passed six Parkway exits, it was dark. Billie Holiday, Lester Young, and Teddy Wilson on the stereo: "The Same Old Story," "I Cover the Waterfront," "Let's Call the Whole Thing Off." I heard Angel murmur with pleasure in the middle of "Am I Blue." Angel prefers rock and *salsa* to jazz and refuses to listen to my tapes except for Billie Holiday.

My mind drifted for a while, meditating on three little girls in blue. Four really.

It was raining again and very sticky. The air conditioner helped some. Angel looked cool and relaxed, as always, in a tropical skirt suit with a satin tee-shirt underneath, de la Renta style.

I changed a twenty at the Expressway tollbooth.

As I cranked down my window Angel told me, "You are very nice to pay Ernie so much money, Easy."

"He'll just blow it doing wine with Snookie, but he sure earned it. You know, Angel, you're the one that really stuck a neck out. You sure you won't take part of that bonus?"

Angel wagged his head from side to side until I thought it would fall off.

"Know how you feel. I've seen more bills shoved in people's faces in the last three days than in my whole lifetime. Makes you tired."

"Papi," Angel said sternly. "You stayed too long in Atlanty City. Did you just tip a dollar to that tollbooth man?"

I had to laugh.

"Everybody gets tipped in Atlanty City," Angel observed, sounding not exactly tired of it.

I stopped laughing, abruptly.

Angel said helpfully, "Roberta's friends need somebody's help so bad, and you helped them good, and now everybody is rich."

"Not everybody."

"Is very sorry about poor Veronica, Easy, and your friend, Charlie."

I twitched in my seat.

"But everything else is okay, yas? You did very good, Easy."

We pulled off at Newark exit 142.

I grunted. "I wish I had your rose-colored glasses, Angel. Half my moves in AC turned around and bit the wrong ankles."

Angel's eyes grew wide and shiny. "Easy, don't."

I shrugged him off. "You know I elbowed you into sticking your neck out for none of your business."

"Oh, Papi."

"Not to mention putting old Ernie in hot water three or four times too."

"Ernie don't mind."

"Let's not forget how I went klutzing around to help Roberta's people, and wound up squashing the last deal my old friend Charlie Faucher had to keep him alive."

"Stop *it*, Easy!" Angel stuck a nail-painted forefinger into each ear and hummed a peppy "Am I Blue."

"Another thing—this is a real beauty—I swagger up to Roger Trimster, tell him I'm his blackmailer. Then, when I'm all he's got, he's so terrified I want him alive to deep fry his ass, that he walks into the ocean and drowns himself."

Angel started to protest, but I interrupted: "Trimster drowned about ten yards from me, and I was too paralyzed by the damned ocean to help him."

"You can't swim!" Angel was furious. "If he throwed himself off a casino, you couldn't fly after him neither. Besides," my friend added triumphantly, "he killed Veronica!"

I shook my head. "It's a toss-up. His daughter's about as likely."

"He was gonna shoot Angel! It was justice, Easy!"

"Justice? That's a way of settling court cases by making deals. I made one. There were no innocents—except maybe me for a while."

Angel's face, as he tried to follow, pupil-like, was so solemn that I smiled.

"Who could do better?" he asked stubbornly.

I shrugged. "In that damn hurricane? Probably nobody."

"See?"

"You know what I do mind? I mind walking away not knowing exactly who jumped where."

"Why?"

"Why? It's a itch."

Angel nodded, puzzled.

"Because, well. Because—why do you think I'm an investigator in the first place? Can't take bobbing around in the middle; like to know where I stand."

Angel smiled with patient incredulity. "You like always helping somebody."

"Yeah? Muff Anglaise—or Veronica Vallee or Ronnie Valentine or whoever she was—sure needed helping. The Cricket's life insurance was a smoke screen; she was asking me for protection. So, the minute I blow into town, she gets capped. Could be I even tipped off her killer."

I turned my grim face on Angel, who was studying the dark blots of Newark whizzing past. He did stop humming long enough to say: "You got a big crush on this Veronica because she's dead now."

"I don't think she would hurt Trimster. She was hustling her piece of the action. They played the hand for her, is all."

"You didn't know her too good," Angel reminded me, wisely.

"Probably nobody did. I think she could be whatever anybody wanted her to be. I never before went for a character like that, but she made it mighty pleasing."

Angel's face flushed girlishly. "Nobody is too old to learn something good."

I grinned at him and nodded.

Angel leaned his Farrah wig closer. "But this one! How could you truss her?"

I couldn't get comfortable in my seat. After a couple seconds, I said, "I guess life's more than trust." I paused. Angel's mouth fell open. He'd never heard the like from me, but it sounded about right.

I thought of something and chuckled. "Muff and old Atlantic City—they both yank you around something awful, but you can't resist trying your luck. I'm not sorry I did."

Angel sing-songed, to ease the bite: "She used you, Easy."

I shook that off. "No more than anybody else, man. She wouldn't hurt me." Angel hissed. The nighttime Newark traffic was heavy and aimless, as always. "Of course, that's one more thing I'm never going to know for certain."

"Then you better not want to," Angel scolded, with just a trace of tenderness. "Sometimes," Angel said dreamily, "bad things are like in a dream after they over. Atlanty City was pretty tricky, Easy, was sometime fun, and sometime we didn't like it. But we are home sweet home now."

At that Angel and I both swiveled heads to look out the side windows at the passing Newark street scenes. And we laughed. Good lord, we roared.

* * *

After I dropped off Angel and then Ernie, feeling itchy and about to launch a wide-lidded night, I skipped my apartment, cruised downtown, and parked across from my office.

At Marlene's windowless desk at the hub of everything, I shrugged off my old British-tailored jacket, plunked into Marlene's swivel chair, and emptied my mail basket one piece at a time. Circulars, routine bills and payment checks; many phone message slips in Marlene's loopy handwriting. Nothing that couldn't wait, except one hand-addressed, five-by-five pink envelope. It was postmarked Atlantic City, last Thursday, the day I drove out of Newark. Felt like a single sheet and something the shape of a silver dollar.

I used my ring finger to poke sand out of my eye. The note was lettered in a round, womanly hand:

Dear Ezell,
There are a few things I didn't mention. You are too nice a guy to come to Atlantic City right now, as everything is breaking into pieces. Besides, as of now I will be all set without Jimmy's insurance money, so there's no reason for you to work on that any longer. Also, some men here know that you and I talked, and it is better for you to stay away. Pretty soon I won't be living in AC anymore. Then I will write and tell you where I am living and you can use the enclosed to raise air fare to come and see me.

It was sighed, "Love and Kisses, Muff Anglaise (Veronica Vallee)." When I shook the envelope, a yellow casino chip bounced off the desk and rolled to the floor. I picked it up and held it under the gooseneck desklamp. It was worth twenty dollars on the tables at City by the Sea.

ABOUT THE AUTHOR

RICHARD HILARY grew up in New Jersey and was
educated at Rutgers—The State University and Harvard. In his formative years, he gained extensive experience in the factories, sheet metal shops, and loading
docks of central Jersey. For seven years he was a cop in
Newark. More recently, he has worked as a big city
Assistant District Attorney and a college professor. He
has lived in Staten Island, Rhode Island, South Dakota,
Cambridge, Berkeley, Los Angeles, Worcester, North
Brookfield, Mass., and Philadelphia, as well as the
Newark area.